HOT PINK

HOT PINK

ADAM LEVIN

McSWEENEY'S RECTANGULARS
SAN FRANCISCO

www.mcsweeneys.net

Copyright © 2011 Adam Levin

Cover illustration by Walter Green

The stories within originally appeared in *Tin House* ("Frankenwittgenstein"), *McSweeney's*
("Hot Pink," "Considering the Bittersweet End of Susan Falls," "Cred"), *St. Petersburg Review*
("The Extra Mile"), *Indiana Review* ("How to Play *The Guy*"), *New England Review* ("Finch"),
and *Guernica* ("Important Men").

McSweeney's and colophon are registered trademarks of McSweeney's,
a privately held company with wildly fluctuating resources.

ISBN: 978-1-936365-21-0

For my sisters, Rachel and Paula Levin

CONTENTS

FRANKENWITTGENSTEIN

9

CONSIDERING THE BITTERSWEET
END OF SUSAN FALLS

25

THE EXTRA MILE

51

FINCH

57

RELATING

MIXED MESSAGES // TWO CONVERSATIONS // BILLY //
A PROFESSOR AND A LOVER // THE END OF FRIENDSHIPS //
CRED // IMPORTANT MEN

85

JANE TELL

97

RSVP

135

SCIENTIFIC AMERICAN

145

HOW TO PLAY *THE GUY*

173

HOT PINK

185

FRANKENWITTGENSTEIN

Bonnie: The Beautiful Body-Action Doll for the Self-Body Image-Enhancement of Toddling and Preadolescent Girls at Risk.™

Dad conceived her gastrointestinal mini-tract a decade ago. Back then, he was employed at Useful Modules in Grayslake, designing low-valence fibrins to lubricate the motors of their robots. We lived in a part of Waukegan that was getting nastier by the hour, but we had premium channels and a VCR, we ate our snacks off paper plates in the family room and laughed at sitcoms together, our legs overlapping under the afghan. Our bikes were worthy of their combination locks and our mom was a sweetheart, packed us lunches every day before going to work, occasionally slipped notes between the folds of our paper napkins: *Who's the smartest and the handsomest? You are!*; *One week till your birthday, a great day!*; *Basketball team, shmasketball team—you don't need them.*

And then Bonnie: The Beautiful Body-Action Doll for the Self-Body Image-Enhancement of Toddling and Preadolescent Girls at Risk.™

We were watching an exposé on eating disorders and it made our father sad. Halfway into the opening montage—a quick-cut stream of dark eye-hollows and flesh-poor pelvic arches, thighs the width of knees and grainy close-ups of mouth-scars; the soundtrack a string of desperate self-state-ments spoken through echo-filters by choked-up teenage girls, *I'm too fat, I hate myself, No one loves me*—Dad brought his hand to his forehead, as if to shade it from the sun, and he kept it there.

By the first commercial break, the twins were sleeping soundly against his shoulders. Mom kissed and whispered them into consciousness, sent the three of us to bed. I fell straight into a nightmare about a hockey team suffocating me in a pileup. This was in the old Chicago Stadium, but it wasn't the Blackhawks who did it. It was the Yang, a team I'd never heard of. I woke up wet and ashamed.

I stayed in my bed for a while, trying to picture good, bright things. I tried cartoons and they turned violent under my eyelids. I tried an-gels, but they were dead people. I wanted to lie on the couch and watch TV, fall asleep to the sound of human voices, whatever they were saying. I was sure that if I went downstairs and told my folks I'd had a nightmare, they'd let me sit with them, but I was just as sure that speaking of the nightmare would make it permanent.

I decided to go down there and tell them it was unfair how, even though I was nine, I had the same bedtime as my seven-year-old brothers. I didn't get to tell them anything.

When I returned to the family room, a pale girl with puffed cheeks and wrecked lips was onscreen, confessing, and Mom was holding Dad's hand. Dad was weeping. He said, "Poor girl. Poor young girl."

I said, "Dad."

He hid his face. I forgot my complaint and Mom sent me back to bed. I slept fine.

In the morning, Dad made us omelets and bacon. "I'm sorry you had to see that," he told me. "No boy should have to see that. I'm gonna make you a special omelet, with extra cheddar."

Timmy and Brian said they wanted extra cheddar, also.

Dad said, "No. Mike saw. You didn't."

Brian said, "What did he see?"

"He saw nothing."

"Nothing nothing or nothing special?" said Timmy. Timmy was existential.

"Nothing nothing," I said.

"What did it look like?"

I said, "It looked like you."

"So then it looked like Brian, too! You're saying we look like nothing, but you're also saying that nothing looks like us."

"Yes," I said.

"Honest?"

It was the last breakfast Dad made for us. That night, he started on Bonnie's mini-tract. Between his nine-to-five at Useful and the hours he spent in the attic laboratory, it got so we saw him only at dinner and bedtime.

After three years of weekend and evening home-lab work, Dad completed the mini-tract and, in a flush of exuberance, drove us down Lake Shore to the auto show at McCormick Place. It was a rainy day, but the sun was out, and as we passed through the Gold Coast, oohing and ahhing at the dripping high-rises and the skyscrapers behind them, Dad told us that, within a month, we'd leave slummy Waukegan and move downtown. He asked Mom which building she wanted to live in and she pointed to a clover-shaped black one next to Navy Pier. "Lakepoint Tower!" Dad said. He shot me a glance in the rearview. "You see that, Mikey? You'll have the lake outside your bedroom window."

At the auto show, I stood rubbing my eyes before a red Lamborghini with doors like bat wings. No one was allowed to touch it. There were ropes.

The following Monday, Dad brought the mini-tract to Good Parent

Educational Toy Corporation. They fawned over it but didn't want to buy it without being sure there was a financially feasible way to rig up the calorie-sensitive infrastructure that Dad promised was forthcoming.

Dad chose to understand Good Parent's enthusiasm as a kind of pledge and, long since sick of manipulating gluten, anyway, he quit his job at Useful to focus all his energy on Bonnie. He cashed out his 401(k) to fund a better home-laboratory. Let his beard go wild and took lunch in the lab. On weekends, we'd put it on a wheely-cart by the door. Knock three times and walk away. Once, I went up there with Brian, and we stayed after knocking. Dad came out.

I said, "Dad."

He said, "No." Then he ducked back inside.

Brian said Dad was a fuckface and I told him to shut up. Then Brian punched me in the stomach and I slapped the side of his head. It toppled him. He was smaller than me. When he sat up, his eyes narrow and wet, he said we were no longer brothers and vowed not to speak to me ever again.

Two years later, I got caught with a hard-on in the shower after gym. I wasn't even looking at anybody, my eyes were closed, but Bill Rasmussen announced the news to the locker room. I could've taken him, easy, and I didn't. It was mostly true what he said about me and I froze up.

When I came home from school, Dad was singing to the twins in the kitchen. Old Beatles songs. I went in there. He crooned at the three of us, clapped beats out on the counter. At first, we held back our laughter because we liked it and didn't want to give him any kind of victory, but he kept going so long, and he won. We had to laugh to stop him. He'd finished Bonnie's infrastructure. "Tomorrow's payday," he told us. He sliced up some apples and made us triple-decker grilled cheeses in a pan.

Timmy, newly vegan, gave his sandwich to Brian. Brian said, "No way this means you get Claudia."

Claudia Berman was a high-haired, flat-chested baton-twirler who lived across the street. Sometimes she called and asked for Timmy. Sometimes Brian.

"I think she likes me," Timmy said.

Brian said, "No one likes you."

"Well, I definitely like her, even if she doesn't like me. She has kind eyes, I think."

"She thinks you're an asshole, Timmy."

When Dad brought the new Bonnie to Good Parent, they slapped him on the back and called him a visionary. Then they said they needed something much simpler: Dad had designed the mini-tract to take any type of food you could jam into the doll's mouth—he figured that little girls would thrill to feed Bonnie the same food that they themselves were eating—but Good Parent figured they would do better with a Bonnie who was only able to digest a perishable, vitamin-enriched protein paste that required refrigeration and could be sold for five dollars a tube. So they told him to dumb down the mini-tract and create a paste. "Something that smells good," they told him.

That night at dinner, Dad gave us the lowdown. "Spilled milk," he said. "Another year. No big thing."

Mom rolled her eyes.

After another couple years, Timmy's studying the Gnostics, Brian's a hand-to-hand weapons geek, possibly dealing, and Mom's on a semester's suspension from Lincoln Elementary for saying "Hispanic" instead of "Latino" at an assembly during Diversity Week. No one in Waukegan is gay and I've lost all vestigial interest in the bodies of women, even movie stars.

And Dad's done just what Good Parent asked him to do, but now they have a problem with the quality of the paste: it's too good. Good Parent needs to be able to count on Bonnie's obsolescence. They want a paste that will slowly destroy Bonnie's insides so that after eleven months Bonnie will break and the little girls will have to buy a new

Bonnie, maybe a new and improved Bonnie, maybe even a Bonnie that can digest real food.

Dad gets back to work and, six cloistered months of labor later, he's invented a nontoxic, corrosive molecule with which he augments the paste. With each successive paste-feeding, the plastic gaskets in Bonnie's mini-tract dissolve a little. It's doubly brilliant because the more Bonnie's gaskets dissolve, the less she can "digest," which means not only that she needs to consume increasingly larger volumes of paste to stay out of the caloric red zone, but that her gaskets wear away at a higher rate as time marches on. When Dad graphs "Paste Consumption over Time" and superimposes it on "Mass of Gaskets over Time," the effect is gorgeous: a lopsided X.

In the week between his completion of the paste and its presentation to Good Parent, he prints out hundreds of these graphs and papers the walls of the house with them. For the hell of it, he adds a speculative z axis titled "Geometric Escalation of Concern" to the graphs he hangs in the family room. It's the most promising gesture he's made since singing "Please, Please Me" in the kitchen, and we all fall under the spell of it. Even Mom. That Saturday, she breaks into her savings to take us shopping for jeans at the outlet mall and we share food-court Chinese off styrofoam platters.

"We're fine," she says. She buys herself new lipstick and gets it all over our faces, our necks.

Good Parent tells Dad that the paste smells too good, that their initial idea of an entirely good-smelling paste lacked foresight, that since the gist of the Bonnie doll is that she'll help prevent girls from acquiring eating disorders, Bonnie's food should definitely smell good at the outset (though not so good that Bonnie would want to binge on it), but when the food is processed and turned into "excrement" or "vomit," it should smell bad—or at least not like strawberries—lest the Bonnie product send a mixed message to its at-risk consumers, which could mean lawsuits. They tell him that as long as he's going to take the time to fix the paste-smell situation, he might as well also figure out a way to cause an excess of hair to form on the bodies of Bonnies who refuse to eat and won't cut back on their overzealous exercise routines.

By now, it's been four years since Dad finished the mini-tract. Our savings are gone and our family is living off my mother's teaching salary. Mom's well on her way to a blackboard-related repetitive-motion injury, the twins are about to turn fourteen, and I'm at the peak of my adolescence and I need Zoloft and better Levi's and I can't stop thinking about cars and how all the other kids get cars when they graduate high school, which isn't true at all but feels true. I've never kissed anyone with tongue and I doubt I ever will.

Dad seems fine, maybe a little sleepless, but otherwise fine, and then he goes out for smokes one day and forgets to wear pants. The bulls haul him back to us. Timmy and I meet them out front.

"This poor, sick man your father?" says one of them.

"Get some fricken slacks on him or we charge his ass," says the other one.

Timmy runs inside.

"Leave our property," I tell them.

"Listen to this pillow-biter! Doesn't know when he's getting a kindness done to him."

"Have a little mercy. He's the son of an indecent exposer: apple and the tree."

"Fruit and the tree's more like it. Stay off the streets of Waukegan."

The cops drive away. Dad goes straight to the attic.

Despite the brush with public indecency, he finishes designing his revolutionary Mustache & Happy Trail SkinStrips the very next day. For his edification, and to show our allegedly continuing support for the Bonnie project, Mom uses her discount to buy him a new hardcover bestseller called *Beyond Fat and Thin: Dispelling the Myths Surrounding Eating Disorders* by eating-disorder specialist Russell Randbert, PhD.

This turns out to be a mistake.

In his book, Randbert argues that girls acquire eating disorders when they feel out of control. He explains that binging, purging, starving, and reckless exercise are not symptoms of a negative self-body image but means by which girls can gain a temporary sense of autonomy over their bodies. The negative self-body image, Randbert says, comes *after* the dysfunctional eating behavior manifests: "I'm too fat" is the easiest explanation a girl has to offer herself for why she is engaging in behavior that only happens to make her thin. "I'm too fat" is not only a "delusion," Randbert quips, but a "delusional motive," as can be inferred by observing that psychotherapies that address body-image issues invariably fail, whereas those that focus on control tend to succeed.

Once Dad's finished with the book, I read it. His marginalia are crackpot for the most part: frowny faces and hanging stick-men, short-fused sticks of dynamite, mathematical equations containing exclamation points. On the inside covers are 3-D diagrams of alien digestive systems, their labels done in block letters: A NINE-CHAMBER YOU-LOSE STOMACH, THIS STUPID ESOPHAGUS, THE WHEREFORE ART MY BOWEL. But then, at the end of the book, fountain-penned in the half page of white space under the acknowledgements, I find this: "Although a given toddling-to-preadolescent girl will, to a certain degree, control her Bonnie, the manner in which Bonnie obsolesces will undermine any *sense* of control the girl could have otherwise acquired through the exercise of Bonnie as self-metaphor. I fail I fail I fail them all." The handwriting is deceptively neat.

I pass the book on to Mom. She skims it. Then she throws it in the fire.

My father—like Nobel, I'd like to think—becomes fatalistic. His creativity gets blocked.

He locks himself in the attic laboratory and bleats, and sometimes there are smashing sounds. He can't figure out how to make a paste that starts out smelling good, ends up smelling bad, and corrodes the mini-tract all the while. He drinks, fights with Mom. He becomes impotent. Mom, in her loneliness, has made of me a reluctant confidant is how I know that. She and I start scarfing pints of ice cream together at midnight. I get cavities, she gets heavy. All of us dread dinner. Dad comes to the table and refuses to eat, saying, "I don't deserve it, I don't deserve your food," while Mom looks to me for shrugs of allied contempt. Our father gets so skinny, the neighbors start talking cancer. We let them talk, fearful that any sympathy they might have for us will lessen if they find out he's insane. We despise him and we don't even fear him.

What makes it worse is how so much of his falling apart gets realized through the attempts he makes to put himself back together. Like some pop-eyed Manson Family ascetic, he invents rules about watching television. For example: he must change the channel once and only once every ten minutes, whether or not a commercial is on. Next it's his bowels: he has to sit on the toilet from 9:30 a.m. to 9:50 a.m. and cannot sit on the toilet at any other time of day, regardless of his needs. Every morning at eleven, he plugs the bathroom sink and fills it with near-scalding water, then plunges the first joint of his pinkie in, holds it there for thirty seconds, and doesn't breathe. He's no fool, my dad. He knows he's making self-destructive gestures and, worse than that, he knows that nearly scalding your pinkie is a half-assed way to go about self-destruction. One morning, I come across him in the hallway outside the bathroom and he puts his arm around me, says, "Mike, your dad's a pussy. A real pussy."

Brian, at the bottom of the stairs, overhears this. "Yeah!" he yells up. "And a fuckface, too. You want to slap me, now, Mike, you scrawny bitch? I don't forget."

Dad says, "Son."

Brian says, "What? You're gonna protect him?" Then he skims a ninja star at the ceiling and tears the stair carpet with a bowie knife.

* * *

By the third year of his inventor's block, Dad can't find the deep end he'd otherwise go off of and he becomes obsessed with the origin of the phrase, convinced that *deep end* refers to the deep end of a pool, which is not a thing he can reconcile with off-ness or on-ness. It's all he talks about, if he talks at all. He doesn't show up at the dinner table anymore. He plucks a rusted chain-mail blouse from a dumpster by the theater and wears it all day without an undershirt, eye-droppers lemon juice onto his chest before bed. One afternoon, he bites a small chunk of flesh off the back of his left hand and, every succeeding afternoon, rips the scab off with his teeth, then breaks out the dropper and does the raw red derm like it was his nipples.

On the eve of my brothers' last day as sophomores, Claudia Berman rings the bell. They barrel down the stairs and Brian trips on the way and says Timmy tripped him. Timmy makes for the front lawn and Brian puts a tackle to Timmy's knees, flips him over, and starts whaling on his face. I run outside to pull the skull-sapper out of Brian's calf-sheath while Timmy, spouting purple from the nose and mouth, Brian's forearm pressed against his trachea, flails his arms around, trying to get hold of something. He gets Brian's ear. The left one. It comes off. Brian falls backward, on top of me, holding his earhole, bleeding less than I'd expect. Claudia screams Timmy's name and runs inside for towels.

It's the end of Brian's alpha. It's the end of Timmy's optimism. It's the end of a lot of things.

Dad takes bedding to the attic and sleeps on a slab.

Mom hits the local singles bars on Fridays.

Months pass.

Brian's prosthetic ear—which the insurance company covers only half the cost of, thus engendering the misappropriation of tuition for my first year of college and destroying, once and for all, any false hopes I might have had of getting even a used Kia—starts coming loose on cold days and finally falls plum off after the Winter Formal Dance, while he's walking to an Inspiration Point–bound Chevy with Claudia, for whom he knows he's consolation meat. I graduate high school, turn eighteen years old, and when I try to enlist in the Coast Guard, they won't have me. As I walk out of the recruiting office, the guy who'd been queued up behind me calls me a homo and I pretend not to hear because no one cares what I do anyway. Timmy wears all black all the time and, with hot irons and scalpels stolen from Dad's lab, he mutilates his thighs and lower abdomen to absolve his guilt about Brian's ear, which Brian keeps milking, the guilt. Mom starts dating a rhubarb farmer from Kenosha, telling me about it. She says he's gentle, and clubfooted, but he loves her.

Our life, by this time, has become a cartoon. Maybe it's an X-rated cartoon, and maybe it would seem more real if, in my bumbling, fleshy way, I weren't trying so hard to make a prime-time morality play of it, but still: if on a certain moonlit evening in Arizona, I'd seen my mother drop off a cliff and go *SPLAT*, I doubt I'd be very surprised to find her cooking eggs in our kitchen the following morning. Rather, I'd be surprised to find her cooking, but if she were standing beside the stove, chewing her nails or talking to herself, I'd only squint a little before I believed it. And yes, it's true that *The Catcher in the Rye* took ten years to write and no one's cured cancer yet, but a Barbie with a working digestive system? We let him turn us into Looney Tunes for a high-concept doll?

On my nineteenth birthday, Dad hands me the card-stock receipt for a six-month subscription to *Hustler*, a block of two-by-four, and a tube of vitamin-enriched protein paste. He invites me into the lab and sits me down before a lathe-drill, props the two-by-four under the bit. Hand on the grip, eyes engoggled, he tells me, "You're eighteen now. It's about time you and your dad had a talk about girls and technology."

"Okay," I say.

"They don't go together," he says. "Look at me, Mike. Do you see?"

I look at him. He looks sick. He looks embarrassed. A pearl of saliva is drying whitely in the cleft of his chin. He smells like Mad Dog and burned plastic.

"I hate you," I tell him.

"I hate me, too," he says.

I start crying, which is pretty typical.

"It's nothing to cry about, kiddo. Well, maybe it is. But wouldn't it be a whole lot worse if I thought I was a good man? It would be irresponsible. It would lack rigor."

He aligns the drill. When he moves, the chainmail against his chest-skin makes a noise like velcro. He picks at his scabs, forgets I'm there with him.

"What do you want, Dad?"

He snaps to, coughs something up and swallows it.

"Manage a restaurant," he says. "Sell insurance. Harvest rhubarb like that Swedish guy. For chrissakes, though, don't try to battle eating disorders with new technologies. Don't create systems. Describe systems. The ideal doll is a girl, so don't bother making dolls or trying to improve girls. I'll tell you what. I'm not God. I'm not even any kind of Frankenstein. When you were born I bawled my eyes out because I knew I couldn't do better. And then the twins. Them, too. But not a daughter. Never had one. How can I describe a girl if I've never had a daughter?"

"I'm gay."

"I guess that makes sense."

"It's got nothing to do with sense."

"Well, either way, I got you the wrong subscription. And I've fastened the wrong drill bit. Do you have a boyfriend?"

"Yes," I lie.

"Is he nice to you? I mean, does he treat you well?"

"He's okay."

"I suppose I've never met him because you're embarrassed to bring anyone to the house… Listen. Don't settle for a bunch of nonsense. You're better than that. I don't deserve to have you as a son. You're a shining example of goodness and tolerance and I'm this crazy piece of shit over here. I'm trouble. It's a privilege to even be despised by you—"

"Dad."

"Ditch that boyfriend and find yourself a good one. Adopt a baby girl. Teach kindergarten. Don't worry about humanity. Love *humans*, boy-o, be close to them. Let humanity work things out for itself. You'll be a happy man. You know you enliven me? You're an endless well of hope!"

He drapes his arm over my shoulders, squeezes. "Do you think you were born gay, or was it the way you were raised?"

"Born," I say.

Then, as suddenly as Kekule's snake became a benzene ring, Dad theoretically solves the problem of the smell of paste. His face twitches.

"Son of mine!" he says. "My son!"

He figures out that changing the makeup of the paste isn't the answer, but that copper-coating small portions of the plastic joints in the mini-tract will cause the digested paste—in its present form—to stink up real bad upon its regurgitation or elimination, and now all he has to work out is (1) how to push forth the hairs in the follicles in the Mustache & Happy Trail SkinStrips that he's embedded in the rubber over Bonnie's upper lip and below her navel, and (2) how to trigger them at the appropriate time, i.e., when Bonnie becomes "anorexic."

To actually sprout the hairs, it's a simple matter of activating microgram weights and polymer pulleys not dissimilar to those used in the mini-tract system. As for the situation-appropriate triggering of the sprouting activation, Dad decides to plant a function on a microchip, the workings of which are a little bit beyond me, but entail the delicate balancing of a paste-intake equation with a limb-movement equation. A large enough imbalance translates to "anorexia" and, depending on the degree of the imbalance, commands certain weights to shift and certain pulleys to pull so that one or both of the embedded Mustache & Happy Trail SkinStrips can do what they were made to do.

Now it's only a matter of time.

*   *   *

One summer evening three months later, our family, minus Dad, plus the limping rhubarb farmer, is eating barbecue at the picnic table in the backyard. Brian sits to the right of Timmy, and whenever Timmy speaks Brian says, "Who's talking? I know I heard a voice, but for some reason I can't tell where that voice is coming from. Funny," he says, "I can't seem to tell where just about any sound I hear comes from."

It's cooling down outside. A rabbit chases another rabbit until he catches her on the cement patio and they have sex until they become distracted, at which point they stop and stare at the sky and become distracted and start having sex. Moths bang their heads on lamps. Squirrels chew. Mosquitoes wobble. Fireflies incandesce.

The farmer's wearing a checked bow tie. He's had his shoes and socks off since he lit the grill, and Mom keeps admiring how "brave" and "open" he is for showing off the naked lump. Cutting into some sausage, he asks me if I'm interested in doing man's work, and Mom, bouncing in his lap so her jowls sway, leans toward me, karate-chop hand at the side of her mouth. She chokes down potato salad and stage-whispers, "Olaf has big plans for you. He's a man of *ideas*." The farmer's eyebrows rise and fall, rise and fall.

"I'm a homosexual," I tell the table.

The farmer says, "Why do you want to go and say something like that at dinner?"

Timmy raises his fork over his head and jams it into the soft side of his own elbow. Misses the arteries. He twists the fork, then pulls it out of his arm and reaches across the table, directing the thing at the farmer. Tines drip blood onto Olaf's sausage. Timmy says, "Don't threaten my brother, Olaf."

"Who said that?" Brian says.

Olaf says, "I wasn't threatening no one, young man."

Timmy drops the fork. "I'm sorry," he says. "I misunderstood." Sucking on his arm, he steps out of his sandals. He goes to the patio and starts kicking it hard, toes first. The rabbits keep pumping.

"Oh, Timmy," Mom says.

"That's the kind of thing," Olaf says. "That temper of yours. Your boy's temper," he says to Mom. "That's the kind of thing lost your other boy his ear, now isn't it." Olaf establishes eye contact with Brian in what seems to be a gesture of solidarity.

Brian says, "Don't pity *me*, you milky fucken lame."

We're quiet for a minute, plate-gazing. It's on me to break the silence.

I tell them, "I'm okay with myself." I tell them, "I believe the world is mostly good, a self-repairing blemish on the face of God, an open system moving away from chaos, toward organization. I believe that each of its many seemingly awful components are essential to its betterment and will, in distant, perfect retrospect, be understood as wholly functional." I'm in the middle of telling them, "To hate him requires us to hate ourselves and we don't need to hate ourselves, we can have a little faith," when there is a cracking sound and Olaf's head smacks the table and Mom screams and Brian stands and Timmy crawls back to us and I look up to see Dad, free of stage armor, holding a blood-covered Bonnie by the waist. The blood is Olaf's. The victory is Dad's. He raises the doll, high, over his head.

It's the first time we've seen her with all her skin on. Dad tosses her to me, and when I catch her against my chest, she nearly undoes the scoop of my arms.

"She feels heavy," I say.

"She feels *very* heavy," Dad says, "but boy is she beautiful!"

I pass Bonnie to Brian, who passes her to Timmy, who says thank you, and Brian doesn't ask who said thank you, and Mom gets smelling salts from the first-aid kit and Olaf snaps awake and asks what happened to my noggin and Mom tells him that he banged it on the patio after tripping on his foot and Dad winks at her and that's when we know they'll patch it up.

* * *

Negotiations take seventeen days. Good Parent offers Dad a touch over half a million for the patents. In the end, he goes with Hasbro for something in the low seven-figure range.

Bonnies line the shelves of all the major chains by Thanksgiving. They cost ninety-nine dollars a pop and come with a free tube of paste. By mid-December, parents across the country take to camping out in toy-store parking lots the night before doll shipments come in. A couple predawn fistfights are reported in Lubbock. A Hasbro truck hijacked at gunpoint en route to St. Louis. A Christmas Eve riot in Denver.

Mom is liposuctioned, chin-tucked, retires early. Brian gets an ear with a built-in phone. Timmy is pierced, tattooed, has velvet-tipped fiberglass Pan's horns implanted in his forehead. I can't decide what I want, so I'm given a red Volkswagen and a condo where I lose my virginity to a skinny fatman who's gone by sunrise. Dad builds a private kindergarten in Evanston, pays me to hang out and tell stories to the kids before naptime. I keep fucking up the happy endings, but they fall asleep anyway.

CONSIDERING THE BITTERSWEET END OF SUSAN FALLS

CHAPTER 130,020

DREAMS ABOUT FLYING

Susan Falls hates the flying dreams. She wakes up and she can't walk, which is beside the point. She can't walk when she wakes from non-flying dreams, either. The flying dreams speak of an unconscious obsession with walking, her therapist tells her.

The therapist tells her about the stages of death and dying, harping mostly on the denial stage. What the rest of the stages are isn't important. What is important is that when the therapist tells her about the stages, he does so, he says, because he does not think the loss of Susan's legs has been properly mourned. To Susan, this is nonsense.

She lost her legs as a baby, in the jungle, to gangrene, after the leopard bit her. So she'd never really had them to begin with, at least not long enough to require her to mourn their loss. Besides, what upsets her isn't that she can't walk, but that she has dreams which would seem to suggest that somewhere deep inside she wants to walk, when nowhere non-deep inside does she.

And tacky dreams at that. The flying is always travel-channel scenic: Susan soaring over the ocean or the mountains, between skyscrapers with puffy-cloud reflections on their windows. It might be different, might point to something real or individual about Susan, if she flew over the Gaza Strip or post-NATO Belgrade. Mazar-i-Sharif. She never dreams of what she wants to, though, no matter how hard she thinks about whatever that might be before she goes to sleep. Last night, for instance, she thought of Carla Ribisi's ass for nearly an hour, and ended up cruising over the Grand Canyon at four thousand feet.

CHAPTER 130,021

THE ACCIDENT, PRETTY TO THINK SO

Susan and her mother are in the all-white kitchen, drinking orange juice, waiting for Susan's father to come downstairs before eating the egg dish that Jiselle, the distant cousin who came to America to be an au pair but could not find a job as an au pair and so has become the cook, has made. Jiselle is on the balcony, smoking cigarettes.

"You don't look so good today, Sus," Susan's mother says. "Bad dreams?"

Susan nods, staring through the glass table at the glass table's frosted glass base. Where the kitchen isn't white or transparent, it's mirrored, and if she looks up, she risks being confronted with a vision of herself first thing in the morning.

"Was it about the accident again?" says Susan's mother.

Susan shuts her eyes with a force that, had she any magic in her, would be great enough to knock the whole penthouse into orbit. Susan's mother likes to talk about the accident. She likes to say, "Susan would do well to talk about the accident, herself." She says it to everyone.

"I asked if you dreamed of the accident," says Susan's mother.

"The accident?" says Susan. "How could I remember the accident well enough to dream about it, *anyway*?"

"Now don't—"

"Don't what?" Susan says. "Don't mention your lackluster mothering style? Your irresponsibility? Don't question the sanity and goodness of a

26

woman who'd not only leave her baby on a jungle floor but let the wounds she suffered by the leopard's fangs fester and—"

"Oh, *the leopard*. Isn't it pretty to think so!" Susan's mother says. Susan's mother sneezes, angrily, and screams for Susan's father.

Susan's father, dressed in beige suit-pants with braces half-braced, his untucked U-shirt flapping at his belt-line, thumps down the spiral staircase to the kitchen. "What is it?" he says. "What's happened?"

"She's talking about leopards again."

"Oh my God."

"Forget it," Susan says. "Forget it."

"Susan, do you need to go back to the hospital?" Susan's father says.

"You're still in the denial stage," Susan tells her father. "Dr. Fleem told me to expect that from you. But what I want to know is: what about me? What about me?"

"Damn that Fleem," Susan's mother says, and to her husband: "Call the Medicar."

"Frances, just hold your horses for just a second here, honey." Susan's father pulls a cigar from somewhere in his pants and fondles it against the beam of a mean halogen bulb. He says, "Now Susan. What was it you were saying? Something about leopards?"

"No. Nothing," Susan says. "I wasn't saying anything about leopards."

"How did you lose your legs, Susan?" Susan's father says.

Susan is crying. Her mother is staring at her. Her mother looks like a bug and Susan does not want to one day look like her mother. "A car," Susan says.

The egg dish that Jiselle made is getting cold and it looks very good, too, very tasty. Last night, Jiselle told Susan that she'd been formulating this egg recipe, experimenting with temperature, testing various sauces, spices, and coagulants for nearly six months, and that it had, at last, become perfect; there was not a similar egg dish all the world round, at least not one Jiselle had heard of, and while it was true that the appeal of eggs for breakfast tended to be their banality, Jiselle believed the dish, novel though it was, would, owing to its deliciousness, prove itself to have serious staying power. Last night, Jiselle told Susan that, in her most private thoughts, she called the thing Jiselle's Delicious Egg Dish and that, of late, she had something of a dream, and this dream (in sum) was of Jiselle's Delicious Egg Dish becoming vastly popular over the next twenty years, worldwide popular, and thereby eventually becoming a banal egg dish itself, at which point the dish's name would be simplified, shortened, to Eggs Jiselle.

And now it was getting cold, Jiselle's Delicious Egg Dish. The auburn-tinged glaze atop the whites was becoming a filmy gel.

"She's only just saying it," Susan's mother says. "She doesn't really mean it. She's only just saying it."

"Now, now, Frances. Susan, tell us more. You said 'a car.' What about a car?"

"I was playing in the street with Pedro. A car ran us over and I lost my legs."

"How old were you?"

"It was last year."

"How old were you, Susan? was the question."

"I was thirteen when the car hit me. It was the day before my birthday. I turned fourteen the day they hacked off my legs."

"Who hacked them off?"

"The doctors."

"Where did the doctors hack your legs off?"

"In a rondavel."

"Susan!" Susan's mother says.

"My legs were infected, Mom, and after lightly anesthetizing me with an orally administered paste of palm wine and pulverized valerian root, the doctors, as you like to call them, chopped off my legs with their rusty machetes in a dung-floored, thatch-roofed rondavel."

"Medicar!"

"Just kidding," Susan says. "It was at Children's Memorial."

"Liar. You're lying. You don't believe what you just said."

"I need to go to school now," Susan says.

"You need to go back to high school, young lady."

"I hate high school."

"High school was the most glorious time of your life."

"I need to go to school."

"Not until…"

"Please, Mommy. I'm sorry. I love you. You didn't leave me to the teeth of that dastardly leopard. Please, let's just eat our Eggs Jiselle and get on with the day."

"Eggs Jiselle! Did you hear that, Frances?"

"She sure can turn a phrase, Mike, can't she, our girl Susan. Little smartypants. How much do you love Mommy?"

"This much."

CHAPTER 130,022

MIDRASH IN THE MORNING, NOWHERE DEEP INSIDE DOES SHE

Susan has the duration of the ride to campus to do yesterday's assignment for Media Studies 761: Consuming God. She takes Genesis Rabbah, a book of midrash, from her bag, and reads a story about God and Adam that her professor has asked her to present to the class this afternoon. He wants her to frame it as "the first ever buyer-empowerment scheme."

The story: Before there was an Eve, Adam was lonely and bored and sad, and, to fascinate him, God revealed the future of the world, taking care, as He did so, to remove all episodes that would occur within the span of Adam's lifetime. Though God's plan worked at first, Adam eventually grew distracted by his loneliness again. God reconsidered showing Adam his own (Adam's own) future life, but judged, for the second and final time, that doing so would be a grave misstep, and instead chose to try His hand at improvisation. Rather than continuing to show Adam what would be, God showed him what could be, were one event that was slated to occur one way to instead occur another way.

If I allow that Adam was able to transfer 70 years of his life to David, then I should probably allow that he was able to transfer more, but chose not to. And if, for the sake of argument, I allow that investing 80 years in D, rather than 70, would have further glorified A's legacy, I would then have to wonder why A didn't relinquish those extra 10 years (1%) of his own time on earth. ?Maybe because A knew the extra glory supplied wouldn't really pay off? ?what would that imply? ?that even a relatively small bit of life on earth (1% of the gross) can be, by a certain calculable quotient, worth more than a higher quality of already assured immortality? ?That A kept the extra ten years because the betterment of your life's story becomes, after a certain point, less valuable than living itself? ?Too pretty to think so?

…Except, if I allow that between the ages of 70 and 80, D's potential contribution to A's glory was not significant enough to

The story of David—who slew Goliath, loved Bathsheba, and, as its strongest king, made of Israel an empire—was particularly moving to Adam, despite his knowledge that it was only a could-be, that David would, as originally foretold by God, die at birth. Only a few words into the Psalms, which God had spelled out for him in clouds, Adam found himself weeping at the thought that David would never write them, and he transferred seventy years of his allotted thousand to David, so that David would survive beyond birth and do everything that, before the transfer, only he could have done.

What Susan believes: Adam gave life to David out of love for David.

What Susan would like to believe: Adam gave life to David out of love for the world—gave David life so that the world would not be deprived of David.

What she is being asked by her professor to spin: Adam gave life to David out of love for Adam. Being that Adam was the first man, Susan plans to tell the class, all men would be of him, and being that Israel, under David's reign, would be the world's greatest kingdom, Davidic-era Israel would be the greatest achievement to come of Adam's creation. Susan would say that Adam, as he read the Psalms in the sky, was not moved as much by their beauty as by how their beauty would affect his legacy. She would say that Adam wept at the possibility that his legacy could be so glorious, yet wouldn't be so glorious if he failed to take action. She would quip, "And therefore, Adam's giving of life would be better described as spending, and better yet as investing, for its purpose was to ensure a future payoff." If the class was with her—they rarely were—she planned to close with a joke about "the intricacies of calculating a time-lost to glory-increased ratio." With or without the joke, she was confident she would get an A.

What Susan Falls is considering for extra credit: how Adam, who was born a man, and who, without his Eve, without knowing he was a male in the male/female dichotomy—and so knowing nothing of human reproduction—could know that other men would come from him, rather than from the word of God, where Adam had come from.

As the limo exits the Drive at 55th, Susan sets the extra credit aside for later consideration and begins to write in the margins of Genesis Rabbah. While doing so, she is struck by the idea that Adam might be a lot like her—his seventy years her lower body, David her brain. Some time, early on, when she knew things in a pure sense, she might have made a deal with God, an investment of her earthly legs in a transcendent mind with high-capacity intellect. It was pretty to think so.

So pretty, in fact, that she doesn't realize the limo has stopped, has been stopped for minutes, until Jake, the driver, lowers the separator and pronounces her name. "Susan," he says, "are you not well? Would you like me to wheel you to class today?"

warrant A's extra 1% investment (over and above investing in ages 0–70), though between the ages of 60 and 70 the extra 1% was warranted, it might imply that the effect and/or importance of a person decreases as that person's age increases. And if I allow that, I should also allow that the extra 1% could have been detrimental. Maybe if you stick around for too long after you've peaked, you retroactively lessen the importance/effect of what you did before and during your peak: Maybe A knew that if D lived past 70, D would have—either by means of wrongdoing or even simple inefficacy— besmirched the memories others would have of him after his death, thereby marring any reflections that would be cast on his earlier accomplishments, which would leave him less cherished overall, and finally decrease the sum of the glory he'd have otherwise added to A's legacy. ?So then D was made to die when he did in order to save his and A's story from being sullied? ?Too ugly not to think so?

CHAPTER 130,023

CONSIDERING THE UTILITY OF BLUE SNOWPANTS

Susan Falls thinks Carla Ribisi has a big ass and that Carla Ribisi's big ass is beautiful and that Carla does not know it. And Carla Ribisi is always wearing blue nylon snowpants. The intended effect of the snowpants is to disguise the bigness of the ass in bigger-ness, Susan Falls thinks. It is a complicated trick. It begins with a syllogism. The first premise is that anyone who wears snowpants appears to have a big ass:

> 1. Anyone who wears snowpants appears to have a big ass.
>
> 2. Carla Ribisi wears snowpants.
>
> ∴ Carla Ribisi appears to have a big ass.

The trick comes of the word *appears*. *Appears* allows for, but does not necessitate, visual trickery. Things that allow for but do not necessitate other things are tricky, and tricky things engender consideration. Things that allow for but do not necessitate trickery itself are even trickier, and these things engender much richer consideration. The richer the consideration engendered by a thing, the longer the time one will spend considering that thing. Consider the following hypothetical situation:

> Susan Falls has just started dating Carla Ribisi, and the two go shopping for a T-shirt for Carla. They go into the changing room and Carla tries on one of two stretchy V-necks she's deciding between, a red one, say, a warm kind of red, like that of the hair under Susan's arms. The T-shirt looks good and Susan Falls tells Carla Ribisi that the T-shirt looks good.
>
> Carla tells Susan Falls that this is the first time she's shared a changing room with another woman since the long-lost days when she used to shop at indoor malls with her mother. Susan

Falls blushes. Carla Ribisi removes T-shirt #1, and, reaching for T-shirt #2, looks at Susan Falls, longingly(?), and says, "Blusher."

Being called on blushing causes dollar-coin-size spots of the same shade of blush as Susan Falls's face to appear on Susan Falls's neck.

Carla pulls her head up through T-shirt #2. "I'm sorry," she says to Susan Falls. "I didn't mean to make you embarrassed when I said you were a blusher."

The dollar coins darken in time with Susan's ecstasy.

Susan's ecstasy is like neither a balloon nor a hat pin, but like a hat pin's entrance and movement, under the guidance of a cotton-gloved birthday clown, through the skin of a balloon.

There is something that is so Goddamned hot about Carla Ribisi considering and, further, discussing any effect that she has had on Susan Falls. Let alone in a Nordstrom dressing room, trying on T-shirts.

T-shirt #2 looks good, but in a different way than the way in which T-shirt #1 looked good.

"So?" Carla wants to know.

"It looks good," Susan says. "It makes your tits look bigger."

"Hmm." Carla doesn't know if she likes that. She has big-enough-looking tits already. Showing them off, she has decided at different times in her past, makes her look trampy. "That's good?" she says. "That it makes my tits look bigger?"

"You have beautiful tits, Carla. The T-shirt just brings it out."

"Do you mean to say that my tits are essentially beautiful, and that the appearance of more of my tits reveals more essential beauty?"

"Yes!" Susan says, now thrilled to damp underthings by Carla's obsessive parsing and analysis of a sentence Susan has spoken.

"Or do you mean to say," Carla says, "that my tits are beautiful because they're big, and therefore my tits, upon looking bigger, appear more beautiful because 'you can't get enough of a good thing'—the good thing being the bigness of tits?"

"Are you making fun of me?"

"Not at all. I'm having fun with you. And attempting to choose between T-shirts at the same time. So which T-shirt's better?"

"I don't know that we can make informed choices about the T-shirts at this point, because now that we've spent so much more time on the one you're wearing than we did on the first one, we're probably invested in the one you're wearing, and—"

"I'm not gonna sweat that, Susan. Which one do you like better?"

"My opinion—"

"Your opinion isn't founded on a bedrock of rigorous analysis and therefore etc. etc. etc.?"

"You *are* making fun of me."

"I'm telling you that I want and will buy the T-shirt that *you* prefer," Carla says.

"Are you sure? Because you're saying it in this way that it sounds like maybe you're making fun of me." Susan Falls begins to shiver, and then she begins to cry—not really, but hypothetically.

Susan's hypotheticals often end sadly and hardly ever make their point with force. Disregarding the ever-present effect that the Wheelchair

Factor has on her confidence, the Sadly Ending Hypothetical Factor is the number one reason for why she can't bring herself to engage Carla Ribisi in conversation. But back to trickery:

The considerer will arrive at two interpretations of "Carla Ribisi appears to have a big ass," each one implicated by the other:

    A. The actual size of Carla Ribisi's ass cannot be
         known at this juncture (snowpantsed).

    B. Carla Ribisi's ass is a mystery.

Susan Falls has, by now, watched enough TV and studied enough social and cognitive psychology, she hopes, to soon fulfill her dream of becoming one half of a powerful and revered creative team at Leo Burnett. Susan knows about attribution. She knows self-perception theory. Susan knows that for every considerer, there is a specific amount of time, designated x, that must be spent considering a thing before the considerer becomes aware that she has spent time considering the thing. Moreover, Susan knows that after the considerer has considered an as-yet-neutral (unvalenced) thing for x, that thing will appear to the considerer—unless she is someone who suffers from terribly low self-esteem or clinical depression—to be a good (positively valenced) thing, for the (non-depressed, self-esteeming) considerer knows she wouldn't spend her time on a thing that wasn't good. Therefore, once **the mystery of Carla Ribisi's ass** has been considered for x, **the mystery of Carla Ribisi's ass** is good. And all good mysteries are good to solve, so **solving the mystery** is also good.

In order to **solve the mystery**—in order to see Carla Ribisi sans blue snowpants—one would have to spend time with Carla Ribisi, time enough to wind up in places where wearing snowpants would be out of the question: dressing rooms, beaches, showers, etc.

If Carla is a smarty—and Susan is sure that Carla must be, for Susan wouldn't otherwise waste so much time gawking at and thinking about her—then Carla, to ensure that any given considerer's x be met or surpassed, would stretch out this getting-to-know-Carla time for as long as possible before letting the considerer see her without snowpants, for in being kept from seeing what Susan will call Carla's **true ass** for x or longer, the considerer, always considering, would work the previously outlined self-perception algorithm, but this time the considerer would transpose **solving the mystery** with **true ass**, itself, such that not only would **to solve** be a good thing, but **true ass (the solution)** would also be good.

If Susan Falls were to create a successful television advertising campaign for Carla Ribisi's ass, the only two things she would have to figure out would be (1) how much time x equals for the average viewer, and (2) how to make the campaign compelling enough to keep the viewer considering it for $\geq x$.

If Susan Falls could pull that off, then even if the viewer were to start with a bias (e.g., "prefers big asses," "disdains small asses," "abjures jacked-up small asses that look bigger than they are"), the bias would, by campaign's end, be made irrelevant; whether im- or explicitly, the viewer would, once her x was met, reach the same conclusion as Susan:

Any ass worth spending all this time on must be some really good ass.

CHAPTER 130,024

AN ACCEPTANCE SPEECH

The other brilliant aspect of Carla Ribisi's blue snowpants is the sound they make when Carla enters a packed lecture hall, tardy, as she just has. Except people in college are never called *tardy*. The tardy go to high school. In college they're *late*, and this is the sort of thing—this usage of *tardy*—that Susan Falls wouldn't want to betray to Carla Ribisi upon their first actual meeting, but might come in handy later on, when Susan decides it's time to coyly let Carla know something that she wants the whole world to know.

Susan wants the whole world to know that she is a fifteen-year-old college freshman, but she doesn't want the world to know that she wants the world to know. She wants the world to see her as the sort of person who would not only make light of such an achievement on her part in conversation, but the sort of person who would *really not* consider it an achievement. She has a statement prepared in explanation of her being a fifteen-year-old college freshman, and she hopes that the topic will come up so that, one day soon, she can make the statement. This is the statement:

"Ah, well... When you're legless, no one wants to play with you, and TV gets boring fast, so all you have are books and time."

CHAPTER 130,025

SHIKKA SHIKKA, A GLIMPSE AT DEATH

Carla Ribisi enters the packed lecture hall, late for Logic I: An Introduction to Propositional Logic. Her snowpants make the snowpants sound. For every person present, the sound is the seed of a tree of uncountable self-perceptions relating to Carla, and, three strides in, Carla sees them all watching her, the professor included. He's clearing his throat, over and over.

Instead of making her way to her usual desk at the back of the lecture hall, she considerately heads to the nearest open seat, which is in the front row, between a deaf boy—in front of whom crouches an interpreter whose frantic signing distracts all hell out of the ASL-fluent Susan Falls—and Susan Falls, in front of whom is a wheelchair.

The interpreter signs, "Lecture interrupted by noise: S-H-I-K-K-A S-H-I-K-K-A," and Susan's mind twirls at the thought of signing sound for a deaf boy; at the thought of a deaf boy reading a sign for a sound; at what must be the sameness, to a deaf boy, of a sign for a sound and the sound the sign stands for. As if a sound were nothing more than the sign that stands for it.

Susan Falls shivers, like in the Nordstrom dressing room, but not hypothetically.

Carla Ribisi, while getting settled, inadvertently knocks loose the brake on Susan Falls's wheelchair. The wheelchair rolls down the moderately sloping floor of the lecture hall. "Oh God," whispers Carla Ribisi.

And Susan's shivering body starts to shake, only, with her mind still twirling, it's as if it isn't Susan's field of vision that's trembling, but that which is *in* her field of vision; the shaking of Susan's body seems to be the shaking of the classroom, and although a part of her knows that it's her body shaking—a part of her knows from experience that classrooms don't shake—the shaking of her body, rather than being expressed by the words *my body is shaking*, seems to be the expression *of* the words *my body is shaking*. And no part of her knows otherwise, not from experience. And the thought of this makes her shake harder.

And harder, until the rolling wheelchair strikes the wall beneath the tray of the chalkboard and clatters, and Susan startles out of the twirl. Stops shaking. Ideas can't get startled, is what she tells herself; they can't shake. Names don't shiver, she thinks. The world is not just a *word* with an *l*. Everything is fine. The twirl was an outcome of low blood sugar is all.

Look at things, Susan thinks, look at the wheelchair.

The wheelchair, having struck the wall, rolls back a few inches, as if the wall had struck it back, thus describing Newton's third law of motion—rather, *demonstrating* Newton's third law of motion... Or rather demonstrating *the effect of* Newton's third law of motion, for the wheelchair doesn't do the demonstrating, does it?—the *motion* of the wheelchair does the demonstrating... Newton's third law of motion, which is the name of a principle described by Newton, explains why the wheelchair describes the *motion* that it describes after striking the wall. And a shiver comes on.

Better to look at Carla, Susan thinks.

"Oh God," Carla says. "Oh no." The shiver wavers, quits. Susan never got to eat her breakfast is all, her Eggs Jiselle, she tells herself, and to quell the last tiny remnant of her panic, she inhales deeply, slows her blood down. What Carla hears is mounting rage.

"Oh God," says Carla Ribisi once more. "I'm really so sorry."

"It's okay, Carla," says Susan. And all her panic is gone.

"It's just, God, I mean, it's just that..."

"Carla?" Susan says.

"I hate today. Anything I do is wrong." Tears tremble in the scoops of Carla's eyelashes. One falls, splats against a thumbnail the color of a robin's egg, is atomized. More follow.

Everyone in the classroom continues to watch Carla Ribisi, even the professor. To defend Carla, Susan Falls glares at anyone who thinks she's strong enough to stand the eye contact. It is a sacrifice. Susan also wants to watch Carla cry.

"Let's leave," Susan says.

"Really?" Carla wipes snot on the arm of the matching blue parka that she hasn't yet removed. The parka's shell is a shiny kind of nylon, iridescent, and the snot is clear and perfectly straight, like some three-inch pinstripe. It performs miracles of refraction with the fluorescent light particles that fall through the grids of the ceiling panels. Now Carla leans in close and whispers, "But," and then she sees the line of snot. "God that's gross. I'm so gross..." She snorts a giggle.

"But what?" Susan Falls says.

Carla, still whispering: "How will we get out of here?"

"Just pull my chair over and we'll go."

"Everyone'll see."

"Fuck them," says Susan Falls. This is the first time, in her entire life, that she has employed an extra-cerebral profanity. Though in fantasy she has often used swear words, she has never spoken one. It feels good, and it occurs to Susan that, as stupid as most people sound when they use profanities, as stupid as she must have sounded just now, the feeling of power that just rushed through her, from inner labia to thyroglossal duct, the trace sensations leftover from just now, just now when she said the word *fuck*, make sounding stupid more than worthwhile.

"Fuck them, then," Carla Ribisi agrees, and it is the hottest mother-fucking thing Susan has ever heard.

CHAPTER 130,026

TWO BOUNCES IN LOGIC

Carla, eschewing the intricacies of the plan, crouches in front of Susan and, at the sign-language interpreter who is staring at her, makes this sound: "Tch."

"Hook your arms around my neck," Carla says.

"Really?" Susan says, but she's hardly gotten it out before she's in mid-air, her stumped thighs at Carla's soft sides, under her unzipped parka. It is two steps to the wheelchair, and so two bounces, from which Susan deduces that the thing rubbing against her is a navel piercing.

"Okay," says Carla. With one arm, she turns the wheelchair around, then lowers Susan into it, slowly, their bellybuttons meeting for a sliver of a second. "Do you need me to push you?"

"Not at all," Susan says. She follows Carla out of the lecture hall.

"Nice knowing you, ladies," says the professor.

CHAPTER 130,027

IN THE HALLWAY OUTSIDE OF LOGIC

"That guy's such an asshole," Carla says.

"He just wants to fuck you."

"I think maybe he wants to fuck *you*."

Susan's first impulse is to insist that what Carla has just said is not true at all. Instead, she says, "He probably wants to fuck us both, simultaneously. If he had it his way, he'd have us from behind, have us each bent over his office desk. He'd slide his dick in and out of your pussy, so he could watch your beautiful ass twitch beneath his sloppy thrusting, and

40

he'd keep his unclipped fingers rhythmlessly whittling away in me, so as not to obstruct the freak-show view of my lower half."

Carla gasps and does a cat stretch. "That made me tingle, what you just said," she says. "What's your name?"

"I'm Susan Falls."

"That's a pretty name. You want to go somewhere and get really fucked up?"

"I have my Moderns in Paris seminar in an hour but... Fuck it. I was born to get really fucked up with you, Carla."

CHAPTER 130,028

A DANCE, A DAMNED GOOD TIME TOGETHER

Carla rents a second-story room from a professor of music on 59th Street, just east of Ellis Avenue. The home is a standardly professorial Victorian, rampless. Carla wheels Susan through the alley and up to the garage. Punching out the command code on the number pad, Carla bounces a little and turns her head to smile at Susan, twice. "That's my Ali Baba dance," she says. The garage door opens. "Have you ever smoked opium?"

Susan considers telling a lie, but chooses not to. "No. Never."

"Good," Carla says. She wheels Susan into a corner of the garage and crouches down in front of the chair, the tip of her ponytail touching Susan's half-lap. "Wrap around me," Carla says. Susan obeys, lets her hands fall where they may on Carla's chest. Carla stands up.

"You're strong, Carla. How'd you get so strong?"

"I speedskate."

Rather than remarking on any number of the positive effects that she imagines speedskating would have on the ass of Carla, Susan utters a simple "Wow," but her face is pressed against Carla's face, and she feels Carla's face get hot, as if Susan *had* remarked on the likely effects of speed-skating. Susan likes that.

Carla brings Susan up the stairs to her room. There aren't any chairs. "Where do you want to be?"

"The bed's fine. If you can get me somewhere near the headboard, so I could lean..." she is saying, but Carla is already getting her somewhere near the headboard so she can lean.

"Good?"

"Good."

"How old are you, Susan?"

"What?"

"You seem older than most freshmen."

"Actually, I'm fifteen."

"Wow, you're like one of these genius kids who basically skips high school, aren't you?"

"Ah well...When you're legless—"

"That's really hot, Susan."

CHAPTER 130,029

OPIUM

It doesn't matter that the opium came as a gift from Dan Batner, this totally evil ex-boyfriend who Carla had met at an MBA mixer she'd accidentally wound up at last semester. It doesn't matter that he gave it to her last week. His reason for giving it to her—to let her know that, had she not decided he was such an evil young man and then told him to stay away from her, she could have still been with the only opium dealer on campus, and likely the only opium dealer in the tristate area, had she not been so cold—doesn't matter.

It doesn't matter, either, that the opium is not opium, but rather Nopium, an incense that Dan Batner mail-ordered for $19.99 per forty-ounce brick off an ad in the back of a glossy head magazine. Nor does it matter that the black brick of Nopium isn't crumbly/gummy in the same way that opium is crumbly/gummy: doesn't matter because any underclassman at the U of C who'd have researched opium's texture on the internet—no U of C underclassmen had ever had opium in hand—would have only found words such as "crumbly/gummy" to describe opium's texture, and words like "crumbly/gummy" could really mean anything within reason if you thought about them hard enough, anyway. Plus, Nopium smells like real opium, which is a smell that anyone anywhere in the world can become familiar with, as Carla and Susan have, by watching the movie *The Wizard of Oz* and imagining the smell Dorothy smelled when she fell into stuporous sleep in the field of poppies when the Wicked Witch of the West said, "Poppies, poppies," and caressed the crystal ball with long-nailed and delicately fingered green hands while winged monkeys cheeped and yapped and giggled.

It doesn't matter that Susan and Carla are smoking incense out of Carla's color-morphing glass pipe, because even if it were real opium, Susan's not inhaling it. She doesn't know how. Inhaling vs. not-inhaling is not a dichotomy she is aware of. And even if she were inhaling real opium, it wouldn't matter, because it is not the drug but the shared will to use the drug, to share the mouthpiece of a pipe, and to ditch class together, and drag ass across campus to Carla's room, which smells like Carla's hair, like almonds and autumn and soap, that matters. The undone inertia of unlikely emotion-laden circumstance, of tears and knocked-loose wheelchair brakes riding on the sound of blue nylon snowpant-legs rubbing one another is what matters.

"I'm so high, Carla," Susan Falls says.

"So am I," Carla says. They are stretched out on Carla's double bed next to one another. "Since we're both so high," she says, "let's pretend we're not."

"As you wish. You know, your room smells so good."

"Doesn't it?"

"Hey, Carla. I've been meaning to ask you. What's your major?"

"I'm undecided."

"What between, Carla?"

"Between psychology and dropping out of college. I like the way you say my name all the time, Susan."

"I think I want to drop out, too. Do you ever take those things off?" Carla giggles.

"Do you?" Susan says.

"Are you coming on to me, little girl?"

"I've never come on to anyone before."

"You want me to take them off?"

CHAPTER 130,030

A LEOPARD

Ten seconds later, Susan says, "No, not yet. Leave them on for a little while."

"Do you smoke cigarettes, Susan?" Carla pulls a pack of Marlboros from a secret pocket inside her snowpants. "Here. Smoke this cigarette with me and tell me how you lost your legs."

Susan drags on the cigarette, but, as with the opium, does not inhale. She says, "I'll tell you, Carla."

"Tell me."

"It was a leopard. A leopard bit my legs in the jungle when I was an infant. I was lucky to survive. Gangrene set in, though, and they had to hack off my legs with a machete to prevent it from spreading."

"A leopard?" Carla says. "Are you making fun of me?"

"Not at all. And I was an infant, so it wasn't so much the leopard or the gangrene, I guess. An infant can't watch out for—"

"Not to interrupt or be crude or anything, but this question just popped into my head, or maybe not, maybe it's been in my head for a while, since because, you know, of what you said earlier, about the desk and everything, and us being high even though we're pretending not to be high maybe provides me the space or excuse or whatever you want to call it to ask you this question, but are the workings of... Rather, can you—"

Carla is blushing.

"Blusher," says Susan.

"Does your…"

"Yes. And I call it my *naz-naz*, which is Farsi. What do you call yours?"

Carla kisses her knuckles smackingly. "Tell me about your leopard," she says.

"It might have been a car," says Susan. "I don't know. Sometimes I think it was a car, and that's what everyone tries to tell me, but I tend to doubt it was a car."

"Why would they tell you it was a car if it wasn't a car?"

"Any number of reasons. Maybe they do it for my benefit or maybe for my mother's. If it was a car, then according to them I was trying to save my box turtle, Pedro, who I'd brought outside to play with, from being run over by the car. But I know otherwise. I know that if it was really a car, it was because Pedro was crushed, either accidentally or on purpose, while I tested the strength of his shell beneath the wheels of my mountain bike, and that Pedro's death destroyed my will to live, so I threw myself into oncoming traffic with suicidal intent. That's too ugly, though, so they say that I fell into the street while trying to save Pedro from being crushed by a car, because that way accidental circumstance—rather than I—can be blamed for my state of leglessness. That's how the lie would benefit *me*. As well, it serves my mother on a couple levels—no mother can be expected to keep an eye on her thirteen-year-old daughter at all times, let alone control the pathway of a wayward box turtle or an oncoming car. However, a mother can and is expected both to keep her infant daughter off the floor of a jungle where hungry leopards live and to raise such a daughter not to have suicidal ideations at the age of thirteen."

"Well, so wait," Carla says, "do you have any memories of walking?"

"I have millions of memories of walking, but I also have memories of dreams, of flying."

"Those were dreams, though."

"But they feel similar enough, dreams and memories, that it wouldn't be rigorous to trust the distinction."

"What about photographs?"

"You can doctor those things," says Susan. "It's all beside the point, anyway. I'm legless. Hopefully I make up for it with brains."

"You make up for it by a long shot," whispers Carla. She is leaning over, separating Susan's bangs with her thumbs. "Does your fancy brain make it up to you, though?" she says.

"Without my fancy brain, I wouldn't be here right now."

"Here where?"

"Here here. Let alone right *here*, able to demand you remove your snowpants."

"I already said I would."

"You said you would before I was in a position to demand it… This is a confusing courtship, at least in light of what I've read so far, but I know it wouldn't be right unless there were a few feints before revelation. We can't just have everything without complications, you and I. There'd be no story without complications. With nothing to overcome, we'd die unstoried deaths. My distant cousin invented a new and wholly novel egg dish that is probably extremely delicious and she can't imagine its immediate success, even though most success, nowadays at least, tends to be immediate. She can't see Eggs Jiselle becoming instantly famous. She sees an extended process where the name of the dish changes over a long stretch of time and respect slowly builds for her, and fame collects at the same turtle's pace, and the Ritz begins serving Eggs Jiselle some ten years down the line, and ten years later Caesar's Palace and Hotel Nikko, and even Spago eventually takes its own stab at the dish, adding rosemary or wasabi or something, and there's a lawsuit over recipe patents or copyrights, which probably don't even exist, but a struggle and a long time and a lot of effort, because if Jiselle imagined it otherwise, there'd be nothing to look forward to looking back on. So if without a story even the fame of an egg dish isn't viable, then how about true love—it would be impossible."

"What about first sight? There's tons of stories about love at first sight."

"In the good ones, though," says Susan, "the love's thwarted by outside forces. And if it isn't, then death comes to one if not both of the lovers as soon as the love's consummated."

"So they never have the chance to betray one another. It's merciful."

"Not entirely, though. The one who lives, if one of them lives, ends up struggling to find meaning in a seemingly meaningl—"

"I don't think this'll kill you too fast, Susan." Carla lowers her head, kisses Susan's neck.

"If it doesn't...killyoufast...it isn't...true... I really should get... I have a presentation to make in Media Stud..."

"Are you dying?" Carla says.

"Yes, please."

Carla gets off of Susan, removes her snowpants. She doesn't have a big ass at all.

"You don't have a big ass at all."

"Would you have preferred a big ass?"

"I might have, but it doesn't even matter. I'm impossibly dedicated to your true ass."

"Have you ever had sex with a girl, Susan?"

"No, Carla, I haven't even been kissed by anybody but you and my mom, and those kisses were so long ago, they might not have happened, even."

"Do you want to smoke more opium before we do? To guarantee we're high? It'll thwart us sufficiently, I think. When we look back, we'll have to worry about the possibility that it was the drug, rather than love, that allowed for the damned good time we're about to have. We'll have to meet again sober to find out for sure. But we'll smoke more opium then, too, and every time after that, and so we'll continue to worry and we'll struggle and struggle, thwarted forever. You can't doubt a plan that pretty, can you? Isn't it a pretty plan?"

"Yes."

CHAPTER 130,031
NOT FRENCH

Jiselle and Susan are on opposite sides of the tiny balcony. A half-tempo electronic rendering of Mozart's *The Magic Flute* is coming through the speakers of the box on the railing. At the end of the overture, Susan says, "Hey, Jiselle, can I borrow a cigarette?"

"*Borrow* a cigarette? What, are you gonna give it back to me when you're done?"

Jiselle thinks this is awfully funny when, really, it's just stupid fucking banter. On the other hand, Susan knows that one asks not to "borrow" a cigarette but rather to "bum" a cigarette for precisely the reason Jiselle has made salient.

Jiselle says, "When'd you start smoking fags, anyway?"

"This afternoon."

"How'd you like the eggs?" Jiselle says.

"They were ungodly," Susan says.

"They were not."

"I didn't actually get to eat them, but Jiselle, let me ask you. In terms of cousinhood, exactly how distant are we?"

Jiselle extends her arms as far as they'll extend. "No blood," she says.

"Wow, your armpits are shaved."

"I'm British, Susan. I'm not French."

"Neither am I. Fuck." Susan puffs at her cigarette.

"Are you gonna inhale on the bloody thing or what?"

"What?"

Jiselle demonstrates.

Susan mimics, coughs, considers.

Her mind twirls at the thought of getting high on opium that never entered her system; at the thought of Adam distinguishing between himself and the world and its future and his own; the thought of a man, not yet slated to die, thinking to give seventy years away; of how to understand the difference between giving and having while alone and immortal in Eden. How you could mourn the end of something you never had a chance to take for granted.

Susan starts to shiver, and she shivers till she shakes, and it doesn't let up when she flops out of her chair. It doesn't let up when her ass hits the floor of the balcony, nor when the impact shocks her spine. Even after the back of her head strikes a corner of her wheelchair's footrest, and even after the back of her head strikes the corner again, and her skull pushes in her brain, she doesn't stop shaking, not for a full seven seconds.

The breathy honking that comes from Jiselle might sound like weeping, but because she keeps sticking her tongue out and saying things like "Good one," and "Joke's up, bloke," and finally, mysteriously, "Bung-o," her dying cousin concludes it's not weeping. And then her dying cousin is dead.

CHAPTER SUSAN
SUSAN

Free-floating three feet over the balcony, disembodied Susan is at once alarmed and relieved that Pedro is not there to greet her. The alarm soon dissipates, however, because disembodied Susan is looking at her disem-Susaned body, at her head turned left-cheek-up, the cigarette she dropped at the start of the shaking burning her hair away, and it is gleefully a shame. Susan knows everything now. She knows, for instance, that while Jiselle, who has run inside to call for help, starts to cry, she is silently repeating, "She *asked* for the fag, I didn't push it on her," and, though she can't seem to express it, or anything else, Susan knows for sure that nothing is inexpressible.

The hair on the head of the body burns away quickly to reveal a red mark Carla kissed atop a freckle just below Susan's left ear.

"How I was pretty, isn't it pretty to think so, how I was pretty to think so, says Susan, thinks Susan," Susans Susan, Susaning.

THE EXTRA MILE

This wheezing heckle, this spluttering raspberry, this vile string of punchlines life. Funny? Sure. But also cruel. "Cruel," you might retort, if you ever said anything, whoever you are, "but funny, too." And I'd tell you the half-full/half-empty line doesn't change the fact of the binary— that you either laugh a lot and feel a little bad, or laugh a little and feel a lot bad. What *I* ask is, where's the solace? All I've got left is this pool and its sundeck and that gaggle of knucklehead schmendricks over there to hone my timing to a sharper brutality against the shrinking, alter-cocker bones of. Our wives are all dead and we sit around warping. We can't re-member what made them laugh. As know-nothing boys, we wooed them like naturals; as men, we killed them with... what? Not killed them. Failed to save them. They died of neglect and the world was destroyed and we stayed in Florida to learn irreverence. That's the whole story, a long dirty joke.

It was time to play cards, so I went to our usual table by the deep end. Everyone appeared to be suffering from mouth pains. After we'd exchanged all our how's your digestions, my friend Heimie Schwartz asked my friend Bill the Goy, "How often did you go the extra mile for your wife?"

"All the time," Bill the Goy said. "Every single time."

I pulled the deck from the box by the ashtray and dealt out a hand of rummy four ways. I neglected to shuffle first. I was in no mood to shuffle.

Our fourth, Clyde the Schlub, who, truth be known, is more of an acquaintance than he is a friend, was stirring Splenda into his mug of iced tea when Heimie put the question to him.

"Clyde," Heimie said, "how often would you say you went the extra mile for your Christina?"

"Always," said the Schlub. "Whenever I got the chance."

We all knew I was next and that I would answer the same way as the Schlub and the Goy. We all knew Heimie had a different answer to the question than the rest of us and that he would offer up his different answer as soon as I gave mine. That is Heimie's rhetorical method. That is how he stirs up a controversy under the umbrella by the pool on an otherwise uneventful afternoon of rummy or canasta, even sometimes cribbage: he creates the promise of consensus, then undermines all hope of consensus with his wild assertions. I do not resent Heimie's thirst for controversy, and in fact think the day tends to get better when it's quenched. However, to my taste, his method lasts a few beats too long. I think: Why redundancy? Why first ask all of us a question we have the same answer to when all you and we really want is for you to get to your wild and controversial assertion already?

I'd had enough of this method, so before he had the chance to ask me his question, I said, "What about you, Heimie? How often did you go the extra mile for Esther?"

At my interruption of the routine, the Goy placed his startled hand on the shoulder of the Schlub and the Schlub spilled a little tea on his cards and his shirt, but Heimie didn't even flinch. He said, "That's just what I wanted to ask you, Arthur."

"I asked you first, though, Heimie," I said. "So you answer first."

"Well," he said, "I'm afraid that before I can answer your question, I'd have to ask you to clarify. I'd have to ask you not to take for granted that I take for granted that both you and I know what it is that the other one of us is talking about when that one of us inquires of the other about this extra mile and how often we went it for our wives. That is to say that I would have to ask you to first define the term *extra mile*."

"You know what it means," said the Goy. "Come on."

"We all know what it means," said the Schlub, licking some tea-drops off an ace of spades.

I said, "Go ahead, Heimie. Define it."

"But I want first to know how you define it, Arthur."

"But you had something in mind when you asked Bill and the Schlub over here."

"Please don't call me 'the Schlub over here,' Arthur," said the Schlub.

"It's a term of endearment," I said. I said, "I call you 'Schlub'? It means I am comfortable calling you 'Schlub.' It means we are acquainted, you and I."

"Okay," said the Schlub, sucking tea-dribble from the stain on his shirt. "But when you say 'the Schlub *over here*,' I feel like maybe I'm being a little bullied, belittled."

"So don't be such a tender-footed sissy," I told him.

"You're right," said the Schlub. "You're right."

"It's true," I said. "So then what did you mean by *extra mile*, Heimie?"

"What did *you* think I meant, Bill?" Heimie said to the Goy.

"Don't redirect my question to the Goy," I said. "I'm asking you, Heimie."

"I'm not too crazy for when you call me 'the Goy,'" the Goy said.

"What is this?" I said. "Is this group therapy for whiners? You want to be the Schlub and he'll be the Goy? You're a pair of goyische schlubs, the both of you. Still, I suppose, if the Schlub over here agrees to it, we could pull a switcheroonie with the monikers—would you like that?"

"Forget it," the Goy said. "Have it how you want it."

"I'm trying my hardest," I said. "Now answer the question you were asked. Establish us some mundanity so that Heimie can shock us in good faith with hot controversy."

"What are you saying to me?" said the Goy.

Heimie said, "He means tell us what you think it means, *extra mile*."

Unable to see clouds for the blockage of the umbrella, the Goy in his shyness studied pinstripes on cloth. "It means *down there*," said the Goy.

"That is a very ambiguous answer," I said.

"*Down there*... and the mouth," added the Schlub.

"The mouth?" I said.

"The mouth and *down there*," said the Schlub. "Add two and two, would you? We're talking about our wives here, may they rest in peace."

"We're talking about an act!" said Heimie. "We're talking about the *extra mile*! And I don't know what you mean by *down there*. Do you know what he means, Arthur?"

"Only vaguely," I said. "In my experience, there's more than one *down there*."

"There's the one *down there*," said the Goy, "and there's the other *down there*. To put the mouth to *the one* is the *extra mile*. To put the mouth to *the other* is filthy and disgusting."

"I agree," said the Schlub.

"I disagree!" I said.

"*I* disagree!" said Heimie, looking a little farklempt. I'd stolen his fire. Or at the very least I'd stolen part of his fire. It was two-on-two now, and he'd expected one-on-three. He said, "And why filthy and disgusting?"

"Because waste comes from *the other*," said the Goy.

"Waste comes from everywhere!"

"But this kind of waste causes illness."

"I was never ill by such waste," said Heimie.

"Nor was I ever ill by it," said I.

"This is filthy and disgusting," said the Schlub.

"Do you eat shrimp?" I said. "The veritable cockroach of the ocean?"

"Yes," said the Goy.

"Do you eat bacon?" said Heimie. "The meat of a beast who rolls in its own excrement?"

"I love bacon," said the Schlub. "It's salty."

"These crazies," Heimie said to me.

"Bacon and shrimp for them?" I said. "Indeed. Maybe even some bacon wrapped around a shrimp, but not *the other down there*, God forbid."

"Shellfish and pork, Arthur?"

"Please, Heimie," I said. "Shellfish and pork, but ass no thank you!"

What did they do, the Schlub and the Goy? They left. We didn't try to stop them. We knew the Goy would return soon enough and, surely, to be rid of the Schlub was a blessing.

"So how often did you go the extra mile, then?" Heimie said to me.

"Which one?"

"Both," he said.

I told him the truth. I said, "Rarely *the one* and never *the other*."

"Same here," said Heimie. "It's regrettable."

"We should've done more," I said.

FINCH

The fifty-third day in a row we hung out, me and Franco got all these grilled cheese sandwiches at Theo's BaconBurgerDog from Jin-Woo Kim, who people call "Gino" cause we're not in Korea or are in Chicago or people are lazy or two of those reasons. Gino's dad Sun's the owner of Theo's, and summer afternoons, he leaves Gino alone there. We went in at three, when the place was the deadest, and Franco said we wanted a grilled cheese sandwich. Right as soon as Gino started making them, though, Franco told him on second thought to make that three sandwiches, so Gino started making a third one too, except then what Franco said was what he'd meant was three apiece, and Gino stopped moving. He was over by the fryer, facing away from us, his hand on the scoop dug into the butter tub.

"What," Franco told him.

Gino got back to work. Grabbed bread and cheese from the rack on the counter.

"For to go," Franco said. He lit up a cigarette.

I passed him an ashtray. A bunch were stacked up on the garbage cans behind us.

"Thanks, yo," he said. "Hey, check this ashtray. Gino's dad stole."

That was probably true—all the ashtrays at Theo's were Burger King ashtrays, the chintzy aluminum kind with crimped edges—and it's not like I was really that tight with Gino, but we sometimes hung out when no one else was available, and I used to have some classes with him up till last year when we started the seventh and they tracked me into gifted, so I didn't want to stand there and trash-talk his dad, but you can't ignore Franco, so I had to do something, so I made a lippy face with my mouth and I shrugged.

Franco shrugged back.

Gino kept cooking. When the sandwiches were finished, he waxpaper-wrapped them, then stacked them in a bag and brought the bag to the register. He said, "Thirteen fifty."

"Nah," said Franco. "We don't have to pay today."

"You do," Gino said.

Franco took the bag. "Today it's on the house," he said.

"It's not!" said Gino. "Pay me. Come on." But what could he do? Franco was sixteen and Gino was my age, plus Franco was big—not tall, but big, and not big like me, but like muscled in a way I bet girls probably talked about. Almost like a man. His mustache wrapped around his chin and wasn't wispy.

He drummed his shaved skull a few times with his fingers, which looked like "I'm thinking, I'm thinking, I'm thinking," then took a frosted cookie from the cookie-tree display and crushed it in his hand inside of the wrapper. He undid the wrapper and dumped out the crumbs, grabbed another cookie, and told Gino, "What."

"Fine," Gino said. There were tears in his eyes. We were ripping him off in his own dad's joint. He gave me this look.

Franco flipped me the cookie.

I stuck it in my pocket, mouthing the words, "I'll pay you back soon." I don't know if Gino saw, but I meant what I mouthed.

On our way back to the alley in back of his ma's, Franco told me, "See? It's all in the voice. That's how you get stuff. Speaking with conviction.

Makes you convincing. 'Grilled cheese on the house, dog! Grilled cheese on the house!' and dude's like, 'Fine, Franco. Fine, man. Good.'"

"I don't think you convinced him, though."

"What you sayin, nigga?"

"I think you scared him cause your size," I said. "And how you crushed that cookie and then grabbed another one like you'd crush that one, too."

"No," Franco said. "The cookie was whatsitcalled—the cookie was fleece—not fleece, it was flair. It was just a decoration—for my conviction. I got this grilled cheese sandwich with my voice. I did it with my words. And it's a valuable lesson in life, my man, that words get you more than fists get you sometimes if you've gotta use the one or the other of them. Feel me?" Saying that last part, he tapped on his temple, which reminded me of a punchline—shot in the temple—and I got so hot to tell the whole joke, I forgot to tell Franco I was telling a joke.

I said, "How do you know Abe Lincoln was a Jew?"

"Lincoln was a white, you big fatso," said Franco.

So I didn't say the punchline cause being called a fatso got me too depressed. It was mean for him to call me it, jokey-voiced or not, but I think that sometimes Franco didn't know when he was mean. He might have known then, though, and felt bad about it too, cause when we got back to the alley he was above-average nice to me for almost five minutes. He gave me a grilled cheese and got his bike, an old Yamaha two-stroke, out of the garage.

He said, "I got something to show you, yo."

Hearing us, Franco III started growling. I hated that Franco III. She was a dalmatian-bull mix and Franco'd trained her to kill on command. It was against the law to have a dog that would kill on command. It was like having a killing machine where you just flipped a switch and someone got killed. You had to make the command secret so that if anyone wanted to find out if your dog was a machine, they couldn't. You had to make it weird, too, so that nobody'd say it by accident in front of the dog. The secret kill-command for Franco III was "Nasal spray." I only ever saw her get told it once—on the twenty-second day in a row me and Franco hung out—but once was enough and I'll never forget it. Franco'd brought her the bones from a full slab of ribs and she was lying on her stomach in the middle of the yard like a nice normal dog, gnawing and crunching and happy to be there. I wanted to even pet her a little. Then Franco told her "Nasal spray," and all the sudden it was like there was nothing else in the world to do but kill me. She was chained to the fence so she couldn't reach me, but I thought she'd pull the posts right out of the ground. She tried to kill me for at least five minutes till Franco said "Scout"—the secret stop-kill command—and then, just like that, she flopped on her stomach and chewed the bones again.

I finished my grilled cheese—completely delicious, Gino used so much butter—and Franco, on his motorcycle, held out the bag like "Go ahead and have another," but then when I reached for it, he pulled it back away and I felt even worse because I got no willpower and now I was reminded. I was supposed to be eating 2,000 calories a day. Before I went to Franco's that day, I already ate 1,570, and then the grilled cheese, and then there'd be dinner, which was gonna be steak because my dad, who's a pilot, was coming home from Asia.

Franco III clanged her chain around and barked. Franco lobbed her a grilled cheese. She caught it in her sloppy pink mouth and tore it up. I watched through the diamond-shaped spaces of the fence.

Franco said to me, "For real, now. Do this no-hands." And I took a step back and he tossed up a grilled cheese medium-high for me to catch in my mouth. I missed it, though. I'm not good at catching. It bounced off my chin and landed in some gravel, but that was no big deal, even though I knew the three-second rule was bull, cause waxpaper blocks out dirt and germs. Before I was able to pick it back up, though, Franco jumped off his bike and ground it around under one of his Jordans, which completely tore the paper. I told him he ruined it. He said he had something to show me so whatever. He only ever had two things to show me.

One of the things was the trick where someone goes, "I got something to show you," and then they give you a charleyhorse. This thing was the other thing. He started the motorcycle up and revved it. The engine was loud like all the other times.

"You hear that?" Franco said.

"Yeah," I said.

Around then's when this fake-red-haired guy came out the gangway side of Franco's house. No one ever went out the front door of Franco's house. I don't know why. This guy came out the gangway side like everyone else. He was probably sixty years old and was really skinny. He wore that light kind of shades you could kind of see eyes through, eyes that kind-of-seeing made you feel like... what? Like you got caught at something scuzzy.

The guy tapped a cigarette out of a softpack, turned into the alley, and walked right up to Franco. He said, "Got a light?"

Franco said, "No. Get the fuck away from us."

The guy made a laughing noise and showed us his palms, then he kept on walking, out of the alley and onto the sidewalk. Before crossing the street, he raised his hands to the sides of his head and patted, like to make sure his pasted-down hair was still in place.

"Why'd you tell him you don't got a light and fuck off?" I said.

"I don't like him," said Franco.

"Why not, though?" I said.

"I don't know. Why? You think he's alright?"

"No," I said. "I think he's a sleaze. But what was he doing in your house, though, the sleaze?"

"Who knows," Franco said. "Probably screwing my mother. Fucken used-car salesman. Parakeet breeder."

I thought "parakeet breeder" was a pretty funny way to say fag, but it didn't make me laugh, cause I didn't like him talking about his ma having sex, especially with a sleaze who colored his hair. I never even really officially met her—she barely left the house—but I saw her take the garbage out a couple of times and she looked used-up, like she belonged in a bathrobe 24-7 and it hurt her teeth to eat. It was a mean thing to say, I thought, what Franco said about her.

"That's not nice to say that about your ma," I said.

"To say what?" Franco said.

"That she's screwing some guy."

"My dad used to say it all the time," he said. "All the time."

Me and Franco became friends the day we saw his dad's ghost. That was the first day of the fifty-four-day run of me and Franco hanging out together, which was also the first day we ever hung out together. At that time, Franco was just friends with Helio who was my friend. Helio had weird chromosomes or genes or whatever and was brown like a Mexican guy, but Italian like most of the rest of the neighborhood, and his stomach wasn't just a six-pack but an eight-. We'd been friends since fourth grade, when he got kicked out of fifth and put in my reading class. Five out of six times, on average, he beat me up in a fight, but that wasn't just because he was strong. About two out of three times, he'd fight me in front of people, which put me off guard because he was funny and girls liked him, too, and so they would cheer for him like he was the home team and I was the away team. Even if I'd been like the home team and him like the away team, though, I don't think it would've changed our outcomes too much, cause it was just people watching that screwed me up. When it was just me and Helio fighting, I won one in two times. That's about seventeen percent of fights won overall compared to fifty percent of fights-fought-in-private won, and considering that me and Helio used to fight, on average, three out of seven days a week for nearly three whole school years, my stats are reliable. Unless I mean significant. I get it confused sometimes, the difference between reliability and significance, and that's one reason why even though I'm supposed to be the junk at math—it's mostly my math skills that got me tracked into gifted—I think that, really, I'm just above-average good at it. Which doesn't even make me feel a little bit bad cause those other guys in gifted are serious pussies. All I'm trying to say is it's highly unlikely that my outcomes against Helio in public versus private fights can be accounted for by freak accident. I tried explaining that to Jenny Wansie once cause we were alone in the nurse's office together and it seemed like she finally liked me to my face a little bit, but then after we were done having our temperatures taken and mine was high and hers was normal, which I think made her mad at me, she said that I was a freak accident, and then when I came back to school the next week from having the strept throat, all her girl friends started calling me "Freak Accident," then they called me "FA," like *eff ay*, and then the guys who were friends with the girls called me "Fa," like *fah*. Some of these guys were on the basketball team, and I beat two of them up for saying Fa to me, but it doesn't do anyone any good to beat basketball guys up because fighting isn't why people like them. It's basketball. And even if I had it in me to make it so they couldn't play basketball anymore, by breaking their fingers or cutting important connective tissue in their legs, it wouldn't do any good, cause it would make them pitiful and me this dickhead. I was in love with Jenny Wansie so hard. Still am. It really broke my heart. It breaks my heart. Sometimes I call her on the telephone and she talks to me about boys she likes. She sometimes calls me "So La Ti Do." I told my ma because I didn't understand. My ma said it was a term of endearment, but my ma thinks I'm the smartest and the handsomest and she thinks that everyone else thinks so, too.

But Helio used to steal cigarettes for Franco is why him and Franco were friends, and one time Franco asked him to steal a can of butane, too, and when we brought all that loot back to Franco in his garage, he offered for each of us to take a cigarette, which Helio did and I didn't do, and that's maybe when Franco and I started our friendship because, right as soon as I said no to the cigarette, Franco said to me that I was a smart kid. He said, "Smart kid." But if that's not when we became friends, it was a couple minutes later, after him and Helio were finished smoking.

We were all just sitting there on Franco's brown couch in the garage, listening to Franco III yelp about her chain being too short, and Helio said, "Can I put the butane in your lighter?"

And Franco said, "I don't got a butane lighter."

"Oh," Helio said.

And Franco looked at Helio like he wanted Helio to ask him a question, but Helio's not so smart—he's smarter than Gino, but he's not very smart, especially about people. One time I called him "Hell-io" by accident because I was yawning while I was trying to say his name, and he thought I was making fun of him, even though I was his best friend. He punched me four times in my back because of it and the next day he called me "fat stuff" in front of Jenny Wansie, which was one of the rare occasions where I really beat him up in a home/away situation.

I said to Franco, "Why'd we steal you this butane if you don't got a lighter that needs it?"

Franco said, "So we could huff it."

"Drugs?" Helio said.

"It's not really drugs. It's a inhalant," Franco said.

"You want us to be huffers with you," Helio said. "You're a huffer," he said. He said it fast and mean, with his lips all twisted. He was scared, and he didn't want us to know. He's tricky like that, Helio, dishonest about his feelings.

Then Franco, who was maybe my friend then, or would be in another couple minutes asked me, "What's wrong with this kid?" He was talking about Helio. Then he said to Helio, "What's wrong with you, kid? You sound like health class."

"I don't want to be a doper," Helio said. He cracked his knuckles and made his eyes squinty instead of saying "Period," like, "I don't want to be a doper. Period."

"Don't be stupid," I said to Helio. "A doper does drugs. This is a inhalant." I looked at Franco to make sure I had it right, and Franco shot me with both of his pointer fingers.

"Exactly!" Franco said. "Now, you huff this butane with us, or you go away. Period. And don't you ever say I'm a huffer again. Got it?"

Helio got it. He hugged himself a little, but he stayed on the couch.

"Here," Franco said. "This is how you do it." Then he did it.

The way you do it is that the butane comes in a long metal can with a straight silver metal tip about three quarters the height of my thumb's length, but a lot skinnier. Then there's the white plastic tip shaped like a construction cone that's about half the height of my thumb's length. The white plastic tip fits over about two thirds of the silver metal tip. Each tip has a hole at the top. When you put the white plastic tip in your mouth so that the top of the ridge at the bottom of it is against the front of your teeth, you push the can into your face until the bottom of the ridge of the tip is against the top of the can, which means the silver metal tip goes inside the can as far as it can and then the butane comes blasting out into your throat. It's cold and tastes a little bit sweet. You have to aim right and huff deeply, or else you get it on your tongue and it tastes fuzzy and bubbly and you have to gag a little bit. If you do it right, things change almost immediately. First, if you try to talk, your voice is very low, which I don't know why, but I think it's because the butane makes your voice box so cold and your voice box needs to be a little bit hot to form more high-pitched noises with the cords it has inside it. That's not so important, but there's a tradition around it. After you're done with your turn huffing, you hand the can to the next guy and say something to show that your voice is frozen low. Since silence in your ears when you're huffing isn't silence but this really warm kind of *wah wah wah* that lasts till the inhalant wears off, what you usually say when you hand the can over is "Wah." Franco went first and demonstrated. He said "Wah" to me, fell back into the couch, and gave me the can. I huffed it for longer than Franco, said "Wah" to Helio, fell back into the couch, and gave Helio the can. Helio let go of one of his shoulders to hold on to the can, but he only took a squirt of it, and I think he got the bubbles cause what he said was "Weh," and it wasn't so low.

Next thing I knew, all the things were gigantic and all the nothings were tiny. I looked at Helio and he was so much bigger than the garage door, I couldn't understand how he got into the garage without cutting some of himself off first. I thought that was funny, and then I noticed I was warm. I tried to put my hand on Helio's shoulder to show him I was his friend and isn't this cool, but it took so much strength to lift up my hand, cause it was not only gigantic, but dense. Everything was dense, even the nothings, and it felt like the couch was slowly moving backward. Franco was the densest and the most gigantic. Just one of his blue eyes was bigger than all of me. I almost said to him, "Franco, you have the biggest blue eye," but right when I thought of it, the butane began to wear off and I thought that might have sounded really faggy. I tapped Helio on the shoulder, and he gave me the butane. I huffed the butane.

"Wahhh," I said.

"That's a boy," Franco said. Then he huffed. Then I huffed. Then Helio did a little.

"Oh. Oh. Oh. Oh," Franco said, and his gigantic hand was on my shoulder. His other hand was pointing. "Dad?" Franco said.

"Your dad's home?" I said. Then I saw. It was a gigantic dense guy who you could see through in some places. His mustache was the same as Franco's, but less black and more thick. He had his hands in front of him, by his waist. His hands were moving around while his wrists stayed still. It seemed like he was either telling some great story, or he was listening to some boring story and saying, "Come on, already, get to the point, already," except he wasn't saying anything.

"Dad?" Franco said. "How are you, Dad? I love you, Dad."

"Pleased to meet you," I said. "This is really amazing. Do you mind if I ask you what's it like in the world of pure spirit, Mr. Iafarte?"

Franco told me, "His name's Domenico."

"You got different last names?"

"Iafarte's my ma's."

"Your ma's?" I said.

"Yeah," Franco said. "We changed it after the hospital. It was a pain in the ass."

"I'm sorry," I said. I didn't know why anyone was in what hospital, or when. I wanted to ask, but I never asked. I don't know why I apologized, either, but I felt like I should apologize. Franco didn't seem to notice, anyway.

Looking at him, I got the feeling that the ghost of Mr. Domenico was sad, but he wouldn't let anyone know because it would make him feel like a jerk if we knew how sad he was because then we'd get sad and it would be his fault. I thought maybe it had something to do with the hospital, that maybe he died in the hospital, from cancer or something, and felt guilty about it. I had no idea, though. That butane spins you out.

"I love you, Dad. Do you love me, Dad?" Franco said.

Mr. Domenico didn't say anything. He started to fade, and then he disappeared. Franco was shivering.

"Helio," Franco said, "that was my dad, yo. Franco I. Did you see him? How big he was? I told you how big he was, right? But I bet you didn't believe it. But now you do."

"I didn't see," Helio said.

"He was right there," I said.

"Bullshit, fat stuff."

Franco said, "Hey. Helio. Go away. Don't come here no more."

Helio sat there for a second, and then Franco III barked and then Helio left. Franco raised up the butane can like how I saw this king in a movie raise a gold cup of wine, and he said, "More for us, Clifford. More for us." Then he rubbed his eyes. It felt good that he called me my name and then called us "us," and by that time we were friends for sure.

My dad didn't like it that I spent time with Franco, but I got good grades so he didn't say I couldn't. I heard him tell my ma that if he told me

I couldn't hang out with that delinquent wop son of a wife-beating degenerate gambler wop, then I'd never learn that that's what he was. A
delinquent wop. When my dad says some guy's a wop it means that the
guy is such a bad guy that he makes all Italians look bad, including us.
Like for instance even Finch, the famous hitman, who's half-Irish—my
dad calls Finch a wop. It's funny because he likes to tell Finch stories.
Everyone around here likes to tell Finch stories. Finch is this hitman who
lives somewhere close, though no one knows where, but if it's not in the
neighborhood then it's somewhere else in Chicago. Everyone says Finch
killed everyone who was ever famous and killed, but that he never got
caught for any of it, which is why they call him Finch. I don't get it, but
that's what they say. A lot of kids think Finch is as fake as Santa Claus.
I don't think so, though, and neither does Franco. Franco told me once
that he sometimes wished his dad was Finch and I said so did I. I think
everyone wished that sometimes. Even though everyone likes to hear stories about hitmen, though, my dad pretended that he didn't like to hear
them because he didn't want to set a bad example for me. When he told
me the Finch stories—like the one about how Finch killed that Nixon
and made it look natural because Nixon was dying and Nixon knew that
Finch killed that Hoffa, and Finch knew Nixon was gonna rat him out
from his deathbed (Nixon's) right before Nixon died if Finch didn't get
Nixon first—my dad didn't say, "I've got a Finch story to tell you, have
you heard this one?" He said, "I got a dumb wop story to tell you. This
story is about that hitman Finch who's just another dumb wop. Ready?"
My dad explained to me about dumb wops at the very beginning of the
summer, on the evening of the seventeenth day in a row me and Franco
hung out, when I saw him after I'd been at the garage all day and I accidentally said to him, "Hey, w'su', nigga." He didn't cuff me or anything
because he's not like that, but he yelled at me about how that wasn't a
good word to use inappropriately. He said that only black people can
call each other nigga and get away with it, just like only Italians could
call each other wop and get away with it. I told him it was different for

blacks than Italians because when blacks say nigga it doesn't mean anything bad, usually, but when my dad says wop, it means something really bad. My dad said that that was unfortunate, Cliff, and very sad. Then he made a sad face and started saying about how he was a Democrat even though lots of Democrats let women kill babies which was wrong but not as wrong as white people calling black people niggas and meaning it badly, but I sort of drifted off, thinking about how I'm Italian and lots of black guys at my school call me nigga, like "Get outta my way, nigga." Or "Look at this roly-poly little nigga here." And I was trying to figure out if they were being totally mean or mean with some niceness mixed in, because a lot of times I can't tell when black guys say stuff to me what exactly they're saying and because even though they called me fat slur words, they always added nigga, and that's what they called each other, so maybe they were saying, really, "Cliff, you're a real fatty, but you're one of us." It was a nice thought. I was having fantasies about being one of those guys because the girls liked them a lot at our school. It went like this, how girls liked you: Number one was basketball players. Number two was guys who got haircuts at salons and listened to music where five guys sing and there's no guitars. Number three was black guys. There was no number four. Some of the real geeky girls liked tough guys but only if the tough guys would be their boyfriends, but those girls were ugly, and they always would be.

After the grilled cheese sandwiches on the fifty-third day, I got home before my dad. My ma said to wash my face and change my filthy clothes because she could always smell it on me when I hung out with Franco and it was horrible. "You smell like that garage, Cliff," is what she said. So I washed up really fast with paper towels—just my pits and my face—and then I changed out of my black T-shirt and into this polo my dad brought back from Laos that was colored baby blue. I changed in the bathroom in front of the mirror, which I forget sometimes how bad it is to do that, because I get stuck there, counting my rolls to see how much bigger I'm getting, and it's always bigger because I got no discipline. And by the time I was done my dad was home, and he didn't give me a hug, and guess why. It was because he was worried I was a fag. He's always worrying about something. Plus I think I looked like a fag in that shirt. Baby blue with a collar.

"What do you and Franco do all afternoon at that filthy garage?" my dad asked me.

"We talk about stuff," I said. "Life and stuff."

"What about girls?" He got right to the point. "Do you talk about girls ever?"

"Not really." I told him not really because first of all it was true. I was always scared that if I talked about girls, Franco would want to go get some girls, and that would mean he'd ditch me, and where would I be for the afternoon? Either fighting Helio or stuck at Theo's with Gino is where. And also the whole Jenny Wansie thing was embarrassing to talk to anyone but my ma about, especially my dad and Franco.

"Do you like girls, Clifford?" he said. When he said it, my ma brought out the steaks, and I hoped maybe he'd forget what he asked. So I cut into the steak and I told my ma that it was some delicious steak. "Hey!" my dad said. "I asked you a question."

"About what?"

"Don't play dumb with me, Cliff. About girls. You like 'em?"

"Sometimes."

"Name me one you like."

"I don't really—"

"He likes Jenny Wansie," my ma said. "You're crazy to worry, Carlo. Your son's the biggest heterosexual on the block."

I know she didn't mean that I was the biggest in size, but it made me sad for a second, because it was true in that way, too. There was this gay guy, Vito, that lived down the street and pretended he wasn't gay, and he was bigger than me, but if you take into consideration age and proportionate size, I was the biggest heterosexual on the block. I wanted to not eat the steak because of all the calories I had before, but my ma got upset when I didn't eat her food and it pissed off my dad. So I ate. I probably ate 4,500 calories that day, which is sick.

"Jenny Wansie. Eh? Eh," my dad said. My dad always says "Eh" when he's embarrassing someone. "Look at him blushing. Alright. Sorry. I didn't think you were gay, Clifford, but I was worried because Lee Anders's son I didn't think was gay either, and Lee Anders walked in on him just the other day. Commiserating with a little Asian kid."

Lee Anders was one of the copilots my dad flew around the world with.

"An Asian kid?" my ma said.

"Gloria, we're Democrats. It doesn't matter the kid was Asian."

"Then why'd you say it?"

"For detail. To add texture to the story."

"He wasn't really Asian?"

"No. He was Asian alright. Till Lee Anders got through with him, and then the kid was just ugly."

"Lee hurt the boy?"

"Boy! He was sixteen years old, for chrissakes. Now, Clifford, I want you to know this: it's okay for people to be gay because we're all Democrats here, but just not for you. It's like saying nigger and being Italian. It's just not right for you."

"How do I know I'm a Democrat?"

"Here's the test: do you think our new mayor Richard M. Daley is a funny guy who makes a lot of clever plays on words when he talks, or do you think he's more like an illiterate, nonsense-speaking midget with a really red face?"

"What do you think?" I said.

"I'm asking you, Clifford."

"Your dad's asking you."

"I don't know," I said.

"There! You're a Democrat. You got an open mind on you. You don't know, so you withhold judgment." He stood up, leaving his fork in his steak, and walked to the other side of the table to hug me and kiss me wet on the cheeks. Then he went back to his steak and said, "Hello, son! How's your summer been?"

I like my dad. He's crazy. "It's been alright."

"Just alright? Have you been seeing a lot of this hot little Wansie I'm hearing so much about?"

My ma was laughing because she likes my dad for being crazy, too. "Clifford doesn't like to talk about little Jenny."

Again with the size. I was the biggest heterosexual and the girl I loved was little. They didn't know. They couldn't. I knew they couldn't, so I didn't let it get to me.

"If he doesn't like to talk about her, it must be serious. Have you gotten to first yet, Cliff?"

"Carlo."

"What? I'm just asking about first. First is just French kissing. Have you been French kissing in the U.S.A., Cliff? Eh? Eh. Eh? Ah, you're too young to remember that song. Pass the mashed, Gloria," he said.

She pushed the bowl of potatoes over to him and everyone was quiet for a minute. I was about to ask my dad to pass me the potatoes when he was through with them, but he started talking, which was good, because one thing I didn't need to do to myself was those potatoes.

"Am I square or what? This day and age," my dad said, shaking his head. "First doesn't mean French kissing anymore, does it? That's just being in the batter's circle, isn't it? What used to be third is now first base. The times they are a-changing. It's fine, though. That's what Democrats stand for."

"Don't be sad, Carlo. You're no square. First is still Frenching, right?" my ma said to me.

Like I knew. You could tell they were so sure I kissed all the girls I wanted to.

"No," I told them. "First ain't Frenching."

"Really, Cliff? What is it, then?" my ma said.

My dad lifted up his eyebrows and did the thing with the finger in the fist. My ma smacked him and then they kissed. My dad was a football player in high school and my ma was a dancer. My dad was cool, though. He had an old hotrod. I've seen pictures. It was a black '67 Chevelle with a blower. He was a badass, my dad. My ma was really pretty, too. She was his Jenny Wansie except that she actually liked him, which made it much better, and then I was born and they were happy about it.

"So?" my dad said. "What's first then?"

"Two guys and a girl," I said.

"Get out," my ma said.

"Are you serious, Cliff? That's kinda disturbing to your father," my dad said. "Frankly, I'm shocked. And with so many Republicans in our Congress…"

"He's making it up," my mother said.

"I'm serious," I said.

"Well, so what's home plate?" my dad said.

I don't know how to explain this, but he had this thing in his voice like I was ruining his life, which I didn't want to do.

I said, "Home plate is when you fall in love with the girl of your dreams and she loves you too and everything's alright."

My dad slapped the table. He lightened right up. My mother grabbed hold of my cheeks because she thinks I like it, which is my fault because I never told her any different. She said, "You're gonna get to home plate one day, Cliff. If not with that little Wansie girl, then with someone smarter and prettier."

"You're a nice boy, Clifford," my father said. "You're gonna be a kind and decent man."

"And you're so creative."

"Creative? This kid's a friggin genius! You know I told Lee Anders about some of the stuff you're learning in those math classes and he didn't believe me? Flat out called me a liar. Said it was bad luck to lie about your own son. Then again, his son's off taking it where the sun don't—"

"Easy, Carlo."

"What? Why does he gotta—Cliff, why do you gotta cry every time someone has something nice to say about you at the dinner table?"

The best thing about huffing was how much you could do. Since it only got you high a couple minutes at a time, the worst that could happen if you did too much—except for death—was you'd get freaked out for a couple of minutes, which wasn't long at all, and so unless your last huff made you have a bad time, you always tried to out-huff that huff this huff. At least that's how I huffed. Franco, too. But I always huffed more than him. Master Glow, Dusted That, Shine Cannon, Ronson—the brand didn't matter. My lungs were deeper cause I wasn't a smoker, plus I wasn't afraid. I'd freaked out a few times, and I'm not saying I liked it, but it wasn't boring either. I never regretted it. Once I thought I was a light getting dimmer in a window. Another time I thought I'd looked up too hard and my eyes were stuck staring inside of my skull. The day after we ripped off all that grilled cheese from Theo's and my dad suspected me of being a fag, which was the fifty-fourth day in a row I hung out with Franco, I was sure Gino Kim was using ESP against me, like to make me remember things we'd done that I'd forgotten. I remembered this one time we bought a bag of tarragon, thinking it was weed—real drugs were impossible to get at our school—and we smoked it in a pipe Gino made by rolling tin foil. The smoke hurt our throats but tasted kind of good. I thought it did, at least. Gino didn't like it. But he liked to eat fish patty sandwiches from McDonald's, so his taste in food smells wasn't reliable— I remembered that too. And I remembered this other time we threw rocks at the slide of a jungle gym for hours. I can't even explain why that was fun, but it was.

I opened my eyes, which I'd forgot were closed, and remembered I'd told Gino I'd pay him back for all the grilled cheese. Thirteen-fifty. And plus the two cookies. Fifteen dollars. But how would I get it? I didn't know how I'd get it. My summertime allowance was ten bucks a week, and I'd given five to Franco for Dirt Gun XL, which is what we were huffing, there on the garage couch in front of the TV. It's the same thing as Dirt Gun, but the trigger you pull to make the nozzle blast the drugs out is black instead of purple, and the can's twice as big—that's why it's so expensive. Franco said "Wah" and rolled it slow across the couch to me. His TV's antenna was missing an ear and the only channel he was able to raise that morning was playing *Three Stooges*, but he hated Moe's voice—he said it made him feel accused—so he'd turned off the volume, and that was fine with me cause the noises the Stooges make give me a headache, but sitting there looking at them tweak each other's noses and make pained faces while I came down from Dirt Gun wasn't any good, so I took a giant huff, not big enough to cause another ESP freakout, but big enough to make me forget about the first one.

Right in that gap between huffing and feeling it, this knocking started up on the door of the garage—not the one made for cars that faces the alley but the one that you enter from Franco's backyard—and Franco III started barking her face off. Once the Dirt Gun came on, though, the wahs were so loud that everything else sounded far away and swirly.

An unhappy-looking fat guy in a suit came in, and the sleaze from the alley from the day before followed him. They stood behind the TV, facing the couch, and the fat guy's mouth was this straight black line, and the sleaze shook his head and said things to Franco. It might as well have been static, though, whatever he was saying. I could tell it wasn't good just by looking at his face, but didn't know what it was cause the wahs drowned the words out. Plus the sleaze's hair, I'd noticed, was the shiniest thing. It was so clean and shiny that the lamplight behind him made his head look on fire. I wanted Franco to see, so I lifted my arm to point the head out, but my arm was dense and heavy, which slowed me down, and before I could even get my index finger straightened, Franco'd jumped to his feet.

The whole couch jerked.

The fat guy's mouth showed small wet teeth and the sleaze pushed at air like "Hold up, take it easy, just please quiet down."

Franco told him, "What!" It was louder than the wahs—the wahs were wearing off fast—and it sounded like his voice cracked when he said it again. "What!" he said. "What!" Then he flicked his lit cigarette, which grazed the sleaze's face. Orange ashes blew around and the sleaze cupped his ear. "Franco!" the sleaze said. "Come on now! Come on!"

Now the fat guy pushed air. "Calm down," he told Franco. "Just sit back down now."

"What!" Franco said.

I'd missed something important. Something big was happening and I didn't know what. I thought I should have known what.

I felt a little sick, then remembered to breathe.

Franco III kept barking her face off.

Then Franco stepped forward and kicked the TV off the crate that it sat on, right at the sleaze, who it caught on the waist. The sleaze shouted "Fuck!" or made the noise *fuh!* and bent forward hard and the TV screen shattered all over the floor.

Franco jumped the crate, tackling the sleaze. The fat guy grabbed Franco's shoulders and pulled. Franco bucked, sent him back into the wall, smacked the sleaze, and kept saying "What!" I was on my feet. I didn't know what I should do. The fat guy caught his balance and dove at Franco. I saw a holstered gun when his jacket flapped up, and I was running out the door, into the yard, like a gifted-track fatso pussy, but I wasn't. I wasn't a pussy. I was doing what I had to.

When she saw me, Franco III went crazy, but I stood just outside the range of her chain and I stared into her eyes—they were all pink with blood and dripping with water—and I pointed my finger and yelled at her, "Easy!" and yelled it again, and guess what happened. The chain sloped behind her and she looked at the ground. She sat on the grass.

I freed her from the fence as fast as I could, and we entered the garage. Cords were straining under Franco's neck skin. His face was this greasy tomato of pain. He knelt one knee on the chest of the sleaze and his other leg was straightened at a nasty-looking angle while the fat guy, behind him, was twisting the chickenwing he had Franco's arm in and saying stuff to him too soft to make out.

I didn't register the fat guy's voice's softness until I'd already said "Nasal spray," though.

Franco III had some distance to cover—most of a garage—and she barked the whole way. The fat guy heard her coming and released the chickenwing. He pivoted quick and, right as the dog hurtled over the crate, he raised both his fists and shouted, "Down!" She hit the ground squealing, already bent to turn, and she re-jumped the crate and pushed her head between my shins with so much force I nearly lost my footing. "Scout," I said, and she laid down flat.

Franco was sitting on top of the sleaze. His face was in his hands. His shoulders were jumping.

The fat guy said to me, "Jesus H. Christ, kid." The walkie-talkie-thing on his belt made that crackle like they do in the movies, and a voice said some numbers.

Then I did run away like a gifted-track pussy. Tried to, at least.

Another cop grabbed me just outside the door. He got me by the elbows and I twisted and pulled, but it wasn't even close. In a million years, with a billion chances, I couldn't have gotten away from this guy. He was bigger than my dad. I just wasn't strong enough. And something about that... something really got into me. It was partly the Dirt Gun—that stuff can spin you out—but only partly, I think. I didn't think it was right that this guy, cause he was bigger, was able to hold on to me. I don't mean it was *wrong* or that it didn't make sense, but... I don't know what I mean. I just hated how it was, and something got into me. I spit on the guy. I tried for his face and what I got was his tie-knot. That was enough, though. He gave me this shake. He couldn't believe it. I couldn't really either. Spitting on a cop.

And then I heard a woman's voice, Franco's ma's voice, a kind of pretty voice that didn't sound like she looked. It sounded much younger, almost like a girl's. She was standing right there, right behind the cop shaking me, and she said to him, "Please, Detective Rizzo, be gentle. This is Clifford Martinucci, Franco's best friend. I'm sure that he's just upset on our behalf."

The cop stopped shaking me. He even let go of one of my arms. I was surprised to hear Franco's ma say my name—I'd never really met her and didn't think she knew me—and more surprised to hear her call me Franco's best friend, which, now that I thought about it, seemed to make sense since we'd hung out for fifty-four days in a row. What surprised me the most, though, was what the cop said back to her.

"Martinucci like the pilot, you're saying?" he said.

And she told him, "His son."

And he let go my other arm.

I didn't know why it mattered I was my father's son any more than I knew what I was supposed to be upset about on whose behalf. I knew enough to keep my mouth shut and wait to find out later, though.

"Baby," Franco's ma said to someone behind me. I figured it was Franco, but nope—it was the sleaze. He limped through the doorway, into the yard, bleeding on the cheek, holding his gut area.

He said, "Here I am, your killed messenger, returned." He laughed a thin laugh.

"Killed?" Franco's ma said. "That's how you talk at a time like this?"

"You know what? Don't guilt me. I was trying to do right by your piece-of-work son—and *for you*—and what happens? He pummels me's what happens. I don't need to feel worse now."

"You what?" Franco's ma said. "A who?" she said. "Pummeled?"

"Look at my face, honey. Look at my clothes."

"That was *Franco* did that?"

"Who else?" said the sleaze.

"Did you do like I asked?"

"I did *just* like you asked."

"Did you tell him you were there for him? Did you tell him you'd be there if he needed to talk, or someone to lean on?"

"Yeah, that's what I told him! I told him all of that shit. I told him we could bond about it. I told him we should. And that's when he came at me! Ask *him*, you don't believe me."

"Him" meant me. I didn't know what to say. I squinted at a patch of yellow grass behind the sleaze.

"Never mind," he said. "Listen. It's feeding time. I'm going."

"Forget about those parakeets, Alan," Franco's ma said.

"They're hatchlings," he said. "It's important to keep them on a very strict regimen."

"We need you here," she snapped.

The sleaze stood up straight and stomped on the ground. "He *jumped* on me, Angela. He knocked me down with a television, and jumped on me and struck me!"

"Yeah, struck you, I struck you," Franco muttered—he was being led from the garage, in cuffs, by the fat cop. "He got struck cause I struck him and next thing's I'll kill him. Go fuck yourself," he said to his ma or the sleaze or all the world.

"Please don't arrest him," Franco's ma said to the fat cop. "He didn't mean any harm. You'd be upset too, you just found out your father died."

"Wait," I said. "Hey," I said.

Nobody waited.

"I won't be pressing charges," the fat cop said, "but we're gonna hold on to him until he cools down. He attacked Mr. Smucci, I think he's on drugs, you just heard him making threats, and we're standing right here. We don't really have any other choice, Ms. Iafarte."

"Hey, wait," I said.

"Are you taking drugs, Franco?" Franco's ma asked.

"Aw, shut up," he told her. "Take care of my dog, please, Cliff, please, okay? She's over by the motorcycle, whining and shaking. I promise she won't hurt you as long as you're nice to her. "

Before I could answer, the fat cop told Franco, "Your friend's gonna be in the car right next to you."

The other cop, Rizzo, said to the fat cop, "You know, this is the pilot's son. Maybe we shouldn't—"

"I know who he is," the fat cop said. He waved around the can of Dirt Gun XL. "Believe me, his dad'll want to know about this. Your dad's gonna hear about this, Clifford," he told me.

I said, "That ain't mine."

"Your dad," I said to Franco. "I don't understand." We were locked in back of the cops' car, waiting. I didn't know for what. The cops were outside.

"It was money," Franco said. "It had to be money. He owed people money."

"That's not what I mean—I mean, we saw his ghost fifty-three days ago, Franco."

"I know," Franco said.

"But he wasn't dead then?"

"No," Franco said.

I said, "But why'd we see his ghost if he wasn't dead, though, you think?"

"Because he was fucking with me," Franco said. "He was always fucking with me." Then he started crying, so I squeezed him on the shoulder and didn't bother arguing. He rubbed his ear around, against my knuckles, which I guess is how you signal "I need a hug" if there's a hand on your shoulder and your hands are cuffed.

I squeezed the shoulder a couple more times.

An Animal Control wagon entered Franco's alley and the fat cop and the other one got into the car.

* * *

The cops split us up when we got to the station. I never got put in a cell or anything. They made me stand in a squeaky hallway off the lobby with a woman cop who was pretty for a woman cop. She gave me a couple LifeSavers, butter-rum-flavored, which are actually really good, and we talked about the Bulls. She didn't know a lot about the Bulls and neither did I, so mostly what we said was stuff about Michael Jordan, and how he was the greatest because of how he dunked or whatever and had expensive shoes, and the cop thought he was handsome.

I don't know what they did with Franco. He told me later that they tied him to a chair and slapped him around to try to get him to confess to having a dog that would kill on command, but they couldn't break him. After that, he told me, his ma picked him up, and on their way out of the station a "special forces homicide cop" took them aside and told them it was Finch who murdered his father. Franco's a liar, though, and he's crazy. I mean, a lot of bad stuff kept happening to him, and it happened in stupider ways than it should have—like I still don't get how his ma thought he'd bond with the sleaze if the sleaze delivered him the news about his dad. About his dad being *dead.* I don't get how anyone's ma could think something like that, but especially not Franco's. Maybe she was crazy, too. Or just temporarily. Maybe she went nuts cause she still loved Franco's dad. Or maybe it was one of those things where you want something to be one way so bad that even though it's the exact opposite way you're still hopeful. And maybe I'd be the same way as Franco if all the same stuff that kept happening to him kept happening to me. But tied him to a chair and slapped him around, though? Come on. And his dad wasn't murdered. He drove into a tree and it might have been on purpose. It was right in the newspaper that afternoon.

I didn't hang out with the woman cop for long. Half an hour tops. My parents got there fast. They entered the station with the ward alderman, Mikey Podesta—I only knew who he was cause the lady cop told me when the three of them walked past our squeaky hallway—but they left with just me a few minutes after that.

At first they hugged me and checked me over to make sure I wasn't messed up or anything, but by the time we got in the car, they were getting pissed. At least he was. My dad, I mean.

"Why did you set that dog on the detective?" he said.

"I didn't know he was a cop," I said. "I was trying to help my friend. Some guy was attacking my friend, I thought."

"Your friend who threw a TV at his stepdad," my dad said.

"He's just the ma's boyfriend, I think—"

"Clifford!" my ma said.

"What?" I said.

"You were high on that Dirt Shooter is why you did what you did."

"I was what on a shooter? I was what?" I said.

"You were high. They saw it right next to you."

"I don't know what you're saying to me," I said. "I don't do drugs. I fell asleep on the couch and when I woke up, there was all this ruckus, and my friend needed help—that's what it looked like—so I went and got the dog to help out my friend."

"You were asleep?" my dad said. "On the couch next to Franco at eleven in the morning?"

"Yeah," I said. "We were watching *Three Stooges*. I hate those guys. You do too. They're annoying."

"That's true," my dad said.

"I don't know why Franco likes that show. It put me to sleep."

"You weren't on Dirt Shooter?"

"What is Dirt Shooter, Ma?" I said. "I don't know what that is."

"I told you he'd never do that Dirt Shooter, Gloria. That was all Franco—I knew it… But you don't hang out in that fucken garage anymore, Cliff, with that wop."

"Why not?" I said.

"You know why not," he said.

I didn't even really want to was the thing—all of a sudden, I was pretty sick of Franco—but I didn't like getting told not to, either. Plus I thought I'd seem guilty if I just said okay.

"Well who's that guy you came into the station with?" I said.

"That's an old friend."

"An old friend who?"

"What's the tone?" said my dad. "His name's Mikey Podesta. He's our alderman. I'd have liked to introduce you if the circumstances were different."

"Why'd Mikey Podesta the alderman go to the station with you?"

"He didn't," my dad said. "He *met* us at the station. He's the one who told us you were there to begin with, and he met us out front."

"How'd he know where I was?"

"The cops called him up."

"The cops called *him*?"

"Yeah," said my dad. "What's so hard to understand?"

"Why'd they call *him*?"

"He's an old friend of mine."

"How do they know who your friends are?"

"They know who *his* friends are."

"Why do they care who he's friends with?" I said.

"Cause he's the alderman," my dad said.

"Why's he a friend of yours?"

"What kind of question is that? What's with all the questions, Cliff?"

"Why do the cops know who you are?"

"I don't even know what you're talking about."

"Before, when they heard my name, one of them said, 'This is the pilot's son.' How do they know who you are? That's weird."

"Weird? Nothing's weird, Cliff," my ma said. "Your father's a pillar."

"A pillar?" I said.

"A pillar of the community," she said.

"A pillar of the community."

"I'm a pilot!" my dad said.

We got to our house. The pillar parked the car and turned around to face me.

"You're not on drugs, right?"

"I'm not," I said.

"You just thought your friend was in trouble, so you helped him."

"Yeah," I said. "Just like I told you."

He studied my eyes, then he said, "I believe you. It's been a rough morning, huh?"

"Yeah," I said.

"Why don't I take you out for lunch and an ice cream or something."

"Yeah," my ma said. "You two should spend some time. Your dad's flying again on Monday."

"How about maybe later," I said. "I want to be alone right now. Think about stuff. I want to take a walk or something."

"Alright," my dad said. "We'll get ribs later, maybe. Or pizza. Whatever."

"Get some lunch, though, Cliff," my ma said. She opened her purse and handed me a twenty. "You can keep the change for that. Eat something good."

I thanked her, and started heading to Theo's, but then I changed my mind and got Burger King instead.

RELATING

MIXED MESSAGES // TWO CONVERSATIONS // BILLY //
A PROFESSOR AND A LOVER // THE END OF FRIENDSHIPS //
CRED // IMPORTANT MEN

MIXED MESSAGES

The message the natives, with hand signs, conveyed was: LEAVE OUR CROPS BE, AND WE WILL GIVE YOU OUR DAUGHTERS.

We hadn't any interest in their crops or their daughters: not their daughters till we realized they were so undervalued, not their crops till we saw that by torching their crops we might teach them to value their daughters more highly.

That our actions could be taken by the natives to mean EVEN TO THE LIKES OF US SEAFARING MEN, THOSE DAUGHTERS OF YOURS ARE OF SO LITTLE VALUE THAT THE PLEASURE WE DERIVE FROM DESTROYING YOUR HARVEST IS PREFERABLE TO THAT WE'D DERIVE FROM THEIR POSSESSION, or perhaps WE WILL TORCH YOUR CROPS *AND THEN* HAVE YOUR DAUGHTERS did not occur to us—these sorts of possibilities simply refuse, in the heat of the moment, to occur with the facility they occur to you later, in your well-appointed quarters, sipping from a magnum of pupu-tree liquor, reviewing the day's events in your log—but such misunderstanding on the part of the natives might in fact provide the correct explanation for why they elected, in the glow of the fires we had put to their crops, to pulp all their daughters' skulls with clubs.

At the time we assumed they were offering us a sacrifice.

TWO CONVERSATIONS

A FALSE START. It meant something to the man it didn't mean to the woman, something it didn't mean to normal people. But that, in itself, was not the problem. It wasn't what drove her mad, so to speak. What drove her mad—*"Drove her mad," so to speak!* the woman thought; *"'Drove her mad,' so to speak," the woman thought!* she thought—came three days later, in their next conversation, when she'd called to clarify the first conversation, a brief conversation, the one in which he had said A FALSE START, which brief conversation she had since realized to have been too easy for him (she had, she'd realized, been too easy *on* him), *too easy* in the sense that she had not *shed tears* till she got off the telephone, had *exhausted all her powers* via *holding back tears* and *controlling her voice and the sound of her breathing*, telling herself—while still on the phone—that weeping, hers, was *what he was after*, and therefore weeping would mean *her defeat*, when that hadn't been, she now reflected, the case at all, but *quite the opposite*, for *failing to weep*, the woman saw now, had signaled to the man her *ready acceptance* of all that he'd said about A FALSE START, which nullified in him any *sense of obligation*, any sense of *his duty* to offer her *comfort*, to *clean up the mess that he'd made* because *mess*? where *mess*? *mess* what? what *mess*? No one had *wept*. No one had *argued*. No one had done anything except to *accept* and stammer about A FALSE START once or twice, and when she called him up, *weeping*, three days later, what *drove her mad* was the way he made it sound as though she was betraying—in calling him, *weeping*, three days later—an agreement they'd made, the way A FALSE START had become *THE FALSE START*, as in "But we already discussed *THE FALSE START*."

BILLY

I had this mutt once. Medium-to-large. A gift from my father, a schmuck. I forget the mutt's name. It had a few before it died and I can't remember what we finally settled on. When we dropped its corpse into the ditch we'd dug, my schmuck father said a prayer to his schmuck higher power in which the mutt's name was mentioned, and I remember feeling confused for a second because the name wasn't the name I was expecting to hear. Whether my father'd used the mutt's most recent name and I'd been expecting to hear an earlier name or it was the other way around I couldn't say, but it sounded all wrong. It sounded wrong to my brother, too, now that I think about it, so that probably means Dad used an earlier name because my brother was not sentimental—he was a mental cripple—and he corrected my father's prayer, and my father gave him a kind of schmuck-type look, though he let the correction stand, and Billy piped down.

Billy was also one of the names of the mutt, not just my brother, who was, understandably, confused by this fact, though it was my brother himself who named the mutt Billy. Billy, now that I recall it, was the mutt's original name, and that, in fact, is part of how the mutt came to have so many different names.

I said the mutt was my mutt, but the mutt started out Billy's mutt, who Dad brought the mutt home for and then told to name it. When Billy named it Billy, I said it was a bad idea and my dad said it wasn't up to me. What he actually said was, "Not your dog," which is how a schmuck talks, but what he meant was what I just said he said—wasn't up to me—and then he left the room and ate some cold chicken.

A few days into having a mutt with the same name as him, which made Billy-my-brother more confused and scared than usual, Billy said he wanted to change the mutt's name, and my dad said he could not change the mutt's name. Said he had to stick with his choice, honor his commitments, the schmuck, though what he actually said to my brother when my brother, mentally crippled, said he'd like to change the mutt's name was, "Can't. Made your bed." I made, in response, a kind of fuck-you face, and my father told me, "Not your dog," so I offered my brother a dollar for the mutt and Billy sold me the mutt and ran off to buy candy and I gave the mutt its second name, which I don't remember, and my schmuck father gave me a kind of schmuck-type defeated look, so I gave the mutt a third name, right then and there, and received another schmuck look, and I gave the mutt a fourth name, and so on, until the schmuck stopped looking at me, which didn't take that long.

The thing about it was, though, I didn't much want the mutt and had bought it only to help out Billy and get at the schmuck, and had, in fact, later offered to sell the mutt back to Billy, newly named, for just a penny, but Billy didn't much want the mutt either, poor mutt. Poor schmuck. Poor Billy. Poor me.

A couple days later, the mutt got sick with something I can't remember, something painful we couldn't afford to treat, and the schmuck, who said it was my responsibility, would neither let me handle his gun nor would he shoot the mutt himself. I'd had enough of this schmuck ruling over me and Billy, and I did what I had to. I raised up a shovel and ended the mutt and raised up that shovel and turned to the schmuck and told him some things had to change around here and I told him he would help us bury the mutt.

A PROFESSOR AND A LOVER

No. A SENSE OF ENTITLEMENT—a phrase better suited to describe the quality possessed by freshmen who park their Jeeps in the handicapped spaces of faculty lots and contest B-minuses with intendedly rhetorical questions like "How do you expect me to be accepted into a top-tier law school if you won't give me an A?"—would not describe the DRIVING FORCE that had led Professor Jon Maxwell Schinkl, medievalist, to drag three fingertips along the curve of moon-faced sophomore Hallie Benton's jawline and speak INAPPROPRIATELY about her mouth. Nor, for that matter, did PERVERSITY describe the DRIVING FORCE. But then no one on the committee had posited PERVERSITY. To accuse Schinkl of PERVERSITY would endanger their whole PROJECT, for PERVERSITY was a HEGEMENOUS concept responsible for SOCIAL BIAS against the likes of furries and N.A.M.B.L.A. constituents, no less so coprophiliacs and gerbilers. (Though to be fair, just last semester THE RIGHT OF GERBILERS TO GERBIL was hotly contested by a special panel comprising six members of the very disciplinary committee before whom Schinkl was presently speechifying, and while it's true that during that panel-discussion—over the two-hour course of which the words NATURAL and UNNATURAL remained impressively unspoken—three of the committee members had defended the gerbiler assertion that GERBILS SEEMED TO ENJOY GERBILING, it is also true that the other three members, while they readily defended THE LEGITIMACY OF THE *DESIRE* TO GERBIL, and even the possibility that gerbils themselves enjoyed THEIR ROLE IN THE PROCESS, were also MADE UNCOMFORTABLE BY THE IDEA OF SPEAKING FOR ANY POPULATION BEREFT OF A VOICE WITH WHICH TO PROTEST ITS OWN OPPRESSION and therefore opined that THE WILL TO MAKE SUCH PROTESTS, HOWEVER FRUSTRATED BY SYSTEMIC LIMITATIONS, IS MORE SAFELY ASSUMED MANIFEST IN GERBILS THAN NOT and that furthermore WHETHER THEIR ROLE IN THE PROCESS IS EXPLOITATIVE OR TRULY CONSENSUAL, GERBILS, AS OFTEN AS NOT, DIE INSIDE THOSE WHO GERBIL THEM. Thereafter ensued a firestorm of fresh debate about the meaning of CHOICE and THE RIGHT TO DIE. The firestorm had raged beyond the bounds of the panel, for the most part via listserv, until just last Monday, at which point Hallie Benton's formal complaint, to the relief of everyone in the college but Schinkl, decisively snuffed it.) No, it was not PERVERSITY the committee had accused him of. Had they accused him of PERVERSITY, they would have been vulnerable to the counter-accusation of HYPOCRISY, an accusation with which they had—each and every one of them—made their careers by uttering skillfully, liberally, without hesitation. Like a master long-swordsman and a long sword, the committee members had wielded HYPOCRISY so many times, had landed so many fatal blows with it, that they almost couldn't have helped but to forge and don the superlative armor they'd forged and continued to don against the accusation. Even if their armor's impregnability was an illusion—even if the armor was, as it were, a little bit pregnable—the members' reputations as masters over HYPOCRISY served to prevent all but their most reckless enemies (doomed from the outset by their recklessness anyway) from testing that armor with the one weapon it was specifically designed to frustrate. No, to stab at their helmets with HYPOCRISY would only serve to humiliate Schinkl further. In pursuing the death of master long-swordsmen, one's only hope is to mount a cliff and take aim with a crossbow, if not a carbine. Yet THE PATRIARCHAL RHETORIC OF ROMANTIC LOVE was all that Schinkl had come to the hearing strapped with, and even if that old cannon *had* retained some firepower, he was far too scared of heights to climb any cliff, and so instead he said a number of lofty-sounding things that smelled of self-pity and resigned.

THE END OF FRIENDSHIPS

That to hide amid the strip mall's dumpster-array and unbox, uncap, and—tipping her head back, squinting against the high summer sun, nozzle whole inches above her lips—empty the tube of frosting she'd stolen from Pattycake's Partystore into herself had provided Danielle Platz, who was lately getting stocky, AN EROTIC CHARGE was not the kind of information her father, Richard, had meant to solicit when he queried their neighbor, Dr. Linus Manx, about whether Danielle had behaved that afternoon on her trip into town with the Manxes. It seemed to Richard Platz the kind of information that a decent human being, psychotherapist or not, shouldn't ever share with another human being about his child—the second human being's. Either one's, actually, come to think of it. And Richard Platz, coming to think of it, had no doubt at all that Dr. Linus Manx would have proffered the same untoward information about Johan Manx, who had after all hidden amid the dumpsters right next to Danielle, sucking down his own tube of stolen frosting, were Johan, rather than budding his way into sequined, lisping, limp-wristed queerdom—Platz had seen him mincing in overtight T-shirts around the sprinkler, dancing serpentinely in their unfinished basement, making pouty faces when he swung on their swing set—also getting stocky. Which is just what Richard Platz, in so many words, said to Linus Manx on the trapezoid of grass that split their two driveways.

CRED

The funny thing about Kelly's body was the way it appeared to weirdly bulge above the puss area whenever she wore clothes, but then was fine (flat, smooth) once she got naked. (This might more accurately be described as the funny thing about Kelly's *pants*, seeing as it had to be the pants that caused the bulge. And yet the pants were normal, Levi's five-oh-whatevers, so it wouldn't be the way the pants were made that was funny, but the way the pants fit her body. Unless it was a funny way she *wore* the pants, i.e., maybe they would have fit just fine if she didn't pull the waist so high or low, or—it didn't matter. What mattered was that the way her overpuss area bulged or *seemed to bulge* when she was clothed, but then didn't bulge or seem to when she was naked, was... funny.) Cort didn't know whether to think of this as a gift or a curse, though. On the one hand, the bulging overpuss area was off-putting, and that kept, he assumed, any number of other dudes from hitting on Kelly, which, for Cort, meant (most likely) a more grateful girlfriend in terms of how she fucked, not to mention less competition. But on the other hand, was Kelly THE ONE? Because if Kelly *was* THE ONE, then hey, great: no downside to a seemingly bulging overpuss whatsoever. If Kelly was *not* THE ONE, though, and Cort would, eventually, be moving on, then couldn't dating her hurt his chances with other girls later? Might not other girls, later, remember him as the guy who'd settled for that girl with the overpuss out to there, and thereby fail to feel flattered enough by his interest in them to give him a shot? And even if, with his native charm (he had a way with words), Cort could overcome that particular hurdle, might not a longer-term girlfriend, at some point further along in their relationship, find herself incapable—upon recalling Kelly's (seemingly) bulging overpuss—of accepting Cort's assurances that she was as attractive as she wanted to be? ("He says I'm not fat, but what does he know? His last girlfriend weirdly bulged above the puss area!") Or, worse, might not the new girlfriend choose to let herself go (split ends, rough knees, dimpled cellulite, etc.), believing that Cort, who had, after all, dated someone with a (seemingly) bulging overpuss, *wouldn't mind*? Well... sure. Of course. Sure. All kinds of retarded stuff *could* happen, thought Cort, but that was only the scratched-up lousy side of a coin whose shiny nice side was all the cred he'd get from girls for going out with Kelly despite her unfortunate overpuss bulge. And if it *did* turn out that Kelly wasn't THE ONE, and that Cort had been suffering the overpuss bulge for a smaller payout than real true love, not only would that land him in the black, karmically, but these cred-giving girls would be all over him, knowing he would never say anything, or even *think* anything, about their bodies to cause them any feelings of insecurity, because, as he'd have demonstrated by dating that girl with the weird bulge above the puss area, Cort wasn't shallow.

IMPORTANT MEN

As he approached me on the sidewalk, I noticed the important man had the kind of face that would look exactly the same with or without a mustache. He was carrying a black-lacquered cane with a diamond-studded handle and I envied him his cane. I imagined thumping my fingertips against it, the sound that would make, and flipping it upside-down to make believe it was the letter *L*. If the cane were mine, I would pretend it was a long-barreled pistol with a diamond-studded grip. I would holster it in the elastic of my jockey shorts and have friends. When I came across a friend, I would pull the cane out of the holster and point it, say: "Gotcha." I could do that as many times as I wanted, and it would never stop being a good joke. I would be what they call "a character." People would want to see more of me. They would say of me, "That character! Always with the cane he pretends is a pistol!" and exchange intimate glances with one another, then wave the whole thing off with both hands and decide to lunch together. "Lunch?" one would say. "Let's," would say another.

The important man continued in my direction, until he was right in front of me. I made myself sideways so he could pass. My fingernails grazed the button on his epaulet. "Pardon," he said, and he was walking away.

Just like the last one.

"Come back," I said.

He waved me off and sped his pace. I went after him. I walked beside him. The heat was unbearable that day. I was sweating.

"I have something to ask you," I said.

He said, "*What's* that?" but he kept walking, like he was scared of me, like I had done something wrong or something dangerous. I was going to ask him if he ever imagined his cane was a pistol, and then say, "Me too," and we would have something in common. But I knew that would scare him and I didn't want that to scare him so I said something *I* thought was scary so we could both be scared together. I said, "The voice of your brother's blood cries out to me from the ground!" and made a movement with my shoulders like I would hit him, and he flinched. That was when another man (bearded) came along. This second man owned the hat shop that we were standing in front of, but he was not wearing a hat and he said to me, "What the fuck? Who the fuck?"

"I don't know," I said. I was ashamed to look at him. I looked at the display window. It was full of breastless, earth-tone mannequins in bowlers and derby hats sitting in folding chairs around a square table, one on each side. There were playing cards affixed to their hands by means of an invisible adhesive, probably the quick-dry liquid variety. There wasn't a single thumb between the four of them and this second man expected me to pretend they were playing poker.

"Who the *fuck*?" the second man said again.

I imagined he knew I didn't understand him and that was why he said it the second time. I think he gave up on me after that.

Still watching the mannequins, I made a thinking face to appease him. Then I started thinking. I thought: They do not have ears and they do not have hair, yet their hats do not fall over their eyes—there must be adhesive. I thought: But a liquid adhesive of the kind affixing the cards to the hands would, if used on the heads, irreparably gum up the fibers in the hats and ruin their potential to be sold well. No, I thought, a liquid adhesive would not be appropriate at all, and therefore the mannequins must have strips of adhesive *tape* between their heads and their hats, and these strips must be looped into O-shapes. Oh, you're stupid. You thought you were smart, but you're stupid, I hate you. There is double-sided tape for sale at stores. There is the law of parsimony. Nothing need be looped into O-shapes—not when both sides adhere with equal potency. You should have thought of that first, but you are not elegant.

The second man said, "Go," and pointed me across the street.

I crossed the street and straddled a construction horse. I watched the second man talk to the first. They spoke like friends. The second man set his hand on the shoulder of the first man and the first man leaned on his cane toward the second man and soon they were laughing. When they laughed, I could see the steam of their gasps converging. I thought: Maybe they don't know each other at all and the second man is the greatest salesman who ever lived, is selling the first man a hat without the first man even knowing that he is being sold a hat. I thought: I wonder if they notice the way their steam is converging. I wonder if the second man does but the first man doesn't, if knowing how to foment this convergence is one of the secrets to being as great a salesman as the second man. Convinced of it, and convinced that the second man, despite his canelessness, was important, possibly even more important than the first, I set out to find someone to mingle steam with. This is not as easy for me as it is for others. It is not as easy as it should be.

I walked a block and found two men talking. I approached the younger one and said, "What the fuck? Who the fuck? Who the fuck? Go." It didn't work.

JANE TELL

This puffy-eyed woman with a bluish dewlap used to order three mugs of coffee at a time every weekday morning at the Highland Park Denny's. When servers gave her looks or told her that refills were free and unlimited, she'd answer at a volume that begged overhearing, "I have trouble waiting." One time I was seated in the booth beside hers and I noticed a white, rectangular pill lying on its side next to one of the mugs. I was all but certain it was a bar of Xanax, a top-three favorite, but I couldn't read the markings. The woman caught me squinting, and I could see by the way that she pinkened and slouched that she thought I was judging her. What did I care? I guess I cared a little. I said, "Is that a Xanax bar?" Then she started talking fast. She didn't love Xanax. It allowed her to sleep well and made her less anxious, but the trade-off was fogginess and boring thoughts, and her boredom made her sad, so she'd chug down coffee till her brain started firing, but then she'd get anxious all over again and require more Xanax. "Unfixable," she said. I nodded sympathetically and looked her in the eyes and, before I'd even gotten the French toast I'd ordered, she'd said she'd gladly trade half her sixty-count bottle for a quarter ounce of weed to anyone who'd take it.

My cost on a quarter was just thirty dollars, and Xanax bars, at that time, went for six apiece, minimum. It was nonetheless dim to consider the offer—I didn't know her—but middle-aged women seemed harmless to me, and I'd been selling marijuana since my freshman year of high school without any trouble.

We settled our bills and went to her minivan. The bull's-eye on the SuperTarget sign across the strip mall flickered, and the woman, eyes averted, digging around in her purse for her keys, asked me, "Can I feel your muscle?"

She had to be fifty-five, sixty years old. I bent my arm and felt stupid about it. Her fingers, which she'd managed to get into my jacket and under the sleeve of my T-shirt, were icy. "You're strong," she said. "Do you want to smoke with me?"

"No," I told her.

Whenever I smoked marijuana, I'd stare, and whatever I'd stare at would seem important. All images became imagery, sophomoric imagery, the symbolic meaning of the non-symbolic things on which my eyes fixed wholly independent of their actual functions. Cigars not just cocks, but primal cocks—the primal cocks of the patriarchs. The last time I'd smoked pot was a year before; a girlfriend had convinced me I could like it again, like I'd used to in high school. When I woke at my desk a few hours later, the new scrolling message on my monitor read IMAGISTIC METAPHORS HEMORRHAGE ANALOGIES WITHIN THE CLUTCHES OF MY HEAVY HANDS. Before I could delete it, the girlfriend saw it, took hold of my shoulders, and told me, "That's trippy plus also creative," then detailed the ways it was trippy and creative, and I counted off a week before breaking up with her. In short, marijuana made me hate everything, but I'd long since quit explaining even that to anyone. Most people, when you tell them you're not into their vice, they either assume you're afraid or don't like them. If you're selling them the vice, they know you're not afraid. Those few who do take what you say at face value see you're different from them, which undermines trust. And my bags were light—I made ten "eighths" of every ounce. If someone ever pulled out a scale, I'd be fucked.

Still, I could have said more to the puffy-eyed woman to nice up my "No," and normally I would have—I'd have said I had an exam in an hour, or was heading to my parents' house to drive them to the airport—but I didn't feel like lying. That muscle-squeeze had siphoned off my will to accommodate. Nice wasn't in me.

"Really?" said the woman.

"Really," I said.

A throaty, clogged sound joggled her dewlap. "It's okay," she said. "It's really okay. I understand I'm disgusting. I'm old. I disgust you." Tears cut trails through her blush and powder. She did disgust me. Her weeping was cunning. She was cueing me to tell her she was young and attractive. What she wasn't doing, though, was backing out of the deal.

The summer I'd worked for him, cold-calling prospects, my father, an insurance man, had more than once warned me, "Brusqueness doesn't help anyone's sales." About that he was right, but the distinction between *not helping* and *hurting* was, I was thinking there in the Denny's lot, a pretty big one, at least when it came to selling drugs.

The flesh-colored tears clung to some fuzz along the woman's jawline, then trembled, elongated, and splatted on the pavement. After three or four splats, she saw she'd failed to cue me.

"You're cruel," she said. "A cruel person," she said.

I watched the wet spot widen on the pavement.

"A cruel person," she echoed. She had had this conversation before. The big distinction between then and now, apart from my being an entirely different human being, was that the last guy had insisted he was not a cruel person. She couldn't figure out what to say to him at the time, but as she'd driven away from him (I could see her chewing her waxy lower lip, jerking her head in tiny, neck-cramping nods), she'd come up with a retort that she'd hoped to use the next time—this time. But I'd fucked it all up for her by failing to protest against the accusation, and now she was stuck repeating herself. "A very cruel person," she said. "You're cruel." By the seventh repetition—by then she was whispering—I started, despite my disgust, to feel bad for her, guilty for repelling whatever small victory she needed to save the face she'd lost the last time.

"Hey, look," I said. "I'll have a cigarette with you."

"Only because you feel sorry for me." She said it through her teeth.

"Do the cruel," I said, "feel sorry for the crying?"

"No," she said. "I guess they don't." All at once, she stopped her crying. "You're a strange kid," she said. "You're clever," she said, and, tagging my shoulder with a friendly open palm, she told me, "Have your ciggy while I roll up a j-bird."

Her minivan's interior smelled of scented kleenex. She pulled a sleeve of papers from a cassette slot in the console and slipped her body sideways through the space between the seats, her forehead smearing across my jaw as she ducked and contorted toward the bench in the back, where the windows were tinted. "Sorry," she said. I stayed shotgun and pulled two "eighths" from my jacket. I emptied one baggie into the other and handed both back to her. She rolled a small joint and licked it shut, her tongue long and coffee-stained, and fired up her lighter. She said, "Should I call you when I get the refill?" I told her my number and she repeated it back to me while writing it down, then continued to write, singsonging, "For wee-eed." Once she'd finished her joint, she tapped thirty pills from an amber bottle into the empty baggie I'd given her, and drove me to my car, ten spaces away. Just like that, I'd made a hundred and fifty dollars.

Fifteen minutes later, traffic-stopped for something, the dunce got arrested for possession. The next day, detectives came by with a search warrant (quiet suburb, bored police force). I'd been waiting for a pizza to be delivered, and I opened the door without checking the peephole. My drugs were stored in my box of comics and there was no way to flush them— I was made to sit in plain view on the couch—and there was no way the cops would fail to check the box, so I told them where to look, thinking my willing cooperation might minimize damages. I told them that, too.

"In your dreams," one said. "This ain't some movie. We don't like you, and that haircut."

"It's a real stupid haircut," another one said.

They trashed my beanbag, sifted the styrofoam filling for pills. Then they dumped my comics out of their dust bags, ripping the covers off both my mint-condition *Lobo* #1s—my first investments. At age twelve, I'd bought two so I could eventually sell one and still have my cake. The purchase occasioned a fight between me and my father. He didn't like the idea that I saw comics as an investment in anything other than my "imagination." From then on, I had to use my allowance to buy them, and my collecting behavior ended pretty quickly, and all for the better—my father'd been right. *Lobo* #1 was a huge bestseller. There were thousands of them in plastic dust bags with cardboard backings, in cardboard boxes in closets. The last I'd checked, they were worth less than half the price on their covers.

The cops found the Xanax and three "eighth" bags—luckily all I had at the time. The lawyer my father hired—old friend, deep discount—had me check into a six-week outpatient rehab program at a clinic in Highwood. They all knew I was faking, except the psychiatrist, Dr. Manx. I'd had Manx as a professor during the previous semester—Behaviorist Methodologies: An Introduction—and he liked me. He told me it was clear to him that I was angry, and that I suffered from chronic stress. In court eight weeks later, I pled guilty to misdemeanor possession, the lawyer argued I was a benzo and marijuana addict, and Manx said I used drugs in order to manage my anger and my stress.

I was a "self-medicator," Manx told the judge, but I was twenty years old, my whole life ahead of me, and now I was clean.

I was fined $2,500 and given three years probation and a one-year prison sentence suspended on the condition I underwent weekly urinalyses and attended a twice-weekly anger-management group at the locale of my choice. I picked Highland Park Hospital. It was nearby and I could piss in their cup on my way out. Plus, the brochures said it was behavior-focused, and I liked B. F. Skinner. I'd been reading him steadily ever since the Manx class.

At the start of the first meeting, Jane Tell sat across the group circle from me. She kept her eyes on her knees, her hands in her lap, and her parted red hair fell thick past her shoulders. She scratched at her palms nonstop. Anyone else so slumped and ticky would have read timid, but Tell seemed spring-loaded, extra-alive. It was impossible not to watch her.

The therapist, in his homemade sweater, spoke the stilted-mushy English of a Martian diplomat. He told us the meetings were broken in two. The first hour was experiential, meaning topics weren't scheduled and we would talk to one another about whatever was on our minds. The second hour was instructional. "Not that I am some kind of pedagogical heavy," he said, "but if you will be patient with me, I think I can teach you one or two things."

Aside from Tell and me, there were two women and three men, squint-eyed office workers in their mid-to-late thirties. They had imitation-leather day-planners and adenoidal difficulties. Their sense of humor was desperate, their jokes delivered in the voices they suppressed during staff meetings. They fell apart for the spoken italic. Indignant up-talking left them in stitches: the *just... okay?* punchline; the biting sarcasm of the *yeah, right!?* The last one of them to self-introduce to the group closed with the phrase, "And kicking the fucking copy machine when no one's *fuck*ing looking, I'll tell you what," and they all laughed wildly at the enunciation of the second curse's first syllable, the fluorescent overheads splotching oily patches on their over-pink faces, high shine in the spit-creeks of their off-white teeth.

Tell said she was nineteen and had dropped out of art school. She lived in Deerfield with her mother and stepfather. She called her mother "Peggy" and her stepdad "the Otter." She fought with them viciously, and they had threatened to kick her out if she didn't get treatment.

I told them I was a junior in college and I'd go to prison if I didn't show up. A few of the office workers expressed discomfort. The therapist praised them for their openness and referred to me as a "mandated client."

"Mandated clients," he said, "tend to be resistant to the group process. Helping them to feel a part of the group is one of the activities that can make the group stronger and more helpful to all its members. We welcome you, Ben."

During the break, Tell approached me at the refreshments table. She bugged her eyes out and nodded me toward her.

"I'm Ben," I said.

She said, "I know your name. Don't be such a Steve."

"What's a Steve?" I said.

"No," Tell said. "Ask something braver."

"You want to hang out?"

"Isn't that what we're doing?"

"Elsewhere," I said. "In the future. On a 'date.'"

"Don't do it with air-quotes."

"On a *date*," I said.

"I've never been on a date."

"Few have," I said. "Let alone with me."

"Where would we go?"

"Denny's," I said. "Or the railroad tracks. Maybe even Denny's *and then* the railroad tracks."

"That's some fancy date."

"You..."

"What?"

"I'm a..."

"What?"

"I'm trying to come up with something to make you laugh, but we keep saying 'date,' and I'm a mandated client, and I'm spending all this energy resisting the reflex to shoot for a pun."

"'Let me take you on a really manly date,' or something."

"Exactly," I said. "You deserve a lot better."

"That's nice," Tell said. "It's a nice thing to say. Probably you can just skip all the funny now and offer me a smoke."

The designated area, on the parking-lot sidewalk, was a bus-stop shelter with columnar ashtrays. I sat on the bench and handed up a Marlboro—Tell remained standing. She bent toward my lighter, hair tucked behind her ears, cigarette lipped. She touched her fingers to my knuckles to guide the fire. Free from the dinge of those overhead fluorescents, I could see she was perfect, except for a round, red scrape on her cheek. Before I had a chance to say anything, she was standing up straight again, offering her hand. I took it, held on. She said, "It was nice to meet you, Ben."

I said, "It was nice to meet you too, Tell."

She started off toward the parking-lot exit and then she returned to me. "We should try that again," she said, "with eye contact." She grasped my hand, said my name a second time, and looked at my eyes. Then she walked away, but not back inside.

Back inside, all the chairs were rearranged to face the wall. In front of the wall was a sketch-pad mounted on a tripod easel. In front of the pad stood the therapist. He said, "It's time to begin the instructional portion of group. I think we're still waiting for someone?"

They'd all seen us walk out together and now they were staring at me like I'd done something to her.

"Tell got sick," I said. "She said she'd be back on Thursday and that she looked forward to it and hoped that none of you would feel insulted by her leaving early."

"Actually," one of the men toward the other end of the chair-line said, "I do feel a little insulted. In fact, very insulted."

"That's pretty fucken ridiculous," I said.

The therapist clapped his hands once and said, "This is a perfect opportunity to learn some anger-management skills." He removed a pink marker from its slot along the bottom of the easel and uncapped it. He wrote:

JAKE: Actually, I do feel a little bit insulted. In fact,
    very insulted.

BEN: That's pretty effing ridiculous!

"We'll come back to this exchange later," said the therapist. "For now, while it's still fresh in our minds, can we agree the transcription is accurate?"

I said, "I didn't say it with an exclamation point."

"Regardless of how you said it," said the therapist, "that's how it sounded. The third word you used signifies aggression. It's important to know that—"

"Signify sniveling for Jake, then," I said. "I think we can all agree Jake sniveled."

A group shrug.

"That's a very subjective analysis, Ben," said the therapist, "and we'll explore it later."

I said, "It's a context-based analysis. And that's the only kind Skinner allows for. I just read about it in *Verbal Behavior*. Isn't this a behavioral therapy group?"

"It's a *cognitive*-behavioral therapy group, stress on the *cognitive*, and you shouldn't be reading Skinner," said the therapist. "Skinner's wrong-minded."

"Skinner's a monster," said one of the women. "He tried to make factories where you brought him your children and he turned your children into various types of professionals."

"Skinner's an ingrate," the man next to me said. "The guy just has no respect for the subconscious. He thinks we don't have minds. And we do have minds and our minds are like computers."

"But really good computers," the woman said.

"The best computers ever," the therapist said.

"The problem," Jake said, "is Skinner thinks thinking doesn't matter. And that's ugly, man. That's truly ugly. Maybe it's Skinner who makes you feel so angry all the time, Ben. Because, like, what happens to free will if thinking doesn't matter? Because what's will, you know? It's free thinking. And, frankly, I freely think Skinner's worldview is an insult to my humanity. For one thing, he should've quit making those rats salivate to buzzers, because it was cruel to do it to those animals. And he definitely should have kept his dumb ideas to himself. He's harmful, actually."

"You're a genius," I said.

The therapist wrote it down like this:

> JAKE: B. F. Skinner's philosophy of human psychology is not only disempowering, but dehumanizing.
>
> BEN: You're a (real effing) genius!

After the meeting, I found Tell waiting in the bus-stop shelter. She took my hand and walked us to her truck in the lot by the cancer ward.

"You missed the instructional portion of group," I said.

She kissed me—pressed me against the front of her pickup and kissed my neck fast, once, with licked lips. Then she tugged on my belt loops and kicked at my insteps. I was thinking: It is not as dark outside as you expected, summer is coming. I was thinking: This is the first time you've ever been kissed first.

I had my hands in her hair, then on her arms, her hips. She squeezed the back of my neck and bit my mouth. Everything about us felt clean and susceptible. Her skin was warm—even hot—beneath my hands, but her face cooled mine like a hotel pillowcase.

Soon she pulled my stupid hair and I opened my eyes. "We're scratching the hood," she said. "You want to see inside? I rebuilt the engine with my uncle."

She popped the hood and showed me some things. I don't know what she showed me.

"Let's go somewhere else," she said. "In yours. I want to drive it."

Tell grabbed a Johnny Cash tape from the deck in her truck and we took my car to Denny's. She put the tape in and drove fast. The first song was "Long Black Veil." So was the second. She asked, "Why'd you decide to buy an auto-tranny?"

I didn't know what that meant. Then I knew, but it took a second: *tranny* was transmission. My car's was automatic. She wanted to know if I could drive stick. I didn't want to admit that I couldn't. "You prefer a *standard transmission?*" I said, with that heavy stress on the *standard transmission* to suggest that what had stalled my response was pleasant surprise, not incomprehension, much less calculation.

Tell said, "See, now, that's why I like you. When you act like a Steve, it's cause you're being sweet and you don't even know it—you think you're working something. I'm gonna cut all your nappy hair off and make you famous. Do you have a little Jewish sister who looks just like you?"

"Leah," I said.

"I bet she's a knockout."

"I don't remember 'Long Black Veil' being this long," I said.

"It's my favorite."

Tell parked us at the far end of the lot, facing the Ford dealership. Before we got out of the car, she started kissing me again. Then we reclined our seats and the tape switched sides and "Long Black Veil" started up again and ended and started up again. We listened to it one more time, then walked to the restaurant.

A few steps outside the entrance, Tell stopped. She said, "I know this'll sound weird, but I want you to do something for me."

"Name it."

She said, "I want you to pick me up by the ankles and swing me face-first into the side of that dumpster."

"Ha! Fuck that," I said, laughing.

"Don't curse at me," she said. "If you think I'm too heavy, I'll stay on my feet and you can swing me by a wrist." At her waist she balled her hands like they were cuffed. "Pick a wrist."

"Quit it," I said.

She said, "I'm serious. I want you to."

I continued to refuse and she continued to ask me. I was crouching beside her, trying to light a pair of cigarettes—it had gotten windy and my lighter was dying—when a semi-truck pulled into the lot. A tall, pale man stepped out of the cab and walked in our direction. He offered me a friendly half-nod in greeting and met Tell's face—she was winking at him—with a closed fist on the chin. Moaning, she fell back into the wall. I dropped the lighter and went forward to attack. I don't know how to fight. I thought I'd punch the middle of the back of his neck. To make that happen, though, I'd have had to jump higher. I missed his neck entirely, barely grazed his shoulder. He spun around and whammed me a fast one to the jaw. The unlit cigarettes popped from my lips, and I sat where I'd stood, like any clown out of Hemingway.

Pointing his finger too close to my eyes, he said, "Sometimes they like it."

"Thank you," Tell told him. "Get away from us now."

He went inside the restaurant. My jaw only tingled. It hadn't started hurting yet. I lay on my back and listened to the highway, the Doppler-shifting buzzings of passing cars. I didn't have a thought. I could have fallen asleep. "Ben," Tell said, and I opened my eyes. Her face was upside down over my own. Blood from her chin dripped into my hair.

"You're bleeding," I said. "He was wearing a ring."

"We're fine," she said. "Just punched. Get up."

She pressed her lips to my swelling jaw and led me through diesel fumes across two parking lots. It did occur to me that Tell's offhanded-ness was worthy of alarm, likely indicative of something bad, something *wrong*, but I didn't feel even slightly alarmed. Her nonchalance detached me from my own observations, turned me academic. It felt almost as if I were reading about her, as if the person pulling on my hand were only describing Jane Tell to me.

I was slow from getting hit and, just as I was summing words to form a question that would address the matter—one no more complicated than "What just happened?"—Tell edged us between the wall of the SuperTarget and the dollar-ride carousel next to the door where we fucked sitting up with our clothes on. That was the only time I got hit and it was the only time that fucking Tell, or fucking anyone, ever felt entirely right. What would normally have struck me as haunting seemed merely striking. Like when you first learn your body is made of cells, or your emotions chemicals. The first time you cheer for a gangster in a movie. Before you realize what you're accepting.

Afterward, I had the sense the sex implicated me in something. I assumed rightly that it was love and asked her to marry me.

I drove Tell to the hospital to get her truck. On the way, I kept thinking I saw my thermostat needle creeping to the right, but then we'd get to a stop, and I'd look a little closer and see it was smack in the middle—it was fine. Tell's truck, on the other hand, refused to start, so I drove us to her mother's.

My jaw was swollen by the time we arrived. Tell's mother, giving it a squint and a head-tilt, said, "What a pleasure to meet you, Ben, now please leave my home," and Tell ripped the fresh scab off the gash on her chin and bled on the rug.

She said, "I'm moving in with him, and then we're getting married."

"Like hell you are," her mom said.

The stepdad, watching Leno and eating baby carrots from a cereal bowl, spoke the word *guffaw* and slapped his knee. "Guffaw," he said. "Guffaw, guffaw."

Tell handed me her scab. "Smoke a cigarette with my mother while I pack up my stuff."

I held out my pack and her mom took two. She tossed one to the stepdad.

Tipping his head back, he leaned forward and caught it, filter-first, in his mouth. Then he clapped.

"She's done this before," Tell's mother said. I lit her cigarette. "You're just the newest nice guy."

"Amen," said the stepdad. "Hey. How about a light, Peggy?"

"How about give me half a second, Steve."

"Your name's Steve?" I said.

"Stephen, actually. With a *p h*," he said. "Steve means something else."

I took a look around the living room, a normal-looking living room: leather couch, reclining chair, steel-and-glass coffee table. A knickknack tray on an oldish-looking bureau. Framed photos in a line on a squat red-wood bench. I found a clay ashtray on a speaker behind me, next to the television. Everything looked normal. I don't know what I was expecting.

"Look at me," Tell's mom said. "See the resemblance?" I looked. She was normal-looking, too. I didn't see much of a resemblance, though. Maybe something around the eyes.

She grabbed the meat of her gut and shook it. She tucked her head and pointed at the second chin. "This is what happens if you get her pregnant, boy-o. And you will. And then you get another one just like her, no matter how sure she is it'll be a son. Shit. And then she leaves you because you're not who you say you are and she goes and gets another one like him." She thumbed the air in the stepdad's direction. "And then that's it. Two, three more lives wasted and another stupid kid walking around, spreading her legs for any guy who'll listen to her sad stories and say it's not her fault. It's wretched. It's wretched and it's inevitable."

"That sounds rehearsed," I said.

She said, "I told you. You're not the first one."

Tell returned with a duffel, a telescopic easel, and an expandable plastic box containing paints and brushes. She set the easel and the box at my feet. "I should grab a pillow," she said. "I like a lot of pillows."

"You don't *own* a pillow," said the stepdad. "I own the pillows."

"I've got pillows," I said.

"I hope that's everything," said Peggy. "Because we're changing the locks tomorrow."

Tell said, "I still have some stuff in my room I want to get. My truck's broken down, though." She opened my fist and took the scab back. She held it out to her mom. "You can keep this until I can get back here for my stereo and clothes," she said. "And then you can change the locks."

"Why are you so disturbed?" her mom said.

"Just please, Mom?" Tell dangled the scab for a second, then reached around her mother to set it on the edge of the coffee table.

"Please!" her mom said. "We *eat* here." She seized the scab between her pink fingernails and dropped it in the ashtray.

Tell drew a set of scissors from a drawer in the bureau.

"Those are mine," said the Steve.

The truck driver was a fluke. According to Tell, the beating he'd dealt her was cosmic evidence that everything was right between us.

"I've *never* gotten Ricked in the suburbs," she said. "Not in public, anyway."

I was sitting on the edge of my bathtub, my feet in the basin, my face between my knees. Tell stood behind me, working the clippers in single strokes from the back of my neck to the front of my head. She wasn't using a guard, and the metal kept warming. Blood was throbbing inside of my ears. The hair she'd used the scissors on lay in a pile in the tub beneath my eyes and I watched it get sprinkled with dead flakes of scalp and thousands of shorter hairs, hard, like wire.

I said, "Can I sit up for a minute? I'm about to pass out."

She turned off the clippers.

There was a burning cigarette on the edge of the sink. I nodded at it and she handed it over.

I told her, "I don't think I want that to happen again. I don't like it. The idea of it... I think it's bad for you."

"It's fine," she said. "And you do like it. You just don't know it yet. It takes some time."

I said, "I don't think you'd be into it if your mom wasn't so... I mean, if you hadn't, when you were a kid or something, suffered some kind of fucked-up—"

She held the little cutting machine in her fist and struck the front of her head with it.

"Hey!" I said.

She did it again. I took it away from her. "Don't start playing with my mind," she said. "I enjoy getting Ricked because it feels good. Don't be jealous."

"It's not jealousy, Tell. It's guilt."

"That's worse than jealousy."

"It makes me fucken scared," I said.

"It, it, it," she said. "Fuck fuck fuck. Enough with all the curses and pronouns," she said.

"You fucken know what I mean by fucken context," I said.

She gave me a laugh and kissed me on the cheek. She said, "Don't be scared."

"What if you get killed?"

"That's sweet," she said. "There's no need to worry, though. They don't want to kill me. They just want to Rick me."

She flipped the clippers back on and I lowered my head.

A couple days later, Tell answered my phone. "Hello?" she said. "Jane Tell," she said. "Well, it's nice to hear your voice, too. One second." She handed me the receiver. "Your father," she said.

He said, "Jane Tell, eh? This explains a lot. We've missed you, been worried, haven't seen you since the trial. We were starting to think you were avoiding us. We are no longer worried about that, or you. At least I'm no longer worried, and your mom won't be either, once I tell her we've spoken. We wrote down a list of things to say to you, though. We worked on it for two afternoons. Ready? Okay.

"One: don't be ashamed about the drugs. Two: we love you. Three: you're either our first- or second-favorite person in the world, depending on the day, because sometimes we like Leah better. Four: we're glad you're not in prison, glad that you're safe, and we trust you not to put us through anything like you've put us through ever again. Five: things like that happen once, and it's excusable, colon: you're young and this is the first time. A mistake was made. You made it. But everyone makes mistakes."

I said, "You're giddy. What's up?"

"What's up? What's up is I just sold a ten-million-dollar term-life policy to an eighty-year-old woman. Biggest single premium I've seen in two years. It fell into my lap, and the world seems like a lucky place today, boychic."

"Congratulations."

"Thank you, but I didn't call to brag about that, though I might have, had we been on normal, or even semi-normal terms. There are still other things I have to say to you, things that aren't bulleted, things your mom and I decided I wouldn't say to you if you were sad when I called. Now that I've heard your voice, the ease in your phone manner, I'm guessing you're involved with this Jane Tell, the evidence being that she answered your telephone—she has a pretty contented-sounding voice, herself, by the way— and so now I'm thinking you aren't sad. I'm thinking you might even be in love, or falling therein. So. Are you ready to hear what you need to hear? I'm saying you're as ready as you'll ever be, and I'm starting.

"You fucked up," he said. "Know that you're someone who fucked up. But know that doesn't make you a fuckup. The difference is a matter of repetition. We will always love you. That is out of our hands. But if you repeat your mistake, we will know you have become a fuckup, and we will not respect you, and not respecting you will be painful for us, more painful than you can possibly imagine, and our pain will be on your head all the way. One hundred percent. Okay?" he said. "Okay," he said.

"So I started reading *Verbal Behavior*," he said, "and I know this Skinner is your new guiding light, and I really do want to understand what you find so intriguing about his work, nor am I saying that I think the book was anything other than an excellent birthday gift for a father to receive from his only son, but I just can't read it anymore. All those terms! Not that they don't make sense. They do. So far, at least, the book makes a lot of sense. It does. But it also gives me a headache and makes me feel a little powerless, which I guess most truths about the world do, right? Maybe that's how we get the sense that they're true? Because they *hurt*? Because despite our desire to deny or ignore them, they're compelling and we can't look away from them or something? Listen to me yammer! What do I know? I'm just a humble salesman who loves his wife. How's the car running?"

"Car's fine," I said. "Don't worry about the book. I'm glad you gave it a shot."

"Good. That's what I wanted you to say about the book, but you probably knew that. It was a *disguised mand*, right? Is that what he calls it? Yes. I elicited your approval without asking for it directly. See? I know what a *disguised mand* is. I'm your father, after all. We share DNA and I'm smart like you. Like a genius. But listen. We love you. Don't be afraid of us. Don't be ashamed. Just don't fuck up again. We're going to give you back to your new girlfriend now. And you know the two of you are welcome in our home, which is your home, any time you want to come by. Okay? Good. Enjoy yourself, sonnyboy." Then he hung up.

I said, "That was my dad."

"He sounds like a nice man," Tell said. She kissed my hand.

We did not again fuck as well as we had at SuperTarget, but there were two more Ricks in as many weeks. One was the AAA guy who towed Tell's truck from the hospital lot to mine. He didn't hit her. He held her by the throat and dug in his nails. I didn't know it was happening. She leaned in through the window on the passenger side and I thought she was tipping him. Once she hopped off the running board, though, I saw her neck—the five blood-beaded crescents, a black smear of grease—and hurled a chunk of gravel at the receding rear windshield. It bounced right off. The Rick stopped and got out.

He said, "You got a problem, guy?"

"You're an ape is my problem! Why don't you—"

"What!"

"He doesn't have a problem," Tell said. "Go away now." The guy did as he was told. Tell grabbed me through the fabric of my shorts—I was hard. She pulled me toward my car, got in, and we fucked. The backseat velour was grimed with old coffee spills and rubbed-in ashes that glommed on my skin and stank like a punk-squat. When we finished, our knees and elbows were gray.

Then Tell wanted ice cream, and we got in front to drive to the mini-mart. I turned the key and the engine turned over, and the thermostat needle was leaning, though it wasn't. I knew that it wasn't, but every time I looked away from it, I sensed it creeping rightward. I laughed a little. Tell said, "What?" I said it was nothing and put the car in drive, and Tell said I was weird and I laughed a little more, and she said I was crazy, and I wondered if maybe that was true, if, more specifically, I was being driven crazy by a tumor in my brain, which seemed highly un-likely, though certainly a lot more likely than usual—why else would I continue to sense the needle leaning? And how could I even "sense" it was leaning if my eyes weren't on it? I couldn't, yet I did. I looked through the windshield and "sensed" the needle leaning, then looked at the needle and saw it wasn't leaning, and then I thought that maybe I was having a premonition; maybe I kept "sensing" the needle leaning because some hidden part of my consciousness, some part that having sex with Tell had unlocked, "sensed" that the car one day—maybe one day soon, even that very evening—that the car would overheat and... what? Blow up? Overheat and blow up.

Right about then's when I noticed I was panicking, that I *had been* panicking, that my heart was in my ears and my stomach my neck. I remembered I didn't believe in premonitions, and I didn't believe any "hidden parts of consciousness" could be "unlocked" (I was a good Skinnerian). And it occurred to me that my "sense" the needle had leaned hadn't caused my panic. Neither had my fears of having a tumor or my death premonition. Those things were only *symptoms* of my panic. The panic preceded them.

The needle wasn't leaning, my brain wasn't tumored, the car was not about to explode—it just seemed they were because I was panicking.

These thoughts, which took only seconds to think, didn't make me feel better, though. They seemed to actually make me feel worse. My breath was too audible. The seat-smell too sharp. The grime on my knees and elbows too… grimy. I was nauseated, pounding-hearted. I put the car in park.

"What's up?" Tell said.

"I'm tired," I said.

"Let me drive," she said.

We climbed over each other.

Riding shotgun was better. My pulse slowed a little, and though my chest was still swimmy, I knew it wouldn't get worse—I knew that I wouldn't actually be sick.

The members of the anger-management group were angry at Tell, who had not returned after the first meeting. They said they felt rejected. They said they felt deeply scarred by the rejected feeling they felt and powerless to do anything about their feelings of rejection since she wasn't there to be confronted. I kept as quiet as I could for three straight meetings and, at the fourth, they began talking about how they felt rejected by me and my silence.

The therapist smelled progress. He encouraged them to express. They expressed. They didn't like that I smoked alone during the break. They didn't like that I didn't address them by their names when we greeted one another at the start of group. They felt like they didn't know me, like they were spilling their angry secrets to an uncaring stranger. Sally, the woman who'd called Skinner a monster at the first meeting, complained that I hadn't seemed happy when she complimented me on my haircut at the second meeting. She said, "It made me feel like I shouldn't have said anything at all. Like in being nice, and showing you that I noticed something about you, I had somehow crossed a line."

"Notice," said the therapist, "that you just said, 'It made me feel like I shouldn't have said anything at all.' Does anyone see anything confusing about that statement?"

Jake said, "It's not a feeling. It's a thought. You can't *feel* like you shouldn't have said something. You can think you shouldn't have said something, though, and then feel sad or mad or glad, or any of the other ones there." He pointed at a new poster depicting forty cartoon faces, each a circle, each expressing a distinct emotion, with a label beneath it, like

GLAD.

"Exactly," the therapist said. "And I want to expand on that: it is truly positive to unpack the sorts of thoughts and feelings that Sally just unpacked. If we don't unpack the thoughts, we soon forget we have them, and all we notice are the feelings, and the feelings make our negative attitudes stronger, only we can't challenge them and make ourselves better people, because we can't point at them and say, 'Maybe I'm wrong. Maybe I shouldn't have felt sad.' Because we can't argue rationally with feelings. Because feelings aren't subject to rationality. Feelings come after thoughts, which *are* subject to rationality. And the good news, of course, is that we can argue rationally with our thoughts. We can say to ourselves: 'Maybe I'm wrong. Maybe I didn't cross a line. Maybe Ben was having a bad day when I told him that I liked his haircut. Maybe it even made his day better that I told him I liked his haircut, but he was unable to express. I should explore this further. I *will* explore this further. There are so many possibilities.' And by doing that, we can argue ourselves out of feeling sad. We can make our negative attitudes that much weaker! And that's good news." He nodded his head.

Everybody agreed it was good news. They nodded their heads.

The other Rick I met was a sales clerk at Pep Boys, where we'd gone to buy whatever part it was Tell thought she needed to replace to get her truck running. He wore his glasses on a chain around his neck. I was in the seat-cover aisle when I saw her follow him to the garage at the other end of the store. I ran after them and, as I came through the swinging doors, I saw him palm-strike her chest. Tell crumpled into the wall behind her and slid to the floor. The guy turned and saw me. He was shrugging.

I swung on him so hard. When I missed, I fell.

He said, "It's alright, buddy. Just take it easy."

He walked back into the shop proper, rubbing the lenses of his glasses with a handkerchief. Tell brought me to the employee bathroom and lifted her skirt in the grease-smudged sink.

"I hate this," I said in her ear.

She said, "It doesn't feel like you hate it."

Still, after that, Tell quit getting Ricked in front of me.

The school year ended and I got a job washing windows and cleaning gutters on the North Shore with a small crew run by the son of a friend of my father's. They were good guys. They didn't try to make me talk a lot. The job paid twenty-five an hour and it tired me out. If it wasn't raining, they'd pick me up at six in the morning in an old Jetta with a ladder bungeed to the roof and drop me back at home around four. I started eating three full meals a day and I came to appreciate sleep. Tell mourned the scrapes and then the calluses on my hands.

In the week or so after the Pep Boys Ricking, I'd panicked in my car another three or four times. I didn't "sense" leaning needles, think I had a tumor, or imagine I'd explode, though. Rather, I'd fear I'd have a panic attack, and my fear of an attack would itself trigger one. I determined pretty quickly that I had become motorphobic, and I knew that the origins of my motorphobia—the automotive-related occupations of the Ricks I'd met and the close proximity of cars to the Rickings I'd witnessed—were nothing more than what Skinner would call "accidental contingencies" of my behavioral shaping. I knew, without a doubt, that cars were not connected in any relevant, causative way to Tell's getting Ricked or my post-Ricking sex with her, and I told myself so whenever I got near a car, but it didn't really help. The panic's irrationality was a fact the way that death is a fact: the more able I was to accept it, the more convinced I became that it wouldn't go away, and, soon enough, as any behaviorist could have predicted, the act of noting the irrationality became, itself, a trigger of the panic.

One morning I would walk toward my boss's Jetta, and five steps away I'd start thinking, "There's nothing to fear, go make your money," and the next morning I'd have to start from six steps away, and seven the morning after that. Overall, though, the Jetta was manageable; the panic was low-grade. Riding in the back of it wasn't any worse than sitting shotgun in my car had been on the night we'd gone for ice cream. Once we started rolling, I'd get a little dizzy and have to crack the window and think about fucking to distract myself from the sickness in my chest, but I wouldn't throw up or pass out or anything.

My own car, however, was much, much worse, and the panic it incited was anything but low-grade, especially when I rode with Tell—the attacks were at least as intense as the first one, and their increasing frequency lowered my tolerance. I panicked in the backseat, thinking about sitting shotgun where the last time I'd panicked while thinking about driving, and I fled the car in under a minute. Then I panicked outside the open car-door, thinking about sitting in the backseat where the last time

I'd panicked while thinking about sitting shotgun, and I fled the car in under thirty seconds.

Within two weeks of the Ricking at Pep Boys, I'd quit the thing entirely.

Tell couldn't fix her truck herself, and even though I was making more money than I had when I was selling pot—more than enough to buy scores of new books I was too tired to read and a cell phone when there was no one I wanted to call—I didn't offer her any money to pay for a mechanic. I wanted to help her out, but the thought of a mechanic got my heart banging and I'd hyperventilate.

She took a minimum-wage job at an art-supply store a couple miles from the apartment. She'd drive my car there on mornings she was running late. Otherwise she'd walk to work and I'd walk to meet her halfway at the tracks or the park at half past seven in the evening.

Sometimes I'd notice she had a new bruise or cut. Sometimes I couldn't tell if it was new or reopened. The first few times, she'd say who'd done it to her: a bank teller, a sculptor, a plumber, a guy who contracted faux-finishing crews out to restaurants and hotels. I'd ask her to stop telling me about it. Then one evening by the tracks she showed up with a new gash on her shoulder she didn't speak of and I asked her who did it.

"I thought you didn't want to know," she said.

I said, "I want to know it's not happening."

"You want me to lie to you."

"I want you to stop," I said.

She said, "I'm there when you come. I see you."

"That's what you always say, but I still feel guilty, Tell. I can't help it."

She looked around for something to hurt herself with, and when she couldn't find anything, she let her legs go out beneath her and landed on the rail, hard, on her tailbone.

I didn't move. I said, "I'm gonna leave you if you don't stop."

"You won't," she said.

She was right. "Then I won't fuck you anymore," I said.

"Sure," she said.

It wasn't all bad. In the evenings, before bed, I'd come out of the shower and she'd sit behind me on the couch, wrap her legs around my waist, rub cold hand lotion into the skin of my knuckles. On Thursdays we had the day off together. Tell would paint small pictures in the living room on the canvas snippets she took home for free from the art store, and I'd smoke at my desk, examining the spines and covers of the books I'd bought. Sometimes I'd re-read bits of Skinner. When the sunlight faded, we'd go for a walk to the tracks or the park. If there was rain forecast for Friday morning, my boss would cancel work, and Tell and I would walk to Denny's after midnight.

At the start of the instructional portion of meeting number thirty, the therapist maniacally flipped through the tear-away pad and said, "This evening, I'm going to let you in on the secret to everything." He stepped aside and pointed to the pad, on which was written:

> JAKE: Actually, I do feel a little bit insulted. In fact, very insulted.
>
> BEN: That's pretty effing ridiculous!

Sally raised her hand and held it in the air to get the therapist's attention. The therapist didn't call on her. Sally's hand stayed elevated until the first time he used the word *constancy*.

According to Skinner, the way to extinguish an undesirable behavior is to stop reinforcing it.

The therapist said, "People act in order to make the world predictable. To maintain constancy. To keep to the simplest and most readable patterns. People don't move toward what we often call *pleasure*. They often

do not move in the direction of what is best for them. It's constancy."
Here, the therapist paused to take a sip from a styrofoam cup of water.

Sally's hand shot up into the air again, and she waved it back and forth
until the therapist said the word *whom*. Skinner found that before a behavior became extinct, it would increase in either frequency or intensity or
both. Take a pigeon conditioned with food pellets to lift its left wing and
peck the bolt on the door of its cage. If you stop reinforcing it with food
pellets, you eventually extinguish the wing-lifting, bolt-pecking behavior. Before the behavior becomes extinct, though, the pigeon will frantically wing-lift and/or bolt-peck.

The therapist said, "Evidence? How about something extreme? How
about take a look at the children of abusive parents. Is being sexually molested what's best for them? Is being beaten something they enjoy? Come
on. Of course not. Nonetheless, when we try to get them away from their
abusive parents, they cling. They don't want to go, guys. They want to
stay with their abusers. Why? I'll tell you why: constancy. Predictability.
A world in which they know when and by whom they'll get beaten and
sexually molested is less scary to them than a world in which they have no
idea about what could happen next." His face smiled. He took a breath.

Sally raised her hand again and waved it furiously, along with her
head. Some of her hair came out of its barrette. She started tapping her
foot and the thing was this: it doesn't matter what kind of pigeon it is. It
doesn't matter if the pigeon has a soul or not. It doesn't matter if I love
the pigeon or if the pigeon loves me. If I give it food for pecking the bolt
with its wing up, it will peck the bolt with its wing up. If I quit giving it food, it will eventually quit pecking the bolt with its wing up. It
doesn't matter if it knows why it has stopped pecking the bolt with its
wing up or if it knows why it ever started pecking the bolt with its wing
up. And once it stops, I can get it to start again by conditioning it with
food pellets.

"They act to stay with their abusers, these kids. Because why? Because constancy. Constancy constancy constancy. Constancy is based on experience. Without constancy, we fear that the foundations of our individual worlds could crumble. Without constancy we face the unknown. So we repeat. We pattern. To maintain constancy.

"How can we apply this knowledge? Well, judging by the interaction between Jake and Ben that we see here on the tear-away pad, I would guess that Ben comes from a background in which honest statements of feelings, e.g."—the therapist pointed to the tear-away pad—"'I do feel insulted,' have been regularly met with abject cruelty. What does this mean to Ben? This means that if Ben had not acted in an abjectly cruel manner when he responded to Jake's honest statement of feelings, Ben's world could have crumbled! Or so Ben would think. Of course it's not true. That's the good news. That's the miracle. It wouldn't have crumbled! Can you see that, Ben? Of course you can't. Not yet. But that's why we're all here."

The therapist's eyebrows climbed to his hairline and he panned his expectant gaze across the six of us. Sally dropped her hand in her lap and left it there.

The troubling thing, for me, about Skinner was this: while the behaviorist is shaping the behavior of his pigeon, the pigeon is shaping the behavior of its behaviorist. Place two video cameras in the lab: one over the shoulder of the behaviorist outside the cage, and one inside the cage over the shoulder of the pigeon. On the first screen you'll see a pigeon doing tricks for food, and on the second a man doling food out for tricks. For the pigeon to receive food, it has to do a trick, that's true, but for the man to receive a trick, he has to dole out food—that's equally true. Granted, there's a cage, and the cage is the man's—he controls the condition called "cage"—so you can accurately see that the behavior of the pigeon is under the man's influence to a much greater degree than the man's behavior is under the pigeon's. That's all in a lab between a man and a bird, though. In the larger world, between human beings, it isn't so easy to know whose cage you're in, or who's in yours. It's hard enough to determine which side of the bars you're on. Maybe you don't even see the bars.

Jake raised his hand.

"Jake?" said the therapist.

"I have something to say to Ben," Jake said to the therapist. "I'm not very patient," he said to me. "When we first met, I should have been more compassionate. I wasn't trying to foul up your constancy, Ben. I was trying to maintain my own. I guess I just get insulted when people walk out of meetings like that girl did."

"Well-said," said the therapist. "Ben?"

I said, "That's ridiculous."

The therapist pointed at the tear-away pad and made some noise. He made the noise "But constancy." He made the noise "And the good news."

"That's ridiculous," I said.

And the therapist pointed at the tear-away pad and made some more noise. He made the noise "But constancy. Constancy." Then he made the noise "And the good news and the good news," and I made the noise "Ridiculous."

We kept going like that for a while, until I felt cruel or exhausted or beaten or trapped or guilty and I made the noise "Constancy."

"Well said," said the therapist.

I didn't know whether Tell would quit getting Ricked if I quit having sex with her after she'd been Ricked, but I knew that she would continue getting Ricked if I continued having sex with her after she'd been Ricked. And I continued having sex with her after she'd been Ricked, and as the summer began to come to an end, I started to wonder if I had it all reversed, if it wasn't so much that she continued getting Ricked because I continued having sex with her as that I continued having sex with her because she continued getting Ricked. And I started to wonder about every guy I saw. The guys I washed windows with. The fools in the group. The therapist himself. Guys on television. Koppel. Jerry Seinfeld. Ricks? All of them? It was possible. And then it was women I wondered about. Not just which ones were Tells—if there were any other ones—but if they thought I was a Steve. I was pretty sure they didn't think I was a Rick. I didn't know what Tell thought. and I was scared to find out and certain that I wouldn't trust her answer if I asked her; she'd say whatever she thought would hurt me least. And what would hurt me least? I didn't know that either. I didn't completely understand the terms. I'd assumed for awhile that there was a continuum: Ricks at one extreme, Steves at the other, me somewhere in the middle. But maybe there were just Ricks and Steves and then an entirely different scale for everyone else. Then again, maybe Ricks and Steves weren't mutually exclusive: maybe certain Steves were also Ricks in certain contexts, and certain Ricks Steves. Were Steves just Ricks who were too afraid to Rick? Was that the only difference? Was I just too afraid? I kept on fucking her after she'd been Ricked, and kept on thinking I shouldn't keep fucking her. Was that the way of a Steve or a Rick? I didn't know what I was made of.

One day in mid-August, it was raining, and my sister dropped by my place. Tell was at work. Leah pointed at my bald head and asked me, "When'd you do that?"

"A couple months ago," I said. I watched a spider crawl out of a crack in the baseboard between us.

Leah said, "It looks good. I have a boyfriend now, and—" and she saw the spider.

She froze in mid-gesture for a second, then jumped over it and got behind me. "Fuck!" she said. "Fuck fuck fuck."

I put it out with my hand.

"Jesus," she said. "Not even a paper towel?"

I made like I was confused and then I wiped my hand on my head. It was the first joke I'd cracked in weeks.

"You're so gross," she said. "Wash your head. I can't talk to you like that."

I went into the kitchen and washed my head in the sink.

"So I have a new boyfriend," she said.

"Is he a Rick or a Steve?" I said.

"His name's Aaron, weirdo."

I said, "How's Dad? You guys are cool, right? You've always been tight."

"What's wrong with you?" she said. I came back into the living room. She was jacking around with the equipment in my window-washing bucket. She peeled the foam handle off my chrome-plated squeegee.

"Stop messing with my stuff."

"Jeez," she said. "Who made these pictures? That girl Dad talked to on the phone?"

"No one," I said. I was being a dick to my little sister like some Steve in a sitcom.

"They gave me money and I'm supposed to take you out for pancakes and tell you about my new boyfriend."

"Okay, but let's walk," I said.

She said, "It's ninety-five degrees outside. And pouring."

"I'm not letting you drive me anywhere," I said.

"Then you drive."

I said, "I don't want to drive. Do you know how much I have to drive for work? I hate driving."

"I thought you only said you were an addict to get pity from the judge."

"I did."

"Then quit acting like a dry drunk. They send their love and say they miss you. Dad especially. He keeps telling us you're becoming a man. 'He's growing up. He just wants space.' It's sad. They think you don't like us anymore. And you should really start calling them back." Then she left and I was glad and didn't want to be.

* * *

We sat on the tracks that night, smoking cigarettes. Jane Tell had a swelling eye. Blood at the corners of her mouth. I was staring hard, wanting to touch her. When I turned away, the string of dormant freight cars across the ditch looked small as a train-set. I had to throw a rock and fall short to get my eyes straight. We finished our cigarettes and I lit two more, handed one over.

"You're a gentleman," she said. She wiped blood from her mouth with her sleeve, her thumb pushed through a tear in the seam of her cuff. "I think I bit my tongue," she said.

I didn't respond, continued to smoke.

She pulled her knees to her chest and worried the drawstrings of her hood. "I'm sick of the tracks," she said. "Let's walk to the park behind the high school."

Tell stood first and pulled me up. We headed toward the school. The moon was orange and the stars were blue and the sky was black. There were slugs in the grass of the outfield. They shined up at us like new dimes, their antennae eyes bent sideways, placidly, stupidly, daring us to put them out beneath our feet. They reminded me of a vacation I'd been on with my father. We'd flown to L.A. and were taking a week to get to Portland in a rented Mustang—a convertible—that he let me drive on Highway 1, even though, at fourteen, I was still months away from getting my permit. "Don't speed," he told me. "If you get in trouble, I get in trouble. We're both breaking laws. Don't get us in trouble." I didn't. We ate good fresh food and saw a couple movies and stayed at motels with cement patios outside their sliding-glass doors that I would go out onto to smoke.

One time I woke up in the middle of the night and wanted a cigarette, but I didn't want to wake my dad, so I kept the light off on the patio. I'd gone out without a shirt, just boxers and Chucks, and I grew cold and I paced. The ocean was washing against the beach across the motel lawn. From under my shoes came other sounds, crackling and squeaking. Something like the screams of pot-dropped lobsters, but in short bursts and pleasant to listen to. I watched the water move and I thought loosely that I was stepping on wet seashells or unripe berries. To make more of the sounds, I ground my feet against the cement with each step. When I finished smoking, I dropped my cigarette on the patio, and there was another sound, a sizzle. I knew something was wrong.

I crouched down and lit my lighter and saw scores of dead snails, their shells in shards that punctured their skin, some of them torn in half, inside out, wet with that substance that trails them. I'd killed spiders before, and silverfish. I had set fire to anthills. I'd won my only fight in grade school by raking the other boy's face over playground gravel. I had done those things to be cruel. This was different. I got sick. The next morning, my father went out to smoke on the patio. He said, "What the fuck is this? You were sick? Are you better? Are you sick? Were you drinking?"

"The snails," I said. "It was an accident. I feel dirty. I really don't want to talk about it."

He said, "You sound like your sister with her spiders, boychic. They're just slugs." They weren't—they were snails. Slugs don't have shells.

The ones in the field lacked shells—they were slugs. Tell hooked her arm in mine. "They catch the moon like bullet casings," she said. "These slugs look like bullets. Don't I pun so cleverly? Aren't I delightful?"

"Stop it," I said.

Our arms came unhooked. She said, "Do you want to hurt somebody, Ben? We could find somebody," she said, "and we could hurt them." She tackled me and put her mouth on my neck. "We could kill them," she said. We rolled around for a little while. At home, later, I'd find blood on my shirt collar and wonder whose it was.

Tell sat up. Her hood was off and some of her hair had come out of its rubberband. Static held it up in front. "I think we're sitting in wet," she said.

"It's the ground," I said. "It's just colder than your body."

"You're so smart," she said. "But if you're so smart, why aren't we

128

plotting the perfect murder?" She had the edge in her voice that meant I wasn't playing well.

"Who hit you?" I said.

"I fell."

"You're a liar, Tell."

"Why won't you fuck me?"

"Because someone hit you."

"Listen to you," she said. "Listen to *that*. You and all that power in your voice. You won't fuck me because someone hit me? You won't drive your car because you fuck me when someone hits me."

This was the point in the fight-routine at which I could either make her cry by shutting down or fix it up by showing some novel form of affection. I didn't want her to cry. I put a slug on her knee.

"Hi there, gross cutie," she said to the slug.

"I want you to meet my family."

"Let's get the car and go."

"We don't need the car," I said. The house was across the street.

I let us in through the side door. I could hear them making noises with dishes. We stopped at the threshold between the hallway and the kitchen. My mom and dad were at the table, eating ice cream. Tell stood behind me.

My mom saw me first. "Ben!" she said. "Come here!"

We walked over to the table. "This is Jane Tell," I said. "We're getting married."

I don't know if it was because they hadn't seen me in so long or because I shocked them with the marriage bit or because she'd pulled her hood back on, but neither of my parents really saw Tell until after we'd sat down and I'd been kissed by both of them.

Then it registered. "Oh my God!" my mom said. "What happened to your face, baby? Ben, what happened to her?"

"I just fell down some stairs," Tell said.

"You *fell down some stairs?*" my dad said. He looked a wish away from flattening me.

"We need to clean those wounds," my mom said. She was frantic. She made for the bathroom down the hall. "I'll be right back," she said.

I said, "I'll come with you."

Tell said, "Don't go, Ben."

I left with my mother. I sat on the second step of the stairway, just outside the entrance to the kitchen, waiting while she made noise with the cabinets in the half-bathroom.

I watched the kitchen through the spaces between the bars supporting the banister. I could see my father's back and Tell's face. She was crying, and through her tears she winked at him. I didn't know if she knew that she did it or why she did it and I couldn't see what she saw. My father's shoulders moved and I couldn't see what he was doing with his arms, and, for a second, everything seemed possible, and the horror of that, of unlimited potential, made me feel so strong, almost as if I were bodiless, and I knew the feeling had less to do with body than with law, that it was lawlessness, and I would have remained lawless had Tell's face not right then been obscured by my father's hairy hand, shaking out the fold of a white cotton handkerchief. She took it, and, rather than putting it to her cheek, she folded it back up and held it in her lap to have something to look at.

"Listen," my father said softly, "I know you don't know us, but we're good people and we would never hurt you. We need to ask if Ben—"

"He didn't," she said.

"If he did," my father said, "it's okay to tell us. We won't harm you. We'll make sure you're safe. You can stay here if you need to."

She shook her head.

"You really fell down the stairs?" he said.

"No," she said. "But Ben didn't hit me."

"Someone else hit you?"

"Could we talk about something else? I'm sorry, I just—"

"Hey," my father. "Hey hey. It's fine. We'll talk about something else. How about... Well, the engagement. I mean, my son's a great kid, but I'm fairly certain he put every last penny he had to his name toward buying you that obscenely lavish invisible ring you're wearing. I mean, do you really think it's good idea to get married before he finishes college and gets a real job?"

Tell laughed for him. She said, "Ben was just kidding about the getting married thing. He likes to exaggerate."

"Well, look," my dad said. "I know you'd rather not talk about it, and I'm trying not to, but I just—I'm a parent, and I feel like I have to tell you that whatever's going on, *whatever* happened, Jane, you don't deserve to get hurt."

My mother rushed past me with a first-aid box and Tell looked up on hearing her. She spotted me sitting there. I ducked back, reflexively, like I'd been caught at something. I didn't know exactly what.

I stayed on the stairway for a little while. My mom turned a brown bottle onto a ball of cotton and pressed the cotton to Tell's bottom lip. My dad offered her some ice cream. Tell declined. My mom told him to get her some anyway. Tell asked her what kind of accent she had and my mom started talking about immigration.

While my dad was getting a bowl together for Tell, he said, "Where's Ben?" and I crept outside to smoke on the driveway and figure out how to say that I loved her so it meant something better than *I accept you.*

By the time Tell came out front, it had been raining for at least twenty minutes and I was on my third cigarette, pacing carefully to avoid stepping on the worms that had come up onto the pavement.

"You wanted to see if he'd Rick me," she said.

"I don't think that's true."

"You know, you could have just asked me if he'd do it, instead of testing me out like a fucking lab rat. I feel like such a piece of shit now. It's your fault this time. Feel guilty."

"I don't think I was testing you out," I said.

"You don't *think* you were?" she said.

"Quit it," I said.

"Quit it and stop it and cut it out," she said. "Smoke. Walk. Park. Tracks. Denny's. All we do is repeat, you know that? Like an error message. Like a beeping fucking circuit board."

I couldn't tell if she was crying or if it was anger cracking her voice.

"Everything repeats," I said.

"Look at these worms," she said. "They think they've saved themselves from drowning in the grass."

Anger.

I said, "Quit analyzing the imagery, Tell. It's manipulative."

"Listen to you!" she said. "It can't be that manipulative if you know to call it imagery." She slammed me on the nose. It broke. "If *I* was so manipulative," she said, kicking my legs out from under me, "you'd be manipulated by now."

Coughing, my face flat on a dead red worm, I said, "I was jealous."

"You just figured that out?" She made for the street. "I'm moving out," she said.

"Wait," I said, "I'll drive you."

Soaked and bleeding and limping beside her, I felt romantic, like I could prove something simple.

Then we were standing next to my car.

"Take me to my mom's," she said. "I'll come back for my stuff tomorrow when you're gone."

I got in the car and started it. I hadn't driven in months and all the dread came on. I closed my eyes and there they were: the trucker and the tow-trucker and the sales clerk with his glasses. Manx. The therapist. A soldier. A café owner. Any number of cops and vice principals. Every man whose face I could remember but for me and my father. They waited in line to leave their impression and Tell told me it was okay, take it easy, she liked it. I opened the door and got sick in the lot.

"I'll drive," she said. "You sit shotgun and by the time we get there, you'll be used to the car. You'll be able to get yourself home."

I kept my mouth shut. I did what she told me.

I tried escaping the panic by thinking of fucking, but every time I closed my eyes I'd see all the men lined up in front of her.

After we'd driven a couple of miles, I covered up my closed eyes with my hands, thinking irrationally—however deliberately—that it might be possible to blot out the images appearing on my eyelids by shielding them against the backlight of the streetlamps. Instead I saw Jane's body bruising, breaking, deforming, her bloodstained hair in a flat-knuckled fist that dragged her along the shoulder of a highway, one swollen eye winking, the other turned to look placidly skyward.

The car struck a pothole. Both my hands slipped, jarred my nose at the break. What had been a redundant, dull, throbbing pain became so suddenly sharp and brutal that I didn't care about anything else. I could only see white.

Soon enough, though, the pain died down and I knew where I was.

I wiggled the bridge of my nose with my thumbs and returned to that state of excruciating relief. When it disappeared, I wiggled my nose again, but it didn't hurt as badly as it had the first time, and the relief wasn't total. I proceeded to squeeze, and then to tap, and then to frantically flick at my nose until those methods became ineffective.

Through all of that, Jane Tell said nothing—either she hadn't seen what I was doing or she'd chosen to ignore it—and she continued saying nothing till I struck my nose with the back of my fist, and she yelled at me to stop. "Just stop!" she yelled.

Blinded, I leaned against my window and bled.

When the relief wore off, I used my fist again.

And Tell again yelled out for me to stop. And again I was blind and leaning on my window. And when I could see again, I could see that Tell wasn't looking at the road, but looking at me, and the car was about to collide with something black. It was too late to stop.

The collision was quiet, a clop without resonance. The thumping of the anti-lock brakes was louder.

We ran to the gasping animal and knelt. It lay on its side on the yellow line, trying to bark, trying to growl, coughing and squealing. "It's breathing," Tell said. Its spine was severed, even I could see that. "There's an all-night vet on Willow," she said.

I called the vet. They didn't have an ambulance.

I called the cops. They told me an hour.

"But it's breathing," I told them.

They told me an hour.

"Help me," Jane said. She was trying to lift it. It made awful, human sounds. Moaning, pleading sounds.

"Let go of it."

"It's a dog."

"You're hurting it, Jane."

I got into the car.

"Just help me," she said.

"Fucken move," I told her, and turned the key. She got out of the way.

Reader, I ended it.

RSVP

The way I heard it, this guy, Donald, who was pathologically shy, wrote the world's greatest love letter—four lines long, a mere seventy words— to a girl called Janet, with whom he'd made slightly longer than average eye contact on at least three separate occasions. (After what may have been the second, he went to the bathroom and discovered in the mirror a smear of red ink on the bridge of his nose.) Donald wrote the letter in flawless calligraphy on supple paper, then folded it into an origami duck, and at lunch the next day—Donald and Janet worked at the same office—he hung back a couple minutes till all of his fellow employees had cleared out, at which point he walked the duck across the room and mistakenly stood it on the chair of Chrissy's cubicle, which shared a partition with Janet's.

Just a couple minutes earlier, Janet, a secret origami enthusiast who was even shyer than Donald, lonelier too, and whose feelings for Donald were entirely mutual, had noticed, on her way out the door to lunch, that Donald had not yet risen from his cubicle. Janet thought that maybe if she could dally long enough to bump into Donald with no one else around, they might finally get up the nerve to speak to each other, or, failing that, they could make some more eye contact, maybe even within the close quarters of the elevator, and maybe, were the elevator crowded enough, she could brush Donald's arm with a shoulder. So Janet lingered by the water fountain, fake-drinking water, and saw Donald place something on her chair. She was instantly sweaty. What could it be? She ran to the ladies' room and washed her hands twice. By the time she returned, Donald was gone. She went to her cubicle, discovered her mistake. Her chair was empty. Donald's gift was for Chrissy. An origami duck. Janet picked it up, turned it in the light. What beautiful work! Not a crease that wasn't straight. Not the slightest hint of an unintended shadow. Under the wings and along the bill's edges, words inscribed in impeccable calligraphy appeared between the elegant folds: *love* and *eyes* and *bashful* and *you* and *glue* and *us* and *forever*. Other words appeared on the sides of the neck and the webbing of the feet, but Janet, remembering they weren't for her, chose not to read them, and, lest she obey her terrifying impulse to crush the duck against her chest and jump out the window, plunging to her death, she set it back down on the seat of Chrissy's chair and left the building, as if in a trance. She walked a block, not knowing to where, then walked another block, still unknowing. In the middle of the third block, she settled on the lake. She would go to the lake and look at the waves, the sight of which always gave her comfort in summer. The lake was east and east was left. She took a sharp left, into the street, where she was struck by a bus and instantly killed.

For lunch, Donald ate some egg-salad sandwiches. He'd prepared the egg salad the night before, as soon as he'd finished folding the duck, and this morning scooped enough to make four sandwiches into a sealable plastic container. He'd carried the container, along with utensils and disposable napkins, in a thermal lunchbox he'd bought for the occasion. The first floor of the building in which he and Janet worked featured a bakery that made his favorite brioche rolls. After purchasing four, Donald brought them to the park across the street, and, sitting on the ledge of the fountain, in the sun, he sliced three in half, spread egg salad on them, and ate them with gusto. He waited until the very end of the lunch hour to make the fourth sandwich, in order to ensure that it would be as fresh as possible. He would, upon returning to the office, as long as Janet didn't seem repulsed by his letter, give her that sandwich. His last girlfriend, Terri, had sworn his egg salad was the finest egg salad she'd ever eaten, and his friend had liked it, too. Donald, if he did say so himself, agreed that he made a mean egg salad, but he hadn't once eaten it in over three years, not since just before Terri and his friend ran off to Connecticut together and became highly paid pharmaceutical representatives. A part of him had been worried that he might have lost his touch, but no sooner had he swallowed his first bite of sandwich than he realized he hadn't.

He returned to the office a couple minutes late. Everyone was there but Janet.

Chrissy never realized the duck was a letter, but she thought that it might have been a gift from Janet, the dikey bookish girl she'd worked with who a bus killed—so sad—so she held on to the duck for sentimental reasons. Chrissy was lucky to be born with her genes and she knew it, too, so she was nice to everyone, including lesbians, just as long as they didn't try anything creepy, since, first of all, lesbians were people too, and secondly she knew that no one stayed beautiful, you got old and saggy, and having a nice body was not a thing that lasted, but having friends was. Those were her values.

When she got home from work on the day Janet died, Chrissy set the duck on her knickknack tray's edge, where it stayed till the first chilly night in fall, when the heat kicked on and the vent blew the duck all over the tray till its bill wedged between a pair of porcelain gorillas in T-shirts, hugging. Then, on the first warm night of spring (by which time Donald had long since hanged himself), Chrissy threw a party which got so fun that a dancing drunk guy fell down hard, knocking the knickknack tray to the floor. With the exception of the world's greatest love letter, all the tray's contents exploded on impact.

"You broke my knickknack tray," Chrissy told the drunk guy.

"You sank my battleship," the guy told Chrissy.

"You *broke* my knickknack tray," Chrissy said.

The guy said, "Knickknack paddy wack, can't you see that I love you?"

He worked the broom and she held the dustpan. The duck looked like garbage and they swept that up, too. They fucked all night long, fucked well for being drunk. The next night, sober, they fucked even better.

When you and I were young and in love, Tom and I would go to a twenty-four-hour diner in a basement at Western Avenue and Augusta. We'd sit at the counter there and eat fried eggs on small croissants nearly every weekday morning before work. Because we were regulars, the cook would occasionally surprise us with cheese squares melted on our sandwiches, gratis.

I still type all my letters and address the envelopes by hand. I still feel about origami the way I feel about mimes, unless you insist Harpo Marx is a mime. Harpo Marx I feel great about.

You were the person who introduced me to the Marx Brothers—you had everything on tape—but I pretended I knew their work to impress you, and dismissed it on the grounds that the Three Stooges were better. That was Tom's opinion and I looked up to Tom. He was a couple years older than me and full of answers. One time I asked him when I'd stop hating my father. ("As soon as he stops being a cock about your friends, or you become a cock and ditch them like he wants you to.") One time I asked him to explain, in plain language, the difference between signs and symptoms. ("You can observe others' signs, like their swollen labia, but not others' symptoms, like the butterflies in their stomach or their *tingles* or whatever.") Another time, right after I'd sent you the one I'd written, I asked him what he thought about love letters. ("This poet called Don who my cousin used to know wrote the greatest one ever, but he gave it to the wrong girl—some dumb, heartless cunt who wasn't even that hot—and she didn't respond and he killed himself.") Then one time I asked him if he thought gay men pretended their penis was someone else's when they masturbated. He said that he didn't know for sure, but the question was a good one, and he supposed that they probably tried to pretend at one time or another. Then he told me that that was like the Stranger.

"That book?"

"You wind a rubberband around your wrist so your hand falls asleep."

"Oh," I said. "Does it do the trick?"

Tom wished to God he knew, but there were never any rubberbands around when he needed one.

I'd been out with you the night before. I took you to see an action movie. You were still an athlete. You were training for U.S. swim team tryouts and I smoked a lot of cigarettes. I had parked on the roof of a four-story lot and, after the movie, you said we should race back up to the car. You thought it was funny to make me run. The race wasn't close—you spared no effort. You were still hunched over, breathing audibly, hands on your knees, when I finally got there. Your hair was tied back with a cloth-covered rubberband the color of a robin's egg. I pulled it off your head to announce my arrival—I could hardly breathe, much less speak—and you spun around and grabbed me, both-handed, by the ribs, and you pressed me to the wall and I pulled you to the concrete and... I'm sure you remember. But you forgot about the rubberband, never asked for it back. Probably because you had many such rubberbands. They come in packs of ten, twenty-five, and fifty, these rubberbands. They tend to have a gold or silver thread running through them. You know the kind I mean. The one I'd taken meant nothing to you.

It certainly meant more than nothing to me, though apparently not enough, or too much to admit. Maybe some combination. I don't know anymore, I probably never did, but Tom was my friend, and I was young and in love, he was older and not-so, and your rubberband was wrapped around the lighter in my pocket. I handed it over.

"Stranger, here I come," he said.

"Wait," I said. "Actually..."

"What?" Tom said.

"Never mind," I said. "Nothing. Let's invent the religion."

We'd often talked, at the diner, about inventing a religion, but we never got the chance. We'd be too hungover or wouldn't have a pen or by the time we'd get enough coffee in us to begin we'd have to head out for work. That day was no different.

"Tomorrow," Tom said. "We're already running late."

That night I met you for sushi on Division where before me was set a miso soup I hadn't ordered. You insisted I try it, but I didn't understand how to eat soup with chopsticks, so you showed me how to drink it straight from the bowl. A beige drop on your lip became a line on your chin and you wiped it away with the cuff of your hoodie, your thumb hooking through a tear in the seam, its chewed-looking nail and bright pink quick.

"Come on," you said, tilting your face to my bowl.

Through the broth I saw the tofu. White cubes of paste, flaking. Mealy chunks of wet cadaver. A substance I'd managed to dodge for years. I hefted the bowl to my mouth and I drank until there was nothing left to drink.

The cubes stayed stuck to the bottom, a blessing.

I asked you if you'd gotten my love letter yet. I asked roundaboutly, weenieishly—how else would I have asked? No one ever accused me of being too direct. I said, "How was your experience at the mailbox today?"

You told me my letter had arrived, that it was typed.

I said, "Yes, but how was it?"

"*Typed*," you said.

"I signed it by hand."

"There's no other way to sign a letter," you said.

"Would you have preferred a duck? Should I have given it to your buxom office-mate instead?"

"A duck?" you said. "I don't work at an office."

You didn't get my meaning—how could you have, really? I didn't feel like explaining. Doesn't matter, I thought. Had it been the letter you deserved to receive, it never would have gotten to you—you were not the wrong girl.

The following morning, at the diner, Tom reported on the Stranger. "The first few times it works pretty well," he said. "I think after a break it'll work well again. For now it's lost its charm."

I asked him for the rubberband.

He gave me a pink one.

I said, "This is pink. It's not the one I gave you."

"The color," he said, "doesn't make any difference. After work the other day, I tried the one you gave me—the blue one. Then I went to the drugstore and bought a twenty-five-pack. I tried green and red and orange. The best time was with red, but only because I'd learned the trick of it by then and I wasn't too chafed. It was my first exercise in mastery, and so it was the best."

"And after that?" I said.

"I tried yellow this morning. Yellow was good, exactly the same as red, really, but not as good as red. Tomorrow or the next day, for the sake of science, I'll try the rest of the colors—there's still purple and black and white and pink—but I'm sure they'll be the same as the red, and just as good. The mind does not forget the mind and the hand does not forget the hand, but the mind forgets the hand and the hand the mind or some shit."

I told him to give me the blue one.

"The blue one's gone, dude. I threw it away. I'm telling you, though—the color doesn't matter."

I explained why it did.

He said, "Sentimental value. You should have told me that before I jizzed all over it. She must really be something, this girl," Tom said. "A firecracker, huh? Atomic pussy. A real hot number. A whip-cracking piece. I hope I'll get to meet her."

"Come out with us tonight," I said. "I think we're going bowling."

"I'm in," said Tom.

Then I asked him for a pen to invent the religion with.

"Okay," I said. "I think first of all it's good to come up with a fetish because—"

"A fetish?" Tom said. "Like sucking on toes?"

"Like a totem," I said. "Some kind of object to worship."

"Oh," Tom said. "You know, that's not bad. The religion catches on, we could get rich selling them."

"Selling them?" I said.

"The totems," Tom said. "Trademarked totems. Little keychain totems. Idols sewn into the garments of every last worshipper. Make a fucken mint."

"I don't know," I said. "I—"

"No. It's good—totems. It's a great idea. But so the first thing we need is to come up with the bad guy. The guy who the totems protect you from, right? Yeah. That's good. Let's start with the bad guy."

We didn't start with the bad guy. We didn't start with any guy. All we had to write on were paper napkins, and the only pen Tom had was a floaty pen: there was a flat ski-slope in the water cylinder and when you turned the pen to write with it, a flat man in a flat ski cap descended the slope in slow motion. The pen was intended to be a souvenir of some place mountainous and fondly remembered. It was never meant to function as a writing utensil. Its cheap ballpoint would roll only under a heavy hand. I tore through the napkin, scratched a line into the countertop. The cook skipped the gratis cheese squares that morning.

That evening, we all went bowling together. We bowled four games, then Tom noticed how late it was. All of us had to be up for work early. Of the three of us, I lived closest to the lanes. Tom, who was driving, mentioned that to us—I'm sure you remember—and he said it made sense to drop me off first. I wasn't sure it made sense, but by then we were only a block from my apartment.

Today, at my mailbox, square envelope in hand, staring down at my many-seriffed, hand-addressed name, I needed a cigarette like never be-fore, and was digging in my pocket with my free hand, blindly, in search of my lighter, when I underwent a sudden, whole-body spasm (I'm fine), and the hand in my pocket closed on everything in there—keys, receipts, change, etc.—then upwardly jerked and dumped it all on the floor. I didn't find the souvenir pen among the spillage—why would I? it's been years—but I thought I should have. I thought it would have been nice to kind of round things out.

I guess I'm probably too old to invent a religion now, too. But thanks for the invitation. I'm regretful, can't make it, best of luck to the both of you.

SCIENTIFIC AMERICAN

1

A crack in the wall behind their bed oozed gel. Neither knew what to do, what it meant, who to call. The man called their painter. "A crack?" said the painter. "A crack oozing gel," the man said to the painter. "I'll be there," said the painter, "at once." He was. He arrived by himself, with a brush, after breakfast. This was on a Sunday, and the man, who'd liked the painter, liked him even better now for coming straight over.

The woman let the painter in—the man was in the bathroom—and showed him upstairs to the crack behind the bed. "Where's the gel?" asked the painter. "I wiped it," said the woman, "and threw it away." Hearing this exchange through the bathroom door, the man blushed for no reason he was able to discern. "Well, this will be simple," the painter told the woman. "Is the paint where I left it?" he asked her. It was.

The painter went down to the closet in the basement, took the can of paint he'd left, and brought it upstairs. He painted the crack till the crack disappeared. He slid the bed back to where it had been, and returned the can of paint to the closet.

The man had fixed coffee. He poured two cups and walked the painter out front. "So you're not in your whites," he said to the painter, who wore a pair of slacks and a button-down shirt. "I was on my way to church when you called," said the painter. "Church," the man said, "that's something, that's something... We really appreciate all that you've done." "Not at all," said the painter, "it's only decent. A brand new house? A nice young couple? A pit bull who acts like a Labrador retriever? A crack in the wall behind the bed oozing gel doesn't fit in that picture—could drive a man crazy. This coffee, by the way, is completely delicious." "Rwandan," the man said. "Rwandan," said the painter.

They briefly discussed the painter's new car, which was silver and German, a car the man was happy to see that a painter—any painter at all, and especially their painter—owned. Prior to this, he'd only seen their painter's van. A high-performance model, this silver German car was. The man had been poised to purchase one himself, just prior to learning that the woman was pregnant, at which point he'd settled on a rounder green car, a larger and Swedish, responsible car. He wanted, the man did, to share with the painter, toward whom he was feeling fraternal warmth, the story of how he'd nearly bought the German car, but because his wife wasn't far enough along yet (she'd miscarried once, and they both feared jinxing) and the story would not be much of a story if he left out the reason why he bought the Swedish car instead, the man decided not to mention it at all. He could tell it some other time. Maybe at the baptism. Yes, at the baptism. The man would invite the painter to the baptism. He ran it by his wife at dinner that night. She agreed that the painter was a likable person, but said it wasn't safe yet to talk about the baptism. They talked about the dog. How handsome it was. The way its muscles rippled its shiny, fawn coat.

The crack returned. The crack oozed gel. That the problem wasn't paint was easy to deduce. The man called their builder. The connection was bad, fuzzing their voices, cutting in and out. "Call me back," said the man. "Sometimes that'll fix it." "_____ ____gel?" said the builder.

"Oozing from the wall behind the bed," said the man. "Gel where?" said the builder, and, "Merf merf merf." "Call me back," said the man. "It's the walls are cracking, or _____merf?" said the builder. "One wall," said the man, "and the paint as well, but it's not the paint. We painted it over. It must be the wall." "I'll send someone merf," the builder told the man. "When?" said the man. "Merf," said the builder. Here the call ended. The man redialed. He went straight to voicemail, waited for the prompt, identified himself, asked the pertinent question, and ended the call. What if the problem was on his end, though? Or what if the problem was a satellite problem? His message would sound like *merf merf merf*. He went to the patio and called once more, left the same message.

Then he drank water from the garden hose, nervously. Why should he be nervous? He shouldn't be nervous. He tightened the spigot and tried to think of something to calm himself down. He thought of some breasts, all the breasts he could picture, their various cleavages, hang-styles, and nipples. His wife had great nipples, pink and uninvertable, a little bit upturned, the best he'd ever seen. He wondered if the mouth of their baby would ruin them, hoped it wouldn't, then feared that he'd never get to find out, that the baby wouldn't make it into the world, would die in the womb, a forbidden thought. A forbidden thought that did not calm him down.

Where was the dog? He slid the door open and called for the dog. The dog came running. He threw toward the fence a short length of rope that was tied in a bone-shape and scented with beef spray. The dog brought it back, laid it at the man's feet, looked up in his eyes, expectant. This dog was a pit bull, a breed that sometime in the mid-1980s, back when the man was still in grade school, had acquired a reputation for killing babies.

"You wouldn't, would you?" the man asked the dog.

It rose on its hind legs and leaned on the man, pressing its paws to his nipples. They danced.

* * *

The builder arrived at noon with a worker. "Let's have us a look at this hole," said the builder. "It's really just a crack," the man told the builder. "A crack, a hole, leaks paste, what have you—needs to be looked at by us," said the builder. At the words *leaks paste*, the worker made a face that seemed, at first, to signify disgust, but the worker was foreign, the man soon determined (the mustache, the hairline, the fit of the pants), an Eastern or Central European of some kind, and what looked like disgust might not have been disgust but firm resolve: steadfast, unbending, workerly resolve to ascertain the source of the problem at hand, and execute, unflinchingly, by any means necessary, the procedures required to solve that problem. Toward the foreign worker the man felt warmth, fraternal warmth. In his country of origin, he'd likely been a scientist, advanced degree in physics, or a structural engineer, and when he'd fled to America, where he didn't know the language and couldn't find a job in his specialized field, he'd had to suck it up and take what he could get, and here he was now, doing just that, the best that he could, making lemonade, no excuses, no whining, no annoying self-pity. That the worker looked like someone who liked his liquor and slapped his wife around (not to say simultaneously, the beatings and the drunkenness)—that was cowardly, nationalistic, Other-fearing stuff on the part of the man. The man rejected it outright, admired the worker. This worker was a person who could work with his hands and his brain the both—a noble person. The man wondered what he drove and hoped it was German. He doubted it was German, but still, it seemed possible, considering the car the painter drove, and the fact that both men were employed by the builder. The man felt grateful. Good men were on the job. He led them upstairs.

"Where's the paste?" said the builder. "I wiped it," the woman said. The woman's voice came through the door of the bathroom. The man, for some reason, was embarrassed, and blushed, and the worker muttered something, and the builder chuckled. "What?" the man said. "It really doesn't translate," the builder told him. "Try me," the man said. "He says, 'The wettest goose squawks loudest in the drought.'" "What's that supposed to mean?" the man said to the builder. "Exactly," said the builder. "No," said the man, "because who's the wettest goose?" The worker, his eyes bright, smiled at the man. "I enjoy your strong animal," he said to the man. "My what?" said the man. The worker looked puzzled, or maybe aroused, and reached out his hand. The man thought the worker wanted to shake, but the worker had reached out to let the dog smell him—the dog had snuck into the master bedroom to be among people, to stand near the man. "He's not supposed to be here," the woman said to everyone; she'd finished in the bathroom; she stood in the doorway. "Are you," she said. "No you're not, are you." The dog sat back and sniffed at the air. The worker said, "Polyp," and shook the man's hand—the man, in his confusion, had proffered his hand. "Polyp?" said the man. "How terribly rude of me," the builder announced. "I come," said the builder, "from a not-so-classy background, which isn't to say my parents weren't gems who helped put me through business school, just that the sociable graces as the wife says aren't exactly most foremost in my noodle, and sometimes I forget to do the right thing. This here is Polyp, best crackman around. What do you say, Polyp?" "Please meet you," said Polyp. "And we you as well," said the woman to Polyp. "I am," Polyp said.

Then he tore down the wall and put up a new one. There wasn't any gel to be found in the wreckage, and Polyp's sledge was bare of gel, too.

The builder told the man, "The painter's free to come in first thing in the morning." "He's a good man, your painter," the man told the builder. "Best painter in town—how's eight o'clock tomorrow?" "Eight o'clock's perfect." "Perfect," said the builder. "I thank you," Polyp said. "You're welcome!" the man replied. He shook Polyp's hand, and the builder's hand, too.

No sooner had the man closed the front door behind them than he remembered his wife had a doctor's appointment; he had to drive her in the morning to her twice-monthly checkup with the obstetrician. The thing to do—the thing he'd normally have done—would be to open the door and shout out to the builder before he drove away, but the idea of that—of turning the knob, pulling it toward him, raising his voice, comparing daily schedules till gaps coalesced—struck the man as repellant, and, all at once, he seemed to himself to be a great imposition, not only on the builder but on his wife, the whole world, even his unborn child. A sense of failure, a sense of being useless, a feeling of unmanliness, of inhumanity, even—a sense that he was less a person than an obstacle, demanding from others to be climbed or jumped over, to be worked around—nearly overwhelmed him.

What could he do, though? Paint the wall himself? He moved money for a living, money on screens, tiny black digits in spreadsheet cells, his skills were abstract, his work was figurative, he bought and sold debt, he grew and shrunk numbers. He hadn't held a roller since the summer preceding his senior year of college, when he worked a few weeks for University Painters, a company from which, he now recalled, he was fired not because he was *bad* at painting walls so much as because he just wasn't very fast. According to the beer-drunks and potheads on his crew, he was overly concerned about primer. "You're a compulsive fucken uptoucher, man," the boss told him. "The tip of your nose should not be white and the tip of your nose is always white cause you look so closely for dings in the wall you just finished priming, your nose pushes up against the wall and removes a patch of primer so that now you've gotta re-prime, and after you re-prime, you do another ding check, and the cycle, it whats? The cycle *repeats*. And repeats and repeats. My advice for you is you should dial down the tight-ass cause that's why you're fired."

He could paint the wall himself.

He bought tarp and a roller at the hardware outlet. The leftover primer and paint were in the basement where the painter had left them. He primed the wall and painted it, untaped the taped parts. His wife said, "Impressive. Didn't know you had it in you. My husband, my man." They embraced beside the wall and ate a late dinner, then the man called the painter.

"Good news," he told the painter. "You've got the morning off. I painted the wall." "Oh, buddy," said the painter, "I'd have been happy to do that." "I'll gladly tell the builder you showed so he'll pay you." "No, no, no—seriously. No need at all. Don't." "An honest man!" the man ejaculated. "Yeah, well," said the painter. "Not to say I ever doubted it!" the man quickly added. "Well, you've still got my number, so you call if you need me," the painter told him. "Will do. Thanks again," the man said. They hung up.

The man called for the dog and they went for a walk. They walked in the park. In the middle of the park, between a couple of hills, they played some fetch with a fallen branch till he tackled the dog and they rolled in the grass, and the dog barked and growled and licked the man's face, and the man growled back and spoke all the taglines he was able to remember the pro-wrestling heroes of his youth once growling, and his arms got scratched, and the grass stained his shirt, but the stains and the scratches were worth it.

The new wall cracked. The crack oozed gel. The couple didn't know who to call. A lawyer? No. The rest of the house did not ooze gel. There were no cracked walls in the rest of the house. They didn't want to sue and they wouldn't sue, wouldn't know what to sue for if they could sue—maybe the crack oozing gel was their own fault somehow—but they knew who they'd sue if they'd wanted to sue, and he was, their builder, a decent man who'd tried his best to do what was right: he had put up the new wall at the first opportunity, not to mention free of charge, and above all he'd done so with total humility, without even hinting that replacing the wall in so timely a fashion was anything more than that which dutiful builders must do for clients whose walls have cracks gels ooze from. Plus the house, on the whole, was a very good house, a strong, handsome house, entirely predictable, completely sound, creakless and dripless, sturdy and sealed, proud in the daylight and safe in the dark.

Things, in short, could be much worse. They had a heart-to-heart over coffee on the patio. They decided he'd keep a close eye on the gel, and, in order to avert any chance of it sliding down into their open, sleeping mouths, the couple pushed their bed against the opposite wall.

2

Every night of the following week, the man sat in a chair in front of the wall in order to witness the crack ooze gel, but every increasingly caffeinated night he fell asleep before the oozing, foiled again, then woke at first light to a gel-covered crack.

Each morning that week, he wiped the gel with a kleenex, threw away the kleenex in the can in the garage, fed the dog and himself, and took the dog for a walk.

On the seventh morning's walk, his eyes were so tender with sleep-deprivation that even the smallest breeze would sting them, but the dog's fawn coat appeared especially handsome, which filled the man with a prideful affection that, sting be damned, he wanted to relish—there seemed so little to relish of late—so he made the decision to walk the block twice instead of just once, and during the latter half of this walk, in the midst of relishing his prideful affection, it occurred to the man that he needn't stay awake to witness the oozing, for he owned a camera, and he chided himself for not remembering it sooner, and commended himself for remembering it at last.

That night he set the camera on the chair in his stead, pressed RECORD, and happily went to sleep beside the woman. In the morning, however, he met with disappointment. The recording of the wall during the hours before sunrise was far too dark for him to even make out the crack; by the time it grew bright enough, the gel had already oozed; he could see nothing more than he'd already seen.

The next night, at bedtime, he set up the camera just as before, but this time he put a flashlight beside it to shine on the crack.

The following morning, to his great surprise, the crack was entirely free of gel.

He proceeded to use the camera-and-flashlight rig three nights in a row, only to discover, three mornings in a row, a crack with no gel. The woman suggested the flashlight (and maybe even the camera) be set on the chair before the crack in perpetuity; she suggested that keeping the crack well-lit (or under well-lit surveillance) might prevent the gel from ever reemerging. The man thought this plan was cowardly and defeatist, but also, he knew, the woman wouldn't understand why it was cowardly and defeatist. The problem, to her, was that a crack oozed gel, and to prevent that crack from oozing gel would, to her, be a form of victory, while to him it would at best be a stalemate, for the crack would still be there (the woman wasn't even *pretending* to suggest that light or surveillance would uncrack the wall), and at worst be a miserable and total defeat because you don't negotiate with terrorists, do you? You don't buy a high-performance German sedan to convey you to work when a baby's on the way (knock wood, knock wood). You don't learn to live with your plight, you end it. The world was a blooming and ever-fertile garden containing the means with which any man, if he was of any use, could solve any problem that might arise as long as he determined to forego half-measures. But because the man knew the woman wouldn't understand how mounting the flashlight or the flashlight-and-camera would be cowardly and defeatist, he suggested that the gel, if prevented from oozing forth from the crack, might gather *in* the wall, causing them troubles they couldn't imagine, and the devil you know, and the devil you don't.

And the woman relented. "Maybe the crack's finished oozing anyway," she said. "Maybe it ran out of gel and stopped."

"It's possible," said the man.

"If the gel comes back, though," the woman said, "and you won't try the flashlight and camera again, you have to promise you'll keep the crack clean."

The man made the promise, the crack oozed gel, and he returned to the previously established routine. Each morning, on waking, he would wipe the crack with kleenex, throw the kleenex away in the can in the garage, feed the dog, feed himself, then take the dog for a walk.

As the weeks went by, the walks became longer, and the man, on these walks, became increasingly vexed by fundamental questions about the gel's origins, namely: had the gel formed first and created the crack, had the crack formed first and created the gel, had they been created simultaneously by a third phenomenon he wasn't aware of, or might they even have been created by a pair of independent phenomena he wasn't aware of? Was it really safe to say the gel *oozed from* the crack? Might it not be the case that the crack somehow *attracted* or *gathered* the gel from somewhere else? From somewhere in the bedroom? From the *air* in the bedroom? The very air the man and woman breathed nightly?

The man elected not to trouble the woman with these questions. They'd only upset her, which would, most likely, be bad for the baby. He hated, however, to hide things from the woman. It revved his vexation. He grew vexed to distraction. He'd find himself thinking of the crack and the gel during meetings with clients, visits to friends. In the middle of an orgasm he saw them on his eyelids. What did it mean? What could it mean? It was gel on a crack. A crack oozing gel. Or gathering gel. Or coalescing with gel by unknown means for unknown reasons. Crack and gel. He lost lots of sleep. Eating seemed a labor. One morning he forgot to shave a section of his face and didn't even notice until after lunch when a certain associate who liked to yank his chain called out to him just outside of reception and told him, "Nice work! You possess my admiration. Rare is the man who can pull off the cheekstache without looking totally crazy and depressed." Was he crazy and depressed? He remembered a talk show that talked about depression. Or maybe obsession. Something psychological. Experts were consulted. They got into arguments. All they could agree on was *break the routine*. *Break the routine* was the moral of the talk show. *Break the routine* was the cure for... something. He'd give it a shot. It was worth at least that.

In the morning, instead of wiping the crack then feeding the dog then himself and then walking the dog, the man walked the dog first. A couple blocks in, it seemed to be working. His mood was improved, jovial even, and so was the dog's; it licked at his hands and bounded and leaped, cast glances at the trees whose leaves had started turning, then cast glances at the man as if to say, "Look! These trees are really great! Don't forget about these!" and accompanied these glances with a kind of sigh that sounded like "*Fff!*"

After returning to the house from their walk, the man fed the dog, and then fed himself, and then went upstairs to wipe the crack with the kleenex. Upon dropping the kleenex in the can in the garage, he noticed that the tips of two of his fingers seemed slightly moist and slightly tacky. Were they, though? He touched them together again to double-check. They no longer seemed to be tacky at all, but maybe they seemed to be a little bit moist. Only a little bit. Maybe it was nothing. But maybe it was something. He triple-checked the fingertips—no longer moist. Maybe it had been something that then became nothing. Maybe some gel had seeped through the kleenex when he wiped the crack but it was such a small amount that it evaporated rapidly. Unless it was maybe just a drop of fruit juice. Or maybe some honey he'd put in his yogurt? But it might have been the gel. And given how quickly the evaporation had occurred, it might have happened before without his ever noticing. He might have touched the gel any number of times. What the fuck was he thinking, standing there like that?

He ran inside the house and scrubbed his fingers. He stared at his face in the bathroom mirror—he still had the cheekstache. In the twenty-ish hours since he'd first been made aware of it, he hadn't thought even once of shaving it off! Was he losing his mind? Was the gel, contact with it—was contact with the gel poisoning his mind? How could he know?

Was there some way to test it? There were tears in his eyes. One of them fell and got stuck in his cheekstache. And then, all at once, he understood what needed doing.

Next morning, the man wiped the gel with some bacon, and went to the dog, who was waiting on the patio.

"Go on," said the man. "Eat the nice bacon. Then we can go on our Saturday errands."

The dog rose on its hind legs and leaned on the man, put paws to his nipples.

The man stepped back. The dog fell to all fours.

"No dancing," said the man, "till you've eaten what I brought you." He gestured with his chin at the dangling bacon, which he held at his side between two fingers.

The dog stepped forward, rose on its hind legs, and licked the man's chin.

From behind him came a noise, a muted chuffing—the laughter of his wife behind the sliding glass door. She was saying something now.

"What?" the man said.

"Merf merf merf wait!" she said.

"What?" the man said.

His wife slid the door open. "I said that he's watching his weight," she said.

"His weight?"

"You know," his wife said. "Because it's bacon."

"Because it's bacon?"

"The Food and Drug Administration doesn't even classify it as meat. That's how fattening it is. That's why he doesn't want to eat the bacon, I was saying. Because he's watching his weight and bacon is so fattening that it's classified by the USDA as a fat, even though it's meat."

"The FDA," the man said, "or the USDA?"

"What?"

"First you said one and—"

"What I meant was—"

"Either way," said the man, "is it really true?"

"What?"

"That bacon is classified not as a meat, as we would likely expect, but as a fat," the man said.

"Well, it's certainly something I've heard," his wife said.

"But have you seen documentation? I mean, is it documented?"

"You know, I don't know. I was trying to make a joke."

"A joke?"

"About the dog watching his weight."

"I don't think that's very funny," the man said.

"I can tell," said his wife.

"I didn't find it funny when you originally said it, and I don't find it funny now, after it's been explained to me."

"Jeez."

"Jeez yourself," the man said, and flung the strip of bacon toward the fence out of pique. The dog brought it back, dropped it on the patio, sniffed it, licked it, chewed it up and swallowed.

"Good *dog*," he told the dog. He turned to his wife. Her mouth was just a line. She'd been stung; he'd stung her. "I'm sorry," he told her. "I'm sorry I snapped at you."

She said, "Why are you feeding him bacon, anyway?"

"I wanted to give him a special treat."

"You should have cooked it," she said.

"I don't think he cares if it's cooked," the man said.

"Uncooked bacon may contain harmful bacteria."

"I doubt there's any harmful bacteria—bacon's cured. And the stomachs of dogs can handle more bacteria than the stomachs of people can."

"Where do you get *that*?" she said. "Have you seen documentation?"

"Touché," said the man.

"That's right," said his wife. "They die from chocolate."

They stared at each other until his wife smiled.

"Maybe..." she said. "Maybe it's his blood pressure."

"What?" the man said.

"The reason he didn't want the bacon before. Because bacon's very salty. Eating too much salt is a cause of high blood pressure."

"Huh-ha!" the man said. "Now that is a good one."

But he didn't mean it. He did not think it was a good one, or even an okay one. What he thought was: I have just fed what may be poison to my beloved dog for no better a reason than to discover whether what I just fed my beloved dog is poison. I may have just set in motion the slow murder of my beloved dog and, in the process of doing so, I lied to my wife and made her feel bad about herself for having made a joke that I didn't find funny. I am a terrible person. I do not want to have fed what may be poison to my dog, nor to have lied to my wife, nor to have made her feel bad about herself. I do not want to be a terrible person. I do not want to suffer the terrible justice that I want to believe is visited on terrible people. I need to get out of here and *think*.

"I'm going to the store," the man said to his wife. "Do you need anything?"

"Eggs and veined cheese," she said. "For veined cheese omelettes."

"You've got it!" said the man. Then he turned to the dog. "Store, boy?" he said. "You want to go to the store?" The dog started to rise, as if it wanted to dance, but before it got tall enough to reach the man's nipples, it fell back on all fours, dipped its head weirdly, then shifted its weight right to left, as if dizzy.

"So cute!" said the woman. "What's he doing? So cute!"

Every night before bed, ever since he'd married his wife, and no matter how tired he was, the man brushed his teeth, rinsed with mouthwash, and flossed. Though he rarely enjoyed performing these tasks, afterward his mouth always tasted clean, and he felt responsible, forward-thinking, and generally adultlike. His uncompromising dental hygiene was good for his wife (kissing in the future as well as kissing today), good for himself (foregoing mouth-pain/dentures), good for his unborn child (forming good habits now to enable him later to more easily set a good example for the child about forming good habits), and good for America (lower dental costs meant lower-cost dental insurance which meant wider coverage). Preventive care, the man believed, was indeed a noble kind of care, maybe even the most noble kind.

Another, newer, thing the man regularly did (he'd been doing it for nearly six months, now) was to execute a two-point turn in the driveway and back into the garage every time he arrived home, the purpose of which was to obviate his need to back *out* of the garage (a task requiring a greater amount of focus and hand-eye coordination—and therefore a greater risk of accidental collision—than that of exiting the garage hood-first) to drive his wife to the hospital when she went into labor. For all the extra effort it took him (the two-point turn; the extra-slow, neck-straining ingress), his routine backing of the car into the garage was, no less so than the diligent, nightly cleaning of his mouth, a source of quiet pride for the man. Each time he thought of it, his spirits lifted.

And so they did (his spirits lifted) when he entered the garage with the dog to go to the store. At the sight of his in-backed, green Swedish car, the man was reminded that, in general, his intentions were good, and he began to feel a lot less terrible. He wasn't a lazy or careless person. Quite the contrary. He was a two-point-turning nightly flosser, someone who was willing to do the harder thing to better ensure the safety and well-being of those he loved. And he remembered—or *imagined he remembered* (the distinction between memory and imagination being as thin a distinction as any, really)—that his reasons for feeding the dog the gel-smeared bacon weren't nefarious reasons at all. It is true he'd been aware that the gel might be a poison, but he was no more aware of its potential toxicity than he was of its potential capacity to enhance the dog's life. Was it so unlikely the gel was *good* for the dog? Might it not have been something healthy, like a vitamin supplement? Or maybe something that, healthy or not, could provide the dog some pleasure, such as that which, say, catnip did for cats? After all, he loved the dog, so even if, in the spirit of adventure and scientific discovery, he'd gotten a little bit carried away and fed it some gel that might be—*might be*—poisonous, he surely must have done so in the hopes that the dog would profit.

"You might still, yet," the man said to the dog.

They were driving around now, the dog riding shotgun, facing the man, and happy-sounding chuffing sounds were chuffing from its nose.

"Profit, I mean," the man said to the dog. "You might profit yet. I remember the first time I drank a beer. It tasted just awful, didn't it, boy? Like a cross between an ashtray and an uncooked potato, but wet—still, I finished it off. I drank the whole can, didn't I? Yep! I drank the whole can down in Billy Toomer's basement, and by the last couple sips, I didn't even mind the taste. I was really very happy, and so were all my friends. We were happy to have beer and happy to have drunk it. Moreover, we were happy to be happy, because all of us, at first, we all hated the taste, and we didn't understand why men enjoyed beer, so all of us were worried we'd make shoddy men, or maybe even that we'd fail to ever become men, except then we understood—or at least thought we understood—why men enjoyed beer. It wasn't the taste. Who cared about the taste? Beer made you happy, boy! Beer made you laugh! That's right! Like that! Chuff chuff chuff! And we giggled like little girls did at church in the movies, and we drank second beers and talked about girls, mostly their chests, and how some of us had put our hands on their chests—not me, of course, this was only seventh grade, and I wouldn't even kiss a girl till junior year of high school—and we talked about how girls—by 'we' I mean my friends— they talked about how girls seemed to really enjoy it, being groped on the chest. There were sounds the girls made. My friends reported gasping sounds, moaning sounds, quiet little chuffing sounds—yeah, just like that—and I remember thinking, even though I didn't say it, that maybe those weren't sounds of enjoyment, but pain. I'd seen people gasp, moan, and chuff from pain. I had, myself, made those sounds when in pain. And I wondered if, maybe, getting groped on the chest was, for girls, like drinking beer was for us. I wondered if maybe the sounds the girls made *were* pained sounds, like maybe they really *didn't* enjoy being groped on the chest, or, more likely—more likely, I recall thinking, because the girls, at least according to what my friends said, kept putting up with the groping—more likely the girls *learned to enjoy it* and just forgot to change the sounds. And then—and this is the important part of what I'm trying to say, I think—then I wondered if I was full of shit. Just completely full of shit, you know, boy? Shit. I wondered if even though I seemed smart to myself and my parents, I was actually pretty dumb, plus completely full of shit. Do you see what I'm saying? I might have been making something out of nothing. That was the first really deep thought I ever had—or, at least, it's the first one I can remember right now—and, just as I had it, I started feeling dizzy. All of us did. Our faces got long and our mouths were dry. Billy Toomer suggested we try drinking more—that the problem we were having, contrary to how it seemed, was that we hadn't drunk *enough*. That we needed more beer to counteract our sick feelings. So we drank more beer, and man oh man did we get sick then! What I'm trying to tell you, though, is I'm sorry I've been acting so crazy lately—I'm sure you've noticed I haven't been myself. What I'm hoping is that bacon I fed you will make you a happier dog, like the way the beer in Toomer's basement, at least for a little while, made me a happier boy. I can't, if I'm honest with myself, say that that's what I was hoping all along—if I'm honest with myself, I don't know what I was hoping—but I'd like to think, I mean I'd *really* like to think that that's what I was hoping, and, more to the point, I am absolutely certain that's what I'm hoping now. You're someone I care about—you're someone who, frankly, I love. And I trust you. I trust you to guard me while I sleep, and to guard my wife, and I trust that when he or she is born, knock wood knock wood, you'll guard our child, too. I hope you won't be jealous. We won't love you any less. And you have my word that if you don't show some signs of being a happier dog in the next little while, I will never feed you that gel again, and I can only hope, if that's the case, that you'll be able to forgive me. And I want you to know that I'm learning from this, it hasn't been a waste, that what all of this has taught me, this whole experience with the crack and the gel—what I've learned from all of it is something I guess I've known, at least in part, ever since that day in Billy Toomer's basement, something I've known all along but forgotten: that there are lots of things that can't be known. *Important* things. And I'm saying I guess that's the point of the journey. By *the journey*, I mean life. Life might actually have a point, I'm saying, and that point is that you just can't know. Or maybe it's less that there's a point to the journey than that accepting that you just can't know some things, especially the important ones—accepting that is the key to enjoying, or *surviving*, the journey. And what a liberating thought that is, boy, isn't it? Do you see what I'm saying? As long as I'm accepting that *I just can't know*, I might as well enjoy believing whatever I believe. This moment we're having right now, for example. I'm talking to you, boy, I'm baring my soul to you, and even though you're incapable of speaking any of the words I'm saying, let alone defining them, I nonetheless believe you understand what I'm saying. I believe you understand what *underlies* all these words. You understand that I'm here for you, boy, that I'm here to protect and take care of you, boy, and you understand I'm sorry I fed you that gel. I don't have any evidence that you understand me—that's true. But I don't have any evidence that you *don't* understand me, either. So why shouldn't I believe it? That you understand me, I mean? I should believe it. That's what I'm getting at. And what's more, I do. I do believe it. And furthermore, boy, I enjoy believing it, and I *should* enjoy it! I *do* enjoy it, boy. And for that I am grateful. Thank you for understanding me, boy. Thank you for being such a—ooh! Shit. Oh no. No."

The dog had vomited, warmly, onto the man, startling the man. In turning his head to examine what had startled him, the man turned the steering wheel hard. The car was traveling forty-nine miles per hour in the highway's right lane, and he had just enough time, before it struck the pylon supporting the overpass, to brake to forty-one, which put the car into a spin, and to wonder if the gel had caused the dog to vomit, or if, as his wife would probably claim, the bacteria on the bacon was the culprit.

<h1 style="text-align:center">3</h1>

The coma seemed to last for about thirty seconds. The man had a vision of the crack oozing gel and thought of a cummy vagina, a "creampie." That's not what it was, though! He felt so dumb, just dumb and *iniquitous* to even think such a thing. It wasn't a "creampie" at all, but a crack. A crack in the wall oozing gel is what it was, and now he noticed how the light was reversed, like a photograph's negative: the gel a bright, pearlescent white, the crack even brighter, the wall black as onyx. He stared at the crack. It was a lovely crack, beautiful, perfect even—its width, its length, its distance from the ground. How could he have missed that? How could he ever have wished it away? What a fool he had been! The crack was a blessing! The crack was a gift! It was there for him—*his* crack. He knew it all at once, and in the most basic way. He knew it the way he knew he loved his dog. Now all he wanted was to tend to it lovingly, to give it a long, tender wiping—but he couldn't. He couldn't move his hands! He couldn't *feel* his hands, much less find a tissue. He needed a tissue. All he needed was a tissue and one working hand on an arm that could reach. This poor, gorgeous crack, he thought, in need of a wipe! But wait a second, wait. He *could* feel his head. He could feel it *inside*—he could feel his mouth. His mouth was so dry. If he could feel his mouth, he could move his head!

The man sprang from his coma, sitting up straight, licking at the air. The side of his head hurt. Everything was white and beepy and glugging. He heard his wife's voice. "Thank God," she was saying. "Thank God, thank God." His sight adjusted. The room he was in was small and over-lit, a hospital room. His wife was huge.

"Thirsty," he rasped.

She brought him a crinkled paper thimble of water, held it to his lips. He sipped and he swallowed. The side of his head hurt. He remembered the dog, the vomit upon him, the stab of panic just before impact.

"I missed you," his wife said. "I missed you so bad."

"I missed you, too. I've been such a fool. I was wrong about the crack."

"Wrong?" she said.

"Yes. I was wrong. I..." He couldn't explain. He couldn't phrase it right, not with any dignity. His knowledge was a private kind—it wasn't even, he now realized, knowledge. It went beyond knowledge, was better than knowledge. What it was was belief. The crack was *good.*

"How's the baby?" he said.

"Still ticking," she said, and patted her belly.

"And the dog?" he said.

"The dog?" she said. "The dog," she said. "The dog," she said, and she burst into tears. In came some nurses. She must have pressed that button.

They told him his coma had lasted three months, that the pain and the scars along his temple and cheek should fade with time. They told him he'd T-boned his car on the pylon. That all of the Swedish airbags had deployed. That the dog, whose mouth had been wide open—they'd found its vomit all over the car and deduced it had been in the midst of heaving when the car struck the pylon—was thrust, face-first, against the man's head. That the thrust was so violent, its jaws snapped at impact and "opened like a book." That nine of its teeth, sunk to the gums, were lodged inside the man's head when they found him. That the dog, most likely, went instantly unconscious and asphyxiated on vomit. That they hoped that's what it was; that that fate was superior to bleeding to death (a much slower way to go). And they told him the EMTs were blown away, had never, in all their careers, seen anything like it. They told him that he should be thrilled to be alive, and twice as thrilled yet, coma and head wounds notwithstanding, to be entirely intact. He was. He was thrilled. He was thrilled and he was grateful.

They wanted to keep him around for a week, but he left in three days. It wasn't the insurance—he had the best insurance. He needed to get back home.

The crack on the wall was a mess of oozed gel that had hardened and crusted, ruptured, dripped, re-crusted, grayed. At its center, the mess protruded from the wall by as much as half an inch, and resembled, more than anything, a volcanic mountain range mapped topographically. The man knelt down on the floor before it, staring intensely, committing the features of the mess to memory; he wanted a stick to brandish at himself on the off-chance he ever grew tempted to abandon his crack-wiping duties (for a carrot, his vision from the coma would suffice).

Once he had the mess memorized, he drove the new car (same model as the old car; their coverage was excellent) to the hardware outlet, and purchased organic natural sponges and a non-abrasive solvent made with berries, milk, and mink-fat that required refrigeration. ("The Lamborghini of cleansers," the salesperson told him. "A little blob'll do you.")

As per the instructions printed on the tube, he applied a dime-size gobbet of solvent to his wetted (with filtered water) sponge, and waited for the solvent to turn from green to silver. Once the color had changed, he held the sponge to the wall an inch above the crack, pressing just enough to allow a few drips, and then he made the magic happen. The entire mess of crusted, hardened gel came off with one gentle, downward stroke of the sponge, and the crack, shimmering and wet, was freed. He blotted up the moisture with a second special sponge and threw both sponges away in the garage. On his way back upstairs, he stopped in the kitchen to pick up a jelly jar. The mess had slid down the wall intact, but had broken in two—mountains and foothills—when it struck the floor. He put the two pieces inside of the jelly jar, screwed the cap tight, brought the jar to the yard, and began, with a spade, to dig a hole in which to bury it.

Through the sliding-glass door, his wife saw him digging and went outside.

"What are you doing?" she said.

"I'm burying this mess."

"Why?" she said.

"It seems like the right thing to do," he said.

"I think it's strange."

"I know," he said. "But I don't mind."

"Can we talk about the crack?" she said.

"I'd rather not," he said.

"Can I just say that I think, with the baby coming soon, I think that we should really consider trying again to replace that wall. I don't know what that gel that comes out of it is, and I'm worried it's doing something to you that I don't like. And I'm worried about what it might do to me or, God forbid, the baby."

The man stopped digging to stand and hug his wife. "The gel," he said, "won't do anything at all to you or to the baby. I would never let that happen. I *won't* let it happen. I will tend to the crack every morning. The wall stays."

"You're insisting."

"I'll put my foot down if I have to. Do I have to put my foot down?"

"No," his wife said. "You don't have to put your foot down."

He raised a leg high and slammed his foot down on the patio. Then he did it again. His wife laughed, kissed his cheek, and went back inside to watch TV. He joined her once the burial of the jar was complete.

But for one brief moment, the man spent the rest of his life feeling ebullient. The crack oozed gel, he wiped the crack, threw the kleenex away, his teeth were clean, his home was lovely, he backed his car in, he thrived at his job, his coverage was solid. His child was born, the child was cute, the child was healthy, his wife was healthy, they had another child, who was also cute and healthy, his investments matured well, and, after the second child started grade school, his wife sold real estate and thrived at her job, and by the time that he and his wife retired, his children were wealthy, and they had their own children, and the man died smiling in the middle of a dream, and his wife collected millions of dollars in insurance, wiped the crack in his stead, bought higher education and condos for the grandkids, lived mostly in her memories, nearly all of which were good, and then she died, too, in her sleep. In the months before her death, she'd had the house remodeled, but she'd let be the wall with the crack in the bedroom, and in her will's only codicil, she made it clear to all her progeny that if her youngest grandchild, to whom she'd left the house, were to alter the wall in any way or fail to wipe the crack with a kleenex as needed (as the years marched on, the gel emerged less frequently), the house would go to her eldest grandchild, whom the youngest despised, and the youngest did nothing to alter the wall, and he tended to the gel on the crack as needed, and he continues to do so till this very day.

The brief moment the man's ebullience faltered occurred on the steps of the church, following the baptism of the couple's first child (named after the dog). The man saw the painter going to his German sedan and realized that although he'd greeted him earlier, they hadn't had the chance to have a conversation. The man felt terrible, not just for having missed a perfect opportunity to be fraternally warmed, but also because the receding painter's posture was slumpy and defeated, which suggested to the man that fraternal warmth was something the painter direly needed, and the man had failed to provide him with it. What a crummy feeling the man had on those church steps! But he made a decision to call out to the painter, and he followed through, and the moment passed, the crummy feeling died, and his ebullience resumed.

No sooner had the man yelled the painter's name than the painter turned from his car and waved. "Don't leave!" the man shouted. "Wait!" he shouted. He walked down the steps and went to the painter. "I wasn't leaving," said the painter. "Just getting one of these." The painter opened the door of his car and, from a cooler on the floor, removed a narrow orange can containing an energy beverage called ZOINKS!!!. "For bravery," said the painter. The man told the painter, "I know just what you mean! I could've used a can of bravery the last time I went to a baptism, also. It was my wife's brother's kid's baptism, and a funny thing—well, not really funny, not funny at all really, but maybe just kind of *interesting* or *strange*, or, I guess, *coincidental*, which I'll get to why in a second—the thing was my wife had just miscarried a few weeks earlier, and we were really upset, especially she was, and then we're at this baptism, her nephew's getting baptized, and holy moly was I not feeling brave. I mean, I was just kind of waiting for her to completely break down, and I was so scared because I had no idea what I'd say. We'd been over it so many times, you know? There's no way to—there's nothing you can say when something like that happens. All you can do is kind of throw your hands up and hug her and tell here it'll be alright, that you'll try again, that as hard as it is—as *impossible* as it is—to make sense of what's happened, you just have to accept it, the way you accept, I don't know, math. Death. The weather. Your metabolism. See? It's not comforting at all, but your role, as the husband, is to hug her every time, and not try to explain it, but I'm saying this in retrospect—at the time, at that baptism, I still thought I could somehow explain it to her, show her the bright side, but I couldn't even explain it to myself and I wasn't able to admit that. Anyway, I could've used some of that energy drink, I think. To keep the spirits up. To be brave for my wife. Though I heard it rots your kidneys or your liver or something. But oh! So the weird coincidence, I was saying—what I've wanted to tell you, ever since you came over to paint the crack and we had that amazing conversation on the driveway, was how I almost bought the exact same car you drive, but last minute decided to buy the Swedish one I drive because the Swedish one's the safest there is—not that yours isn't safe, but the Swedish is *the safest*—and the reason I bought the Swedish one instead of yours is that we had a baby on the way, the baby you just saw baptized thirty minutes ago, and because of the miscarriage during her first pregnancy, my wife—and, look, I'll admit to it too—my wife and myself *the both*, we were superstitious about telling people she was pregnant because we thought it would jinx us somehow. Counting our chicken before it hatched, as it were, huh-ha! I mean, you like to think of yourself as a sane, scientifically minded person, but the truth is you're not. And by *you*, I mean *me*, you know what I mean? But so how's the car? Is it still an exciting car to own?" The car, the painter told the man, was fine. More than fine, actually. Maintenance was easy and, unless his calculations were off, he got even better mileage than promised, especially on the highway. "What I want to talk to you about, though," he said, "is something I feel really bad about—it's why I needed to get all this bravery in me." The painter turned the narrow orange can upside down, and a single, hot pink drop of ZOINKS!!! splashed onto the concrete surrounding the sewer grate. The painter went on: "That crack in your wall that you called me about? You know how it came back even after I painted it? The paint was bad. Now, I didn't know that when I painted the wall, or even when I repainted the wall. I mean, I knew it wasn't great paint like in the rest of the house, and I felt a little guilty, but I didn't know just how bad it was. But that's not even an excuse, because by the time you had that second wall put up, I *did* know how bad it was, and I didn't say anything about it to you, not even when you called me, and you're *such* a nice guy, with *such* a nice family, so I just want to come clean with you, and that's what I'm gonna do if you'll let me. Your builder, who pays me—and I'm implicated, too, don't get me wrong—but the builder is a shyster, and a serious cheapskate, and there's this guy who works for him, a foreign guy, Polyp, you might have met him—he wears his pants funny, makes weird faces— this Polyp's a jerk, even worse than the builder, and just a couple days before I finished painting your house, Polyp says to the builder, who's building like twenty other houses in your development alone, he says to the builder he wants a raise, an unheard-of-type raise, like fifty percent. And not just for him. Polyp tells the builder his whole crew wants a raise, and if the builder, Polyp says, refuses to give them this raise, they're gonna walk away, just like that, leave the builder in the lurch, and not only that, but there's this veiled threat that's in there, because if you want to know how a fresh-off-the-boatsky chucklehead like Polyp, who, by the way, is also a degenerate gambler and a part-time pimp—if you want to know how a guy like Polyp gets such a plum job building houses for nice couples in the suburbs, I'll tell you this much: it's not because he *doesn't* have crooked uncles in the unions who know how to set structure fires that look like acts of God. So what can the builder do? Take a personal loss to pay Polyp's crew? Well, yes, he could do that, he could make less money, but like I said he's a shyster, so instead of cutting into his profits, what he cuts is corners. All kinds of corners. Luckily, like I said, this all happened just a couple days before we finished your house, so the only corner left to cut there was the paint, and not even all the paint, just the paint in the master bedroom. The paint we used for the rest of your house was good, but the brand that we used in your bedroom was this recently banned Indonesian brand of paint. The builder got hold of hundreds and hundreds of cans of it for cheap from I don't know where—probably Polyp's uncles. The thing about this paint, though, was some of it was tainted with mold or bacteria or something—I never got it straight—but some of it was tainted with something weird and Indonesian that, first of all, cracks sometimes, to varying degrees, and second of all, sometimes, especially in the dark, it attracts some other kind of mold or bacteria that causes that paste stuff to form. Thus: banned. Now, I'd never seen this paint before I painted your bedroom, but the builder, who supplies me with my materials, he brought me two cans of it with the labels stripped off, which should have told me something, but I refused to imagine what that something could be. The first can must not have been tainted, though, right? Because the rest of your bedroom walls didn't crack, right? But the second one, which I barely used—the one I left in your basement closet—that was the one that your cracked wall got painted with. Anyway, after I painted over the crack in your wall, I saw the builder the next day, and I told him about your pasty crack because I figured he owed me money for going over to your house like that on a Sunday, especially considering how that jerk Polyp was getting such a big raise and I was getting nothing. And that's when he came clean about how it wasn't just cheap stuff in those label-stripped cans, but tainted Indonesian stuff. And he told me that if you ever called me again, I had to call *him*, and he'd go out there himself to smooth things over with you and replace the wall, because some of those other houses we used the tainted paint on? The newer houses that we used *only* the tainted paint on? Some of them had wall-cracks oozing pastes and gels like your one wall did, but then a couple of them—the walls were actually, like, *crumbling*. And so the builder, he was scared that if he didn't replace the tainted-painted walls, something terrible would happen— some kid would eat the pasty stuff and die, or a wall behind a crib would crumble violently and a pointy chunk would fall and spear a fontanel or something, and then the jig would be up. Not just for him, but for me, too—I'd painted a lot of those walls myself. Lucky for us, the one thing you can always count on the owner of a newly built home to do is com-plain. So every time there's been a complaint about a crack, the wall gets replaced and I paint it using good stuff. If it's any comfort, you probably got hit by the taint less badly than anyone else. I want you to know, though, that I'm sorry for using cheap paint in your bedroom to begin with, but what I'm even much sorrier for than that is that I didn't say anything to you about the paint being tainted that night you called me, after you'd painted the wall yourself, especially because I assumed, at the time, that you'd used the tainted paint I'd left in your basement, which obviously you didn't because the crack didn't come back, right? But please accept my apology, man. I am humble before you, and I'm telling you the truth now. I was just really afraid that I'd ruin my reputation or even go to jail is why I kept quiet, and I consider you a friend, even though we don't know each other that well—that conversation we had on your drive-way about cars, and that killer Rwandan coffee we drank together... I feel like we bonded, and, above all, I just hope you appreciate the risk I'm putting myself at here, in telling you all this stuff that could really, if the wrong person found out—it could really ruin my entire life—and I hope you can forgive me… Why are you looking at me like that? What's that look mean, man? What is that? You laughing? Are we okay? Are you laughing because we're okay or because…?"

The man took a step forward and hugged the painter. "What a man!" he told him. "What a decent man you are! What a true friend!"

And what a tale! That the painter would be willing to speak all those lies—Polyp a *jerk*? The builder a *con-man*? The painter, himself, *plying his trade in a dishonorable manner*? Please! Oh please! Likely story! Get out!… That the painter would be willing to tell all those big lies—and to do so with such artfulness; *the crack didn't come back, right?, the risk I'm putting myself at here*, etc.—in order to convince the man to repaint the wall, or *replace* the wall… Clearly the man's wife had not been as okay as she'd seemed with the attention the man continued to lavish on the crack, and, still worried that the gel could endanger their child (she was a dutiful mother), had, from desperation (a desperate need not only to try do everything in her power to protect their child, but to, at the same time, continue to be seen by the man as nothing less than the loving, faithful, and above all *supportive* wife she and he the both [the man and his wife] knew that she was), called up the painter, prior to the baptism, and concocted, or asked him (the painter) to concoct, this crazy story of tainted paint and crumbling walls in a last-ditch effort to rid the home of the gel and the crack from which it oozed, and, clearly, the painter had agreed to tell the man the made-up story in order to ease the strain he (the painter) imagined the crack might be putting on his good friend's (the man's) marriage.

Not even for a *second* had the man believed the painter, though. He knew better than that.

He squeezed the painter tighter.

"I'm glad you're not angry," the painter whispered.

"Life is so good," the man whispered back.

HOW TO PLAY *THE GUY*

Vet Prospective Jennys

To play *The Guy*, first you need a Jenny.

Get a girl. Not a child. A mid-to-late-adolescent girl you can loom over. Make sure she looks slutty and abused, too. Bangs, spray-cast to the sky with something shiny. Bangles and bracelets, enough to make noise when she scratches herself. Lots of eye shadow, some glitter in it. A low threshold for startling, paired with a strong tendency to wince when startled. Slam the car door and see. Lip gloss with a powerful fruit scent. If lipstick, then the kind that comes off in flakes. A T-shirt with a violent graphic, tied in a knot at the bottom, its crew collar scissored to create flaps of mock V-neck so that, when she bends forward, the flaps open and you can see the tops of her breasts. Kind of fat is okay, even preferable, but avoid morbid obesity like you would the AIDS. It draws too much attention. The buffalo hump is a no-go. So is a stomach that smiles in more than three places when she sits.

Which brings us to midriff. If she's sporting midriff, make sure the midriff is either too flabby or too sucked-in-looking. If her midriff is good, have her keep it covered. Unless she has an ugly face.

Shorts are actually better than a miniskirt. She should look like the kind of slutty-looking girl who says that girls in miniskirts look slutty.

Before teaching her the activities she will synthesize (see subseq.), stand her before a full-length mirror for an hour and have her repeat the following while she looks deep into her own eyes: "Remember that girl in the miniskirt? What a slut." And if she's kind of fat, have her also repeat: "That one girl was such a fat-ass it sickened me. It sickened me." The repetition of these words will eventually move her.

If she's wearing jeans: black or stonewashed. Never blue. She should be a girl who uses her jeans to assert her individuality, a girl who refers to herself as "pretty unique." I think how tight goes without saying, but just in case: tight. If not jeans, then spandex. Never sweatpants. Sweatpants send the wrong message.

This girl you've gotten: the more she looks like she might be your sister, the better. But do not worry this point too hard. You would be surprised to discover how many girls can pass for your sister.

What She Needs to Learn and How to Teach Her

Teach the girl how to hold a strip of her hair to her lips as if to kiss it or fake a mustache and to periodically chew and suck on the ends of the strip. Teach her how to tilt her head forward so that whatever's in front of her gets looked at from the tops of her eyes. Teach her also how to bob her head from side to side in a slow, even manner that bespeaks an inner state of intense deliberation.

For a girl whose startle-threshold is especially low, mastery of the side-to-side head-bob can, at times, be difficult. Be patient. She is starting from a place of neurological disadvantage. Jerkiness of the neck is to be expected. Offer her encouragement in whispers. Stand behind her, your hands on her shoulders, lightly massaging them. Tell her she is the best you've ever seen. Tell her she can do it. Encourage the use of a metronome. Speak figuratively to her. Talk of challenge. Of rising up. Talk of rising up to meet challenge. When necessary, use metaphors with bird and cage components. If frustrated with her for taking too long, get a grip

on yourself. Mix your metaphors for sagacity. Know the truth. The truth
is that, unlike the side-to-side head-bob, which, like the waltz or the cha-
cha, can be learned by anyone, a low startle-threshold is like a pretty face:
a girl either has one or she doesn't. Count yourself lucky that your girl
does, that her childhood was the kind that gets etched all over the twitch-
muscles. Applaud yourself for the choice you've made. Other girls may
be faster head-bob studies, but you can bet they don't wince like yours.

After she has mastered each of the activities separately, it's time for her
to put them together, to learn to kiss-chew the hair-strip tips while bob-
bing her forwardly inclined head from side to side in a slow, even manner.
How will you know when she has mastered the activity-synthesis? You
will ask yourself: Is she communicating cautious determination? If the
answer is no, then she must continue to practice. If the answer is yes, then
it is time to walk her.

Walk toward each other. Have her look at you while you walk toward each other. Begin at a distance of no fewer than thirty paces. With
each gap-closing step, your sense that she is cautiously determined about
something having to do with you should increase.

After ten successful, consecutive walking trials, she is Jenny. You will
call her Jenny and she will respond to Jenny. You will maintain your
given name until your Steveness/Rickness is determined by Jenny at the
moment of truth.

The Right Friend

Now you must choose the right friend. Who the right friend is de-
pends exclusively on what you look like. Ask yourself: Do I have the face
of a kind stranger? Do I have the look of the jackal? The eye of the tiger?
Am I a funny-looking person or a serious-looking person? Am I wide
or narrow? Am I a handsome devil? A sort of pretty boy? Am I blond?
Does my posture suggest a threat? Does my facial hair? Am I plagued by
the horse-face? The wall-eye? The lonely eyebrow? The liver-lips? The

no-lips? Do I wear boots in the winter or shoes? Am I bespectacled? Is my musculature chiseled-looking? Do I have ass? The right friend will be the one who has the least in common with you physically. The only caveat here is height. Like you, the right friend must be taller than Jenny.

Find Out Who You Are

Once you have chosen the right friend, introduce him to Jenny. Bring him to her house. Spend time doing something nonsexual with one another, but in relative proximity. Be kind to one another. Form social bonds. Help generate a sheltering ambience. Enjoy yourselves.

When Jenny tells you how the world has randomly brutalized her person, hesitate: do not immediately express your righteous indignation. Early expressions of righteous indignation will stifle Jenny, will end her stories early. Silence was forced on her person, and you must remain silent until she's finished telling you about it.

If you are someone who has trouble keeping quiet, then, prior to your introduction of the friend to Jenny, you should stand before a mirror for an hour and repeat the following while looking deep into your eyes: "Experiential symmetry is a minor form of justice." The repetition of these words will eventually silence you.

Once Jenny has finished telling her stories, the temptation for you to compete with the friend in a contest of righteous indignation will be powerful. Do not be ashamed. Compete. However, keep in mind that less is more. The low-decibel utterance of a single, well-chosen word—especially one preceded by a clicking sound from the mouth—will beat a fist-to-chest yelling routine nine times out of ten.

After you are done enjoying yourselves, make plans for another get-together at Jenny's the following evening, then take the friend back to his house.

The following evening, at the designated time, pick the friend up from his house and bring him to Jenny's again. When you get to her front step, make sure that you and the friend are standing next to each other and that you are equidistant from her door. Ring her doorbell. This is the moment of truth. When Jenny answers the door, who does she look at first? If it's you, congratulations. You are Rick. If she looks at your friend first, sorry, but you're Steve. It is Jenny's nature to gravitate toward, and say hello first to, the more dominant of any two males to whom she has previously been introduced. To protest this is to undermine *The Guy*. Remember: whether you're Rick or Steve, you're the one who chose Jenny. So have a little faith in yourself. Have a little faith in your own judgment, in the choices you've made. You have picked the right girl and she has seen you for who you are.

If Steve

It is not easy being Steve, but you must not forget that Steve is important. And you are not necessarily going to be Steve for the rest of your life. The next Jenny might choose you over the next friend. Jennys and friends come and go. In that respect, *The Guy* is not very different from the world at large. Suck it up: be the best Steve you can be. And once you find Geoff, you might forget you're Steve, anyway. So shake Rick's hand and congratulate him for being Rick. Thank Jenny for being so perceptive. Tell her she has done a good job. Tell them better their Steve than someone else's Rick. Be sincere. Believe what you tell them.

If Rick

You are more handsome than Steve. Life has been gentler with you. Your father thinks more highly of you than his thinks of him. Where Steve stammers, you enunciate. Where Steve bumbles, you glide like a Dutch speed-skater. You bound up the creaky stairways Steve falls down. Under the spell of your gaze, Jenny becomes a blushing, shrinking thing. Steve averts his eyes when she catches him staring. Yet Steve cares for you and you must remember not to lord your Rickness over him. He is not, after all, Geoff. And if you try to make Geoff of him, you risk everything, the old loneliness.

Cement the Image

Now it is time to stand in a bathroom and practice Tableau. Make sure to wear shoes for verisimilitude. Make sure the bathroom's mirror is wide enough to hold the image of the three of you standing side by side. Make sure its lower border is low enough to capture Jenny from the waist up. Your best bet is to go to the home's master bathroom.

If the home's master bathroom does not have a mirror of proper proportions, then Steve will inform Rick of the problem. If Rick doesn't know what to do next, Steve will suggest that the three of you go to his house or Rick's house in search of the right mirror. It will be up to Rick to decide which house to try first. If neither Rick's house nor Steve's house has the right mirror, go to the nearest indoor shopping mall. Go to the men's room in the food court. Most men will not protest Jenny's being in the men's room, but if a man protests, Rick will look at the man blankly, saying nothing, and Steve will take a half-step in the man's direction. The protesting man will then retreat.

Stand side by side before the mirror—Jenny in the center, Rick to her right, Steve to her left. If Rick is the one who looks like Jenny's brother, his arm should be around her shoulder. If Rick is not the one who looks like Jenny's brother, he should hold Jenny's hand.

Rick's free hand, his right hand, should be raised three inches above his head. The raised hand's index finger should point forward, in the direction of the mirror, the direction from which Geoff will come later on. Every three to five seconds, Rick should stab the air with his finger.

Steve's hands will stay in the front pockets of his pants. Steve will watch his feet until the moment after Rick stabs the air, at which point Steve will look to the spot where Rick's finger is pointed, then return his gaze to his feet.

All the while, Jenny will communicate cautious determination via the engagement of the activity-synthesis described earlier.

Practice Tableau until it conveys a sense of urgency, imminent justice, and the threat of violence. You will know you have acquired mastery when Steve feels important. Steve's feeling of importance is indicated by facial flush and heavy breathing. When these indications manifest, Rick and Jenny will have a perfect opportunity to acknowledge the importance of Steve. They should do so. Acknowledging Steve's importance will engender group cohesion. Rick should begin with, "How do you feel, Steve?"

To which Steve will reply, "I feel important."

And Jenny will say, "You *are* important," then glancingly touch the flat of her hand to Steve's forearm, and add, "to me. You're important to me."

And Rick, a rare smile stretched across his face, both hands raised to invite a pair of high-fives that should culminate not in slapping sounds but quiet finger-laced graspings, will say, "Now let's find Geoff! Let's do this thing."

Go where Rick says to go. Once you have gotten there, get in Tableau. Convey urgency, imminent justice, and the threat of violence.

Geoff

Who is Geoff? Whoever Rick says he is.

How is Geoff? Geoff is by himself.

Why is Geoff? Geoff is for Jenny who Geoff is because of.

Where is Geoff? He is moving toward the three of you, probably at the nearest indoor shopping mall, riding the escalators. But that is up to Rick.

Play

Now it is time to play *The Guy*:

It is time for Rick to choose a Geoff and indicate his choice of Geoff to Jenny, Steve, and Geoff by aiming his jabbing finger in the direction of Geoff and saying, loudly, "Is that the guy?"

From this point on, the three of you, whether by escalator or foot, will continue in Geoff's direction, so long as he is facing you, and you will not deviate from Tableau.

Rick will repeat, "Is that the guy?"

And Jenny will say, "I don't know."

And Steve will look up at Geoff, then back at his feet.

As the team closes in on Geoff, Rick, making sure to jab his finger in time with the question, will say, "Is that the guy?"

And Jenny will say, "I can't tell."

And Steve will look up at Geoff, then back at his feet. And the team will continue to close in on Geoff.

Repeat these moves in sequence until Geoff either runs away or is standing within two feet of the three of you, at which point Rick will say to Geoff, "You're the guy."

And Jenny will say, "No, he's not the guy."

And Rick will say, "Lucky for you, guy."

And Geoff will go away.

Steve will then whisper, "It's okay," and say, "We'll find him, Jenny," and ask Rick, "Isn't that true?"

And just as Rick, with his jabbing finger, indicates the new Geoff and says, "Is that the guy?" Jenny will touch Steve on the cheek to shush him. Steve will beam.

FAQ

What if Geoff protests in the fashion of "I didn't do it," before Jenny tells Rick, "No, he's not the guy"?

Ignore Geoff. Continue on as if he hadn't said anything.

What if Geoff sasses Rick?

If Geoff sasses Rick, Steve should move half a step in Geoff's direction, and Rick, from behind, should wrap his arms tightly around Steve's shoulders and say quietly, "Cool out, man," and then loudly, "We'll get his ass soon enough." And Steve should say, "Okay, Rick," and go limp in Rick's arms and half-step back into Tableau. Once the team gets within two feet of Geoff, Rick should push Geoff's forehead back with his jabbing finger twice: once when he says, "You're the guy," and again when he says, "Lucky for you, guy."

What if Geoff sasses Steve?

If Geoff sasses Steve, Steve should affect a neck-and-shoulder tick while Jenny and Rick pretend Geoff didn't say anything, unless what Geoff says is pretty funny. If what Geoff says is pretty funny, then Rick should let a single chuckle escape and Jenny should bat him lightly on the shoulder, in a tsking manner.

What if Geoff sasses Jenny?

If Geoff sasses Jenny, there is no other option but for Jenny to follow Rick's "You're the guy" with "Ohmygod, he *is* the guy," at which point Rick and Steve should commit acts of imaginative violence on Geoff, while chanting, "That's what you get, guy. That's what you get for messing with Jenny."

What happens if Rick chooses a Geoff who actually did something brutal to Jenny in real life?

There is no such thing as a Geoff who actually did something brutal to Jenny in real life. Jenny doesn't exist in real life any more than Rick, Steve, or Geoff. However, the girl who plays Jenny (i.e., Jenny's person) does exist, and if whoever's playing Geoff (Geoff's person) did something brutal to Jenny's person, then he should be treated the same as if he had sassed Jenny, except that during the chant, the word *Jenny* should be replaced with the girl's given name. If, for example, the given name of the girl who plays Jenny is Samantha, then Rick and Steve should chant, "That's what you get, guy. That's what you get for messing with *Samantha*." Jenny should at no point after the violence feel obligated to describe the brutal thing the guy did to her person.

What happens if Jenny says Geoff is the guy and Rick doesn't believe her?

It doesn't matter what Rick believes. The guy is whoever Jenny says he is. It is fundamental. Where Rick chooses Geoff, Jenny chooses the guy, and Steve... does what is required of him.

What happens if Rick chooses a Geoff who thinks he (Geoff's person) actually did something brutal to Jenny's person, when really he did something brutal to someone else?

If Geoff's person did something brutal to someone else, but Geoff thinks that his person did something brutal to Jenny's person, then Geoff should be treated as if he sassed Jenny. If Geoff apologizes prior to the acts of imaginative violence, and in so doing addresses Jenny by the name that belongs to the girl whom Geoff thinks Jenny is, then the chant should incorporate that name. For example, if Geoff says, "I'm sorry, Nadine," then Rick and Steve, while they perform imaginative violence on him, should chant, "That's what you get, guy. That's what you get for messing with *Nadine*."

What happens if, after Rick tells Geoff, "Lucky for you, guy," Geoff offers to help look for the guy?

If Geoff offers to help look for the guy, Rick should say, "Thanks for the offer, but this is our thing, guy." It should be noted that this is another opportunity for Rick to make Steve feel important, thus engendering group cohesion. If Rick wants to make Steve feel important, he should wink at Steve while voicing the second clause ("but this is our thing").

What happens if Geoff, in the course of playing The Guy, *beats Rick and Steve into submission?*

In this case, Geoff will have become the man. Steve will be the first to admit it. He will say to the man (formerly Geoff), "You are the man." And Rick will apologize to Steve and Jenny. He will say, "I'm sorry." And then he will say the same to the man, and add, "I mistook you for someone else, and I have failed my friends. I hope you will take my place by their side in this noble search for justice we have undertaken." Then Rick will slink off, never to be seen by Steve or Jenny again, lest he risk becoming Geoff, or worse, the guy, and Jenny will ask the man to be Rick, and so will Steve. If the man accepts, he will be taken to the men's room to practice Tableau. If the man refuses, then he will be pleaded with by Steve and, if he still refuses, he will be bid peace and farewell, and Jenny and Steve will bid one another peace and farewell and go away from one another forever, or a very long time, long enough to heal and to acquire the hope that is necessary to found a new team.

Can the guy be the man?

Yes. Whether or not Geoff remains Geoff or becomes the guy (whether by sassing Jenny or having, as his person, done something brutal to her person or to someone he thinks she is), he gets to be the man if he beats Rick and Steve into submission. It is only fair.

What happens if Rick says that Steve is Geoff?

If Rick says that Steve is Geoff, then Steve has to go away forever, never to be replaced, thus dissolving the team, unless Jenny rebuts by stating that Rick is the guy, in which case Steve can:

   a. tell Jenny to keep her mouth shut about Rick, because Rick is the man, at which point Rick has the chance to revoke Steve's Geoffness by stating, "I made a mistake. I'm sorry," and thus re-cohere the team,

or

b. agree with Jenny that Rick is the guy and state that he (Steve) is in love with Jenny, effectively dissolving the team, then move forward to attack Rick for being the guy, and then:

    i. get beaten into submission by Rick, and left there by both Rick and Jenny, who will have gone their separate ways,

or

    ii. beat Rick into submission, thus exposing the lies upon which the team and all its many games were predicated.

HOT PINK

My friend Joe Cojotejk and myself were on our way to Nancy and Tina Christamesta's, to see if they could drive us to Sensei Mike's housewarming barbecue in Glen Ellyn. Cojo's cousin Niles was supposed to take us, but last minute he got in his head it was better to drink and use fireworks with his girlfriend. He called to back out while we were in the basement with the heavy bag. We'd just finished drawing targets on the canvas with marker. I wanted small red bull's-eyes, but Joe thought it would be better to represent the targets like the things they stood for. He'd covered a shift for me at the lot that week, so I let him have his way—a triangle for a nose, a circle for an Adam's apple, a space for the solar plexus, and for the sack a saggy-looking shape. The bag didn't hang low enough to have realistic knees.

When my mom yelled down the stairs that Niles was on the phone, I was deep into roundhouse kicks—I wanted to land one on each target, consecutively, without pausing to look at them or breathe, and I was getting there; I was up to three out of four (I kept missing the circle)—so I told Cojo to take the call, and it was a mistake. Cojo won't argue with his family. Everyone else, but not them. He gets guilty with them. When he came back down to the basement and told me Niles was ditching out, I bolted upstairs to call him myself, but all I got was his machine with the dumbass message: "You've reached Niles Cojotejk, NC-17. Do you love me? Are you a very sexy lady? Speak post-beep, baby."

I hung up.

My mom coughed.

I said, "Eat a vitamin." I took two zincs from the jar on the tray and lobbed one to her. She caught it in her lap by pushing her legs together. It was the opposite of what a woman does, according to the old lady in *Huckleberry Finn* who throws the apple in Huck's lap to blow his fake-out. Maybe it was Tom Sawyer and a pear, or a matchbox. Either way, he was cross-dressed.

The other zinc I swallowed myself. For immunity. The pill trailed grit down my throat and I put my tongue under the faucet.

"What happened to cups?" my mom said. That's how she accuses people. With questions.

I shut the tap. I said, "Did something happen to cups?"

"Baloney," she said.

Then I got an inspiration. I asked her, "Can you make your voice low and slutty?"

"Like this?" she said, in a low, slutty voice.

"Will you leave a message on Niles's machine?"

"No," she said.

"Then I'm going away forever," I said. "Picture all you got left is bingo and that fat-ass Doberman chewing dead things in the gangway. Plus I'll give you a dollar if you do it," I said. "You can smoke two cigarettes on that dollar. Or else I'll murder you, violently." I picked up the nearest thing. It was a mortar or a pestle. It was the empty part. I waved it in the air at her. "I'll murder you with *this*."

"Gimme a kiss!" she sang. That's how she is. A pushover. All she wants is to share a performance. To riff with you. It's one kind of person. Makes noise when there's noise, and the more noise the better. The other kind's a soloist, who only starts up when it's quiet, then holds his turn like it'll never come again. Cojo's that kind. I don't know who's better to have around. Some noise gets wrecked by quiet and some quiet gets wrecked by noise. So sometimes you want a riffer and other times a soloist. I can't decide which kind I am.

I dialed the number. For the message, I had my mother say, "You're rated G for *gypsy*, baby." Niles is very sensitive about getting called a gypsy. I don't know what inspired me with the idea to have my mom say it to him in a low, slutty voice, but then I got a clearer idea.

I dialed the number again and got her to say the same thing in her regular voice. Then I called four more times, myself, and I said it in four different voices: I did a G, a homo, a Paki, and a dago. I'm good at those. I thought I was done, but I wasn't. I did it once more in my own voice, so Niles would know it was me telling people he's a gypsy.

My mom said, "You're a real goof-off, Jack."

Cojo came upstairs, panting. "Tina and Nancy," he said.

I thought: Nancy, if only.

Cojo said, "They might have a car."

It was a good idea. I called. They didn't know for sure about a car but said come over and drink. I kissed my mom's head and she handed me money to buy her a carton of ultralights. I dropped the money in her lap and pulled a jersey over my T. Cojo said it was too hot out for both. It was too hot out for naked, though, so it wouldn't matter anyway. Except then I noticed Joe was also wearing a jersey and a T, and I didn't want to look like a couple who planned it, which Joe didn't want either, which is what he meant by too hot out, so I dumped the jersey for a Mexican wedding shirt and we split.

A couple blocks away from the Christamestas', this full-grown man walking the other way on the other side of the street looked at us and nodded. It's a small thing to do but it meant a lot. It meant we were feared. My lungs tickled at the sight of it. I got this tightness down the center of my body, like during a core-strength workout. Or trying to first-kiss someone and you can't remember where to put your hands. Even thinking about it, I get this feeling. This stranger, nodding at you from all the way across the street.

It was late in the afternoon by then, and tropical hot, but overcast with small black clouds. And the wind—it was flapping the branches. Wing-shaped seedpods rattled over the pavement and the clouds blew across the sun so fast the sky was blinking. It opened my nose up. The street got narrow compared to me. The cars looked like Hot Wheels. And in my head, my first thing was that I felt sorry for this guy who nods. It's like a salute, this kind of nod.

But then my second thing is: you better salute me, Clyde. And I get this picture of holding his ears while I slowly push his face into his brains with my forehead. I got massive neck muscles. I got this grill like a chimney and an ugly thing inside me to match it. I feel sorry for a person, it makes me want to hurt him. Cojo's the same way as me, but crueler-looking. It's mostly because of the way we're built. We're each around a buck-seventy, but I barrel in the trunk. Joe's lean and even, like a long Bruce Lee. He comes to all kinds of points. And plus his eyes. They're a pair of slits in shadow. I got comic-strip eyes, a couple black dimes. My eyes should be looking in opposite directions.

I ran my hands back over my skull. It's a ritual from grade school, when we used to do battle royales at the pool with our friends. We got it from a cartoon I can't remember, or a video game. You do a special gesture to flip your switch; for me it's I run my hands back over my skull and, when I get to the bottom, I tap my thumb-knuckles, once, on the highest-up button of my spine. You flip your switch and you've got a code name. We were supposed to keep our code names secret, so no one could deplete their power by speaking them, but me and Cojo told each other. Cojo's special gesture was wiping his mouth crosswise, from his elbow to the backs of his fingertips. Almost all the other special gestures had saliva in them. This one kid Winthrop would spit in his palms and fling it with karate chops. Voitek Moitek chewed grape gum, and he'd hock a sticky puddle in his elbow crooks, then flex and relax till the spit strung out between his forearms and biceps. Nick Rataczeck licked the middle of his shirt and moaned like a deaf person. I can't remember the gestures of the rest of the battle royale guys. By high school, we stopped socializing with those guys, and after we dropped out we hardly ever saw them. I don't know if they told each other their code names. They didn't tell me.

Cojo's was "War," though. Mine was "Smith." It's embarrassing.

I coughed the tickle from my lungs and Joe stopped walking, performed his gesture, and was War.

He said to the guy, "What," and the guy shuddered a little. The guy was swinging a net sack filled with grapefruits and I hated how it bounced against his knee. I hated that he had them. It made everything complicated. My thoughts were too far in the background to figure out why. Something about peeling them or slicing them in halves or eighths and what someone else might prefer to do. I always liked mine in halves. A little sugar. And that jagged spoon. It's so specific.

The guy kept moving forward, like he didn't know Joe was talking to him, but he was walking slower than before. It was just like the nod. The slowness meant the exact opposite of what it looked like it meant. I'm scared of something? I don't look at it. I think: If I don't see it, it won't see me. Like how a little kid thinks. You smack its head while it's hiding in a peek-a-boo and now it believes in God, not your hand. But everyone thinks like that sometimes. I'm scared my mom's gonna die from smoking, the way her lungs whistle when she breathes fast, but if I don't think about it, I think, cancer won't think about her. It's stupid. I know this. Still: me, everyone. Joe says "What" to a guy who's scared of him, the guy pretends Joe's not talking to him. The guy pretends so hard he slows down when what he wants is to get as far the hell away from us and as fast as he can.

Joe says, "I said, 'What.'"

"I'm sorry," the guy says.

"Sorry for what?" Joe says, and now he's crossing the street and I'm following him.

I say, "Easy, Cojo," and this is when I learn something new about how to intimidate people. Because even though I say "Easy, Cojo," I'm not telling Cojo to take it easy. I'm not even talking to Cojo. I'm talking to the guy. When I say "Easy, Cojo," I'm telling the guy he's right to be scared of my friend. And I'm also telling him that I got influence with my friend, and that means the guy should be scared of me, too. What's peculiar is when I open my mouth to say "Easy, Cojo," I *think* I'm about to talk to Cojo, and then it turns out I'm not. And so I have to wonder how many times I've done things like that without noticing. Like when I told my mom I'd kill her and waved the empty thing at her, I wasn't really threatening her, it was more like I was saying, "Look, I'll say a stupid thing that makes me look stupid if you'll help me out." But that was different from this, too, because my mom knew what I meant when I said I'd kill her, but this guy here doesn't know what I mean when I say "Easy, Cojo." He gets even more scared of Joe and me, but he gets that way because he thinks I really *am* talking to Joe.

I say it again. I say, "Easy, Cojo."

And Cojo says, "Easy what?"

And now the guy's stopped walking. He's standing there. "I'm sorry," he says.

"Cause why?" Cojo says. "Why're you sorry? Are you sorry you nodded at me like I was your son? Like I was your boy to nod at like that? I don't know you."

"I'm sorry," the guy says. The guy's smiling like the situation is all lighthearted, but it's like yawning after tapping gloves on your way back to the corner. A lie you tell yourself. And I'm thinking there's nothing that's itself. I'm thinking everything is like something else that's like other something elses and it's all because I said "Easy, Cojo" and didn't mean it, or because this guy nodded.

I think like this too long, I get a headache and pissed off.

I put my arm around Cojo. I say, "Easy, Cojo."

"Fuck easy," Cojo says to me. And when Cojo says that, it's like the same thing as when I said "Easy, Cojo." I know Cojo isn't really saying "Fuck easy" to me. He wouldn't say that to me. He's saying "Fear us" to the guy. But I don't know if Cojo knows that that's what he's doing with "Fuck easy." That's the problem with everything.

"Give us your fruit," I tell the guy.

"My—"

"What did you say?" Joe says.

"Easy, Cojo," I tell him.

Then the guy hands his grapefruits to me.

I say to him, "Yawn."

He can't. Cojo yawns, though. And then I do.

Then I tell the guy to get out of my sight and he does it because he's been intimidated.

Nancy Christamesta is no whore at all. And I'm no Jesus, but still I want to wash her feet. Nancy's so beautiful, my mind doesn't think about fucking her unless I'm drunk, and even then it's just an idea: I don't run the movie through my head. Usually I imagine her saying "Yes" in my ear. That's all it takes. Maybe we're on a rooftop, or in the Hancock Building Signature Room, the sixty-ninth-floor one, looking at the city lights, but the "Yes" part's what counts. It's a little hammy. I've known her since grade school, but I've only had it for her since she was fourteen. It happened suddenly, and that's hammy too. I was eighteen, and it started at the beach— sunny day and ice cream and everything. Our families went to swim at Oak Street on a church outing and I saw her sneak away to smoke a cigarette in the tunnel under the Drive. There's hypes and winos who live in there, so I followed her, but I didn't let her know. I waited at the mouth, where I could hear if anything happened, and when she came back through, she was hugging herself around the middle for warmth. A couple steps out of the tunnel, her left shoulder-strap fell down, and when she moved to put it back a bone-chill shot her posture straight and a sound came from her throat that sounded like "Hi." I didn't know if it was "Hi" or just a pretty noise her throat made after a bone-chill. I didn't think it was "Hi," because I was behind her and I didn't think she'd seen me. I wanted it to be "Hi," though. I stood there a minute after she walked away, thinking it wasn't "Hi" and wishing it was. That was that. That's how I knew what I felt.

Now she's seventeen, and it's old enough, I think. But she's got this innocence, still. It's not she's stupid—she's on the honor roll, she wants to be a writer—but Joe and I were over there a couple months earlier, at the beginning of summer, right when him and Tina were starting up. They went off to buy some beer and Nancy and I waited in her room. Nancy was sitting in this shiny beanbag. She had cutoff short-shorts on, and every time she moved, her thighs made the sticking sound that you know it's leg-on-vinyl but you imagine leg-on-leg. I had it in my head it was time to finally do something. I lay down on the carpet next to her, listening, and after a little while I said, "What kind of name is Nancy for you, anyway?"

Nancy said, "Actually, I think Nancy's a pretty peculiar name for me. But I always thought that was because it's mine."

See, I was flirting. I was teasing her. It was my voice she was supposed to hear, not the words it said. But it was the words she heard, and not my voice. It was an innocent way to respond. And I didn't know what to do, so I told her she was nuts.

She said, "No. Listen: Jack... Jack... Jack... Does it sound like your name still?"

It completely sounded like my name, but I didn't say that because hearing it was as good as "Yes" in my ear and I wanted her to keep going. I wanted to tell her I loved her. Instead, I said *it*. I said, "I love it." She said, "Jack... Jack...Jack. I'm glad, Jack Jack."

If she didn't have innocence, she'd have heard what my voice meant and either shut me down or flirted back at me.

When we got to their house on the day of the nodding guy, she was sitting on the stoop with a notebook, wearing flip-flops, which made it easy to admire the shape of her toes. Most people's toes look like extra things to me, like earrings or beards. Nancy's look necessary. They work for her.

Joe went inside to find Tina.

Nancy said, "What's with the grapefruits?"

I said, "We intimidated a man. It's all words."

"I don't like that spoon," she said. "I clink my teeth. It chills me up." She was still talking about grapefruits.

"They're not for you," I said. "They're for your parents."

"What's all words?" she said.

I said, "You don't say what you mean. You pretend like you're talking about something else. It works."

"A dowry goes to the groom, not the other way around," she said.

I said, "What does that have to do with anything?"

She said, "Implications. Indirectness. And suggestion."

Was she fucking with me? I don't even know if she was fucking with me. She's a wiseass, sometimes, but she's much smarter than me, too. And plus she was high. I would've taken a half-step forward and kissed her mouth right then, except I wasn't also high, and that's not kosher. Plus I probably wouldn't have stepped forward and it's just something I tell myself.

"Come inside with me," she said.

She kicked off her sandals and I followed her to the kitchen. It's a walk through a long hallway and Nancy stopped every couple steps for a second so that I kept almost bumping her. She said, "You should take your shoes off, Jack. And your socks. The floor's nice and cold."

That was a pretty thought, but getting barefoot to feel the coldness of a floor is not something I do, so I told her, "You're a strange one." Nancy likes people to think she's strange, but she doesn't like people thinking that she likes them to think that, so it was better for me to say than it sounds, even though she spun around and smacked me on the arm when I said it, which also worked out fine because I was flexed. I was expecting a smack. I know that girl.

In the kitchen, Cojo was drinking beer with Tina and Mr. Christamesta. Mr. Christamesta was standing. He's no sitter. He's six foot five and two guys wide. I can't imagine a chair that would hold him. He could wring your throat one-handed. If there was a black-market scientist who sold clones derived from hairs, he'd go straight for the clog in Mr. Christamesta's drain whenever the customer wanted a bouncer. That's what he looks like: the father of a thousand bouncers. Or a bookie with a sandwich-shop front, which is what he is. But it's a conundrum after you talk to him, because you don't think of him like that. You talk to him, you think he's a sandwich-shop owner who takes a few bets on the side. Still, he's the last guy in Chicago whose daughter you'd want to date. Him or Daley. But a father-in-law is a different story.

He said to me, "Jack Krakow! What's with the grapefruits?"

I didn't want to think about the grapefruits. The grapefruits made me sad.

I said, "They're for you, sir, and Mrs. Christamesta."

"You're so formal, Jack. You trying to impress me or something? Why you trying to impress me, now? You want to marry my daughter? Is that it? My Nancy? You want to take my Nancy away from her papa? You want to run away with her to someplace better? Like that song from my youth? If. it's. the. last. thing. you ev-er do? You want to be an absconder, Jack? With my daughter? So you bring me grapefruits? Citrus for a daughter? What kind of substitute is that? It's pearls for swine, grapefruits for Nancy. Irrespectively. It's swine for steak and beef for venison. You like venison? I love venison. But I also love deer, Jack. I love to watch deer frolic in the woods. Do you see what I mean? The world's complicated. It's okay, though. I am impressed with your grapefruits. You have a good heart. You're golden. I like you. Just calm down. We're standing in a kitchen. It's air-conditioned. Slouch a little. Have a beer."

He handed me a bottle. I handed him the grapefruits. He's got thumbs like ping-pong paddles, that guy. He could slap your face from across the country.

What sucked was, grapefruits or no, I *was* trying to impress him, and I *did* come for his daughter, and he wouldn't be so jolly about it if he knew that, so I knew there was no way he knew it. And since he didn't know it, I knew Nancy didn't know it, because those two are close. So I was like one of these smart guys like Clark Kent that the girl thinks of like an older brother. Except I'm not smart. And my alter-ego isn't Superman, who she loves. At best I'm Smith, who no one knows his name but Cojo.

The one good thing about Mr. Christamesta going off on those tangents was it got Nancy laughing so hard she was shaking. She pushed her head against my shoulder and hugged around me to hold my other shoulder with her hands. For balance. And I could smell her hair, and her hair smelled like apples and girl, which is exactly what I would've imagined it smelled like in my daydreams of "Yes," if I was smart enough to imagine smell in the first place. I don't think I have the ability to imagine smell. I never tried, but I bet I can only do sound and sight.

An unfortunate thing about Nancy's laughing was how it drew her mom in from the living room. She's real serious, Mrs. Christamesta. So serious it messes with her physically. She's an attractive woman, like Nancy twenty years later and shorter-haired—see her through a window or drive by her in the car, it's easy to tell. If you're eating dinner with her, though, or at church, and she knows she's being looked at, the seriousness covers up the beauty. It's like she doesn't have a face, just her eyebrows like a V and all the decisions she made about her hairstyle. My whole life, I've seen Mrs. Christamesta laugh at three or two jokes, and I've never heard her crack a one.

"You, young lady," she said, "and you, too," to Tina, "have to quit smoking those drugs."

That got Nancy so hysterical that I had to force myself to think about the grapefruits again, about that guy coming home with no grapefruits and acting like he just forgot or, even worse, him going back to the store and getting more grapefruits and then, when he got home, making this big ceremony around cutting them or peeling them, whatever his family did with them. I had to think about that so I wouldn't start laughing with Nancy. If I laughed, it would look like I was laughing at Mrs. Christamesta. And maybe I would be.

"It's because you give them beer," she said to her husband.

"Is it you want a beer, honey?" he said to her.

She bit her lip, but took a seat.

He got up real close to her and said it again. "Is all you want is a beer?" He crouched down in front of her chair so his shirt rode up and I saw his lower back. His lower back was white as tits, and not hairy at all, which surprised me. He held her neck, and touched those paddles to her ears. "Is it you want a grapefruit?" he said. "I'll cut you a grapefruit. I'll peel you a grapefruit. I'll pulp it in the juicer. I'll juice it in the pulper. Grapefruit in segments, in slices, or liquefied. And beer. All or any. Any combination. All for you. Am I not your husband? Am I not a good husband? Am I not a husband to prepare you citrus on a sunny weekend in the Windy City? Have I ever denied you love in any form? Have I ever let your gorgeous face go too long unkissed? How could I? What a brute," he said. "What a drunken misanthrope. What a cruel, cruel man," he said. "I'll zest the peel with the zester and cook salmon on the grill for you. I'll sprinkle pinches of zest for you. On top of the salmon." Then he kissed her face. Thirty, twenty times.

That was the fourth time I ever saw Mrs. Christamesta laugh. Or the third. And thank God, because I was done feeling sorry for that nodding guy. I lost it so hard that when the laughter was finished with me I was holding Nancy's hand and she was tugging on the front of my shirt and I didn't remember how we got that way.

I made a violent face at her, all teeth and nostrils. For comedy. Then she pinched me on my side and I jumped back fast, squealing like a little girl.

"Fucken girl," Cojo whispered. But he didn't mean it how it sounded. It was nice of him to say to me. Brotherly.

Mr. Christamesta threw a key at me. "You okay to drive?" he said. "You're okay," he said. He kissed his wife's neck and we went out the back door. To the garage.

The Christamestas have two cars. Both of them are Lincolns and both Lincolns are blue. I tried the key on the one on the left. It was the right choice.

Cojo called shotgun, but he was kidding. I held the shotgun door open for Nancy and Cojo tackled Tina into the backseat.

We stopped at the Jewel for some patties and nacho chips, and then we were on our way.

I forgot to mention it was furniture day. Two Sundays a year, Chicago's got furniture day. You put your old furniture in the alley in the morning, and scavengers in vans take it to their houses and junk shops. If no one wants it, the garbage trucks come in the afternoon and they bring it to the dump. That's what makes it furniture day—how the garbage trucks come. That's why there were garbage trucks on a Sunday.

One of them had balloons tied to its grille with ribbon. We got stopped at a light facing it. Grand and Oakley. We were going south on Oakley. That light takes forever. Grand's a main artery. It's dominant. Grand vs. Oakley? Oakley gets stomped.

There were white balloons and blue ones and some yellows. I don't know what color the ribbon was, but I knew it wasn't string because it shined.

Nancy said, "Do you think it's a desperate form of graffiti, Jack?"

Jack. I checked the rearview. Tina had her feet in Joe's lap. Joe was pretending to look out his window, but what he was doing was looking *at* the window. It was tinted, and he was looking at Tina's legs, reflected. Tina has good legs. You notice them. You feel elderly.

I said to Nancy, "It's probably the driver had a baby."

She said, "I think maybe some tagger got his markers and his spray-cans taken, and he was sitting on the curb out front of his house, watching all the trucks making pickups and feeling worthless because he couldn't do anything about it. He didn't want to write 'wash me' with his finger in the dirt along the body since there's nothing original about that, and he didn't want to brick the windshield because he wasn't some-one who wanted to harm things, but still he found himself reaching down into the weeds of the alley to grasp something heavy. He needed to let the world know he existed, and without paint or markers, bricking a windshield was the only way he could think to do it. Except then, right then, right when he gets hold of the brick—and it's the perfect brick, a cement quarter-cinderblock with gripping holes for his fingers, it fits right in his hand—he hears his little sister, inside the house. She's sing-ing through the open window of her bedroom, above him. She's happy because yesterday was her birthday and she got all the toys she wanted, and it reminds the boy of the party they had for her, how he decorated the house all morning and his sister didn't even care because all she really wanted was to unwrap her presents—the party meant nothing to her, not even the cake, much less the decorations—and so this boy races inside, to the hallway in his mom's house, and tears a balloon-cluster from the banister he tied it to, then races back out front, decorates the grille of the garbage truck."

Finally, the light turned green. If you're Oakley, you get about seven seconds before Grand starts kicking your ass again.

I said, "It could be the driver got married."

Nancy said, "And maybe it wasn't even today. Maybe it was some-time last week. Maybe those balloons have been there for nine, ten days because the driver thinks it's pretty. Because he understands what it means, you know? Or maybe because he doesn't understand what it means, because it's a conundrum, but it's a nice conundrum, something he wants to figure out."

"It could be his son," I said. "It could be it was his son got married or had a baby," I said.

Nancy said, "Oh." And I knew I shouldn't have said what I said. She was trying to start something with me and I kept ending it. She wanted me to tell her a fantasy story. I'm a meathead. A misinterpreter. Like hot pink? For years I thought it was regular pink that looked sexy on whoever was wearing it. And that Bob Marley song? I thought he was saying that as long as you stayed away from women, you wouldn't cry. Even after I figured it out, it's still the first thing I think when it comes on the radio. It's like when I'm wrong for long enough, I can't get right. I had a fantasy story in my head, but I didn't say it. And why not?

We were merging onto the Eisenhower when this guy in a Miata blew by us on the ramp and I had to hit the brakes a little. Everyone cursed except Nancy, who was spaced out, or pretending to be. Then we got quiet and Joe said, "What kind of fag drives a Miata?"

And Tina said, "Don't." Tina goes to college at UIC. She was a junior, like I would have been. "Don't say fag," she said.

"Fag faggot fag," Cojo said. "It's just words. It's got nothing to do with who anyone wants to fuck." He took out a cigarette. He said, "This is a fag in England." He lit the cigarette. He said, "I know fags who've screwed hundreds of women. I know fags who screw no one. Have a fag," he said. He gave the cigarette to Tina and lit a second one for himself. He said, "That rapist Mike Tyson's a fag. And my cousin Niles. He's screwing his girlfriend even as we speak to each other here in this very car. There's fags who like windmills and fags on skinny bicycles. I know fags who fix cars and fags who pour concrete. Regis Philbin's a fag. Kurt Loder and that fag John Norris. Lots of TV and movie guys. Rock stars. Pretty much all of them. So what? It's a word. It means asshole, but it's quicker to say and more offensive cause it's only fags who say asshole like it's any kind of insult. Even jerk's better than asshole. Asshole's a fagged-out word, and fag's

offensive. And it should be offensive. I want it to be offensive. Someone
calls me a Polack? I'm offended. But I'm a fucken Ukrainian, you know?
I don't give a shit about the Polish people. No offense, Krakow, but I don't
give a fuck for your people. Someone calls me Polack, though, I'll tear his
jaws off at the hinge. And cause why? Cause he's saying I'm Polish? No.
Cause he's saying Polish people are lowlifes? No. He's trying to offend
me is why. When he's calling me Polack, he's calling me fag. He's calling
me asshole. So fine. You're pretty. Okay. You smell good. You say smart
things to me when you're not telling me the right way to talk. Good
news. I like you. I want to spend all my money on you. I want to take you
on vacation to an island where there's coconuts and diving. Miatas are for
assholes if it makes you more comfortable. But the asshole in that Miata's
got fagged-out taste is what I'm telling you."

Tina said, "You've thought about this a lot, Cojo."

"I got a gay cousin," he said. "A homosexual. Lenny. He fucks men,
and that's not right and it makes me sick, but that's not why he's a fag.
He's a fag because whenever someone calls him fag, it's me who ends
up in a fight, not him. He's a fag because he won't stand up for himself.
Imagine: your own cousin a fag like that. That's how it is to be me. Not
just one but two fags in the family—Lenny the homofag and don't forget
about Niles the regular fag who all he does is chase girls—but I'm the
only one can say it, right? About how my family's got some fags in it,
I mean. Don't you ever bring it up to me. It's like a big secret, and tell the
truth it makes me uncomfortable to talk about, so let's just stop talking
about it, okay?"

Joe was always talking to girls about Lenny. Sometimes Lenny had cancer and sometimes he was a retard. In 1999, he was usually Albanian. But
there wasn't any Lenny. I know all Joe's cousins. So do the Christamestas.
Lenny was fiction. But I didn't say. If he did have a cousin Lenny, and
this Lenny was a gay, Cojo would defend his cousin Lenny against people
who called Lenny fag. So Cojo was telling a certain kind of truth. And
it never really mattered to Tina, anyway. She'd just wanted to know Joe

cared what she thought of him, and the effort it took him to come up with that bullshit about fags and assholes—that made it obvious he cared. And Joe is definitely crazy for Tina. He discusses it with me. All the things he wants to buy her. Vacations on islands with sailboats and mangos, fucking her on a hammock. They'd still never fucked, but they mashed pretty often. So often it was comfortable. So comfortable they started in the backseat of the car, which was not comfortable for me, sitting next to Nancy, who's staring at the carton of patties in her lap while the sister gets mauled. I hit as many potholes as I could. The Ike's got thousands.

Finally we arrived at the wrong barbecue. We were supposed to go to 514 Greenway and we went to 415. It was my fault. I wrote it down wrong when Sensei Mike told us at the dojo on Friday.

But 415 was raging. Fifty, forty people. Mostly middle-aged guys wearing Oxfords and sandals. Some of them had wives, but there weren't any babies, which always spooks me a little, a barbecue without babies. Like if you ever had a father who shaved off his mustache.

It took us a few minutes of looking around for Sensei Mike before we noticed this banner hanging off the fence. It said HAPPY TENURE, PROFESSOR SCHINKL! By then, we all had bottles of beer in our hands. The beers tasted yeasty. They were from Belgium. That's what set the whole thing off.

The four of us were half-sitting along the edge of the patio table, trying to decide if it was more polite to finish the beers there or take them with us to look for Sensei Mike's house, when this guy came up and made a show of adjusting his sunglasses. First he just lowered them down the bridge of his nose so we could see one of his eyebrows raise up. But then he was squinting at us over the frames and he had a hand on his hip. He stayed that way for a couple of wheezy breaths, then tore the sunglasses off his face with the other hand and held them up in the air behind his ear like he was gonna swat us. Instead, he let the shades dangle and he said,

"Hmmmmmm." The sound of that got the attention of some other people. They weren't crowding up or anything, but they were looking at us.

The guy said, "Hmmmmmm" again, but with more irritation than the first time. Like a whining, almost.

"How you doing?" Cojo said to him. Nancy leaned into me, but it was instinct, nothing to make a big deal of. Tina held her beer close. Cojo was smiling, which is not a good thing for him to do around people who don't know him. His smile looks like he's asking you to stop making him smile. It's got no joy. It's because of his smile that I retrieve the cars when we work the lot together. If customers tip, it's usually on the way out.

Real slow and loud, the guy said, "How's. your Belgian. beer?"

So the beer was his and he was attached to it in some sick way. Like fathers and the end-piece of the roast beef. He wasn't anyone's father, though, this guy. He was being a real prick about the beer is what he was, but it was the wrong barbecue and he was harmless so far. He was tofu in khakis. About as rough as a high school drama teacher. Still, he could've been Schinkl for all we knew, so he didn't get hit.

"You want one?" Cojo said. He said, "I think there's one left in the cooler by the grill."

The guy stared at Joe, just to let him know that he'd heard what Joe said but was ignoring him. Then he spun on Nancy. He said, "Is that *ground chuck* in your lap, young lady? Do you mean to wash down those patties of *ground chuck* with my imported. Belgian. beer?" He poked the meat.

I said, "Hey."

"Hay's for horses," he said, the fucken creep.

A woman in the crowd—they were crowding up now—said, "Calm down, Byron."

He poked the meat again, hard. Busted a hole in the plastic wrap. Nancy flinched and I had that fucker in an armlock before the meat hit the ground. Joe dumped out his beer and broke the bottle on the table edge. We moved in front of the Christamestas, like shields. I had Byron bent in front of me, huffing and puffing.

I didn't want the girls to see us get beat down, but I thought about afterward, about Nancy holding my hands at my chest and wiping the blood from my face with disinfected cottonballs, how I could accidentally confess my love and not be held responsible since I'd have a serious concussion.

Byron said, "Let go."

"You got a thin voice," I told him.

I pulled his wrist back a couple degrees. His fingers danced around.

Every guy in that yard was creeping toward us, saying "Hey" and "Hey now." There were too many of them, broken bottle or no. All we had left was wiseass tough-guy shit. "Hey," they said. And Joe said, "Hay's for horses," and I forced a laugh through my teeth like I was supposed to. They kept creeping. Little baby steps. Tina whispered to Nancy, "Can we go? Let's just go."

"Just let go of me!" Byron said. "Let go of me!"

I said, "What!"

He shut his mouth and the crowd stopped moving. They stopped right behind where the patio met the grass. That's when it occurred to me the reason they weren't pummeling us was Byron. They didn't want me to damage him. And that meant that I controlled them. I thought: We got a hostage. I thought: All we have to do is take him out the gate on the side of the house, get him to the car, then drop him in the street and drive off. I was gonna tell Joe, but then Nancy started talking.

"Do you guys know Sensei Mike?" she said.

This chubby drunk guy was wobbling at the front of the crowd. He said, "What?" But it sounded like "Whud?" That's how I knew he was a lisper, even before he started lisping. Because he had adenoid problems. The first lisper I ever knew in grade school had adenoid problems. Brett Novak. He said his own name, "Bred Novag." Mine he said, "Jag Gragow." When people called him a lisper, I didn't know what a lisper was, so I decided he was a lisper not just because of what he did to *s* sounds, but because of what he did to *t* sounds and *k* sounds, too. So I thought this chubby drunk guy was a lisper, because I used to be wrong about what a lisper was and so "lisper" is the first thing I think when I hear adenoid problems. But since the chubby guy turned out to be a lisper after all, my old wrongness made it so I was right. It was like if Nancy wore hot pink. The color would look sexy on her, and because it would look sexy on her, I'd say it was hot pink, and I'd be right, even though I didn't know what I was saying. I'd be right because of an old misunderstanding.

"Sensei Mike?" said Nancy. "We came for Sensei Mike." Her voice was trembling. I could've killed everybody.

The guy said, "Thenthaimigue? Ith that thome thort of thibboleth?"

This got laughs. The crowd thought it was very clever for the lisper to say a word like *shibboleth* to us.

But fuck them for thinking I don't know *shibboleth*. Some people don't, but I do. It's from the Old Testament. In CCD they told us we shouldn't read the Old Testament till we were older because it was violent and confusing and totally Christless, so I read some of it (I skipped Leviticus and quit at Kings). The part with *shibboleth* is in Judges: There were the Ephrathites who were these people who couldn't make the sound *sh*. They were at war with the Gileadites. The Gileadites controlled all the crossings of the Jordan River, and the main thing they didn't want was for the Ephrathites to get across the river. The problem was the Ephrathites looked exactly like the Gileadites and spoke the same language, too, so if an Ephrathite came to one of the crossings, the Gileadites had almost no way of telling that he was an Ephrathite. Not until Jephthah, who was the leader of the Gileadites, remembered how Ephrathites couldn't make the *sh* sound—that's when he came up with the idea to make everyone who wanted to cross the river say the word *shibboleth*. If they could say "Shibboleth," they could pass, but if they couldn't say it, it meant they were an enemy and they got slain. So *shibboleth* was this code word, but it didn't work like a normal code word. A normal code word is a secret—you have to prove you know what it is. *Shibboleth*, though—it wasn't any secret. Jephthah would tell you what it was. What mattered was how you said it. How you said it is what saved your life, or ended it.

I said to the lisper, "I know what's a shibboleth, and Sensei Mike's no shibboleth. And you're no Jephthah, either." It came out wormy and know-it-all sounding. I sounded like I cared what they thought of me. Maybe I did. I don't think so, though.

"Are you jogueing?" he said. "Whud gind of brude are you? Do you *offden* find yourthelf engaging in meda-converthathions?" He pronounced the *t* in *often*, the prick, and on top of it, he turned it into a fucken *d*.

All those guys laughed anyway. It was funnier to them than the *shibboleth* joke. It was the funniest thing they'd ever heard.

And I was sick of getting laughed at. And I was sick of people asking me questions that weren't questions.

I pulled on Byron's arm and he moaned. Cojo slapped him on the chops and the lisper stepped back into the crowd to hide.

The crowd started shifting. But not forward. Not in any direction really, not for too long. It swelled in one place and thinned in another, like a water balloon in a fist. It was in my fist.

I saw the lisper's head craned up over the shoulder of a guy who'd snuck to the front, and that's when I knew.

They didn't stop creeping up at the patio because they were scared of what I'd do to their friend and his arm. They stopped at the patio to give us space. They stopped at the patio so I could do whatever I'd do to Byron and they could watch.

I said to Nancy, "You and Tina go get the car, okay?"

Nancy reached in my pocket for the keys and whispered, "Be careful." Then Tina kissed Joe. The girls ran off. It could've been a war movie. It could've been Joe and I going to the front in some high-drama war movie. It was a little hammy, but that didn't bother me.

As soon as I was sure the girls were clear, I asked Joe, with my eyes and eyebrows, if he thought we should run for it.

He told me with his shoulders and his chin that he thought it was a good idea.

Then I got an inspiration. I started yelling at the top of my lungs: "AHHHHHH!"

The whole crowd went pop-eyed and stepped back and stepped back and kept stepping back. I got a huge lung capacity. I think I yelled for about a minute. I yelled till my throat bled and I couldn't yell anymore. Then I dropped Byron, and we took off.

Nancy was just pulling out of the parking spot when we got to the car. Some of the sickos from the barbecue ran out onto the street, and one of them was shouting, "We'll call the police!"

We still didn't know Sensei Mike's right address and the girls decided it was probably better to get out of Glen Ellyn, so we headed back to Chicago. When we got to the Christamesta house, Tina and Joe went inside and I followed Nancy around the neighborhood on foot, not saying anything. I don't know how long that lasted. It was dark, though. We ended up at the park at Iowa and Rockwell, under the tornado slide, sitting in pebbles, our backs against the ladder. Nancy opened her purse and pulled out a Belgian beer. I popped it with my lighter and gave it to her. She sipped and gave it back. I sipped and gave it back.

I've told a lot of girls I was in love with them. There's some crack-ass wisdom about it being easier to say when you don't mean it, but that's not why I didn't say it to Nancy. I didn't say it because every time I've said it, I meant it. If I said it again, it would be like all those other times, and all those other times—it went away. And silence wasn't any holier than saying it. Just more drama for its own sake. All of it's been done before. It's been in TV shows and comic books and it's how your parents met. And there's nothing wrong with drama, I don't think. And there's nothing wrong with drama for its own sake, either. What's wrong is drama that doesn't know it's drama. And what's wrong is doing the same thing everyone else does and thinking you're original, thinking you're unpredictable.

I said, "Maybe it's cause he wanted racing stri—" and the sound cut off. My throat was killing me from the yelling and it closed up.

Nancy said, "Your voice is broken."

And that was an unexpected way to put it, drama or no.

I swigged the beer again and told her, all raspy, "Maybe it's racing stripes. The guy wanted racing stripes."

"What?" she said.

"Don't 'what' me," I said. I gulped more beer. I said, "He wanted to paint racing stripes and the city wouldn't let him. There's a code against painting stripes on city vehicles. So every day he ties the balloons on the grille. And maybe that's a half-ass way to have racing stripes, but then maybe he figures stripes on a garbage truck aren't really racing stripes to begin with, so he doesn't mind using balloons. Or maybe he does mind, but he keeps it to himself because he's not a complainer. Maybe he just keeps tying balloons on the grille, telling himself they're as good as racing stripes, and maybe one day they will be."

"That's a sad story," Nancy said. She carved SAD! in the pebbles with the bottle of beer.

"How's it *sad*?" I said.

Under SAD! she carved a circle with an upside-down smile.

"It's not sad," I said.

She said, "I don't believe that."

"But I'm telling you," I said.

She said, "Then I don't believe you, Jack."

And did I kiss her then? Did Nancy Christamesta close her eyes and tilt her head back, away from the moon? Did she open her mouth? Did she open it just a little, just enough so I could feel her breath on my chin before she would kiss me and then did I finally kiss her?

Fuck you.

ACKNOWLEDGMENTS

Many of the stories in here were begun—and a couple or three of them finished—while I attended the Syracuse University MFA Program in Creative Writing. My time there was invaluable to me, and to this collection. It was also inexpressibly joyful. Thank you, teachers: George Saunders, Arthur Flowers, Mary Karr, Mary Gaitskill, Christopher Kennedy, Mary Caponegro, and Brooks Haxton. And thank you, early readers, workshopmates, and alumni pallies: Christian TeBordo, Salvador Plascencia, Eric Rosenblum, Phil LaMarche, Thomas Yagoda, Erin Brooks Worley, Keith Gessen, Ellen Litman, Laura Farmer, Miciah Bay Gault, Stephanie Carpenter, Rebecca Curtis, Adam Desnoyers, Jeff Parker, Nina Shope, Christian Moody, Sarah Harwell, Courtney Queeney, Chris Narozny, Christopher Boucher, and Daniel Torday.

Thank you, Eli Horowitz, for always showing me—or at least trying to show me—what I've been failing to see. This book is better than it was before you read it.

Thank you, Adam Krefman, Juliet Litman, Michelle Quint, and the rest of the McSweeney'ses for all the energy you've put into making this and the last one happen.

Thank you to the editors of those publications in which stories from this book originally appeared: Jodee Stanley, Jordan Bass, Rob Spillman, Danit Brown, Elizabeth Hodges, and Michael Archer.

Thank you, Adam Novy and Sid Feldman, for not telling me to go away when I was young and annoying(er) and didn't know what to read.

Thank you, family, Atara and Lanny and Paula and Rachel Levin, for way too much to even pretend to begin to name—for all those things that make you the second-hardest people in the world for me to properly thank.

Thank you, Leslie Lockett, Leslie Lockett, Leslie Lockett, Leslie Lockett, Leslie Lockett, Leslie Lockett, Leslie Lockett.

ABOUT THE AUTHOR

Adam Levin is the author of the novel *The Instructions*, a finalist for the 2010 National Jewish Book Award for Fiction and winner of both the 2011 New York Public Library Young Lions Fiction Award and the inaugural Indie Booksellers Choice Award. For his short stories, Levin has won the Summer Literary Seminars Fiction Contest, as well as the Joyce Carol Oates Fiction Prize. His fiction has appeared in publications including *Tin House*, *Esquire*, and *New England Review*. He lives in Chicago, where he teaches Creative Writing at the School of the Art Institute.